IN THE SHADOW OF THE TOWE

A NOVEL

BY DAVID MENON

This is for Vicky, Sophie, Nathan, Charlie, Heidi, Lauren, Allana, Jonathan, Jaime, and Kat …. For keeping my juices flowing with their flat whites!

Every writer needs a particular coffee shop where they can go and dream up their work and make copious notes that eventually turn into a novel. The branch of Costa's in St. Annes, Lancashire is my such place of inspiration. If ever you're in the area, it's on Clifton Drive South, between the M&S supermarket, and the Travelodge. Pop in and Vicky and the team will all do you proud!

And outside Costa's say 'Hi! How are you?' to Adrian who will be selling copies of the 'Big Issue' magazine. And buy one!

And in the evening, if you fancy a good curry then 'Zest of India' at Squires Gate or 'The Curry Leaf' at Bispham, both of which are featured in this story, will both serve you well.

David was born of an English mother and an Indian father, neither of whom brought him up. He spent his childhood in Derby but has since lived all over the UK, and also for several very happy years he lived in Paris. He's currently based in St Annes, Lancashire. He loves to travel, he loves Indian food closely followed by French, he's into politics and current affairs and all the arts – books, films, TV, theatre, and music. He's a seriously devoted fan of Stevie Nicks who he calls 'the voice of my interior world'. He worked as cabin crew for BA for over twenty years, he was an events' organizer for the Labour party, and he teaches English to Russian kids at activity camps in Finland and Estonia, although that is currently on hold. He likes a gin and tonic in the evening, followed by a glass or three of red wine with his dinner. Well, that doesn't make him a bad person.

And he once made a cheese sandwich for the actress Julia Roberts!

David has a YouTube channel on which he's progressively posting videos to do with his work. You can subscribe to it at 'David Menon Books'.

You can also go to David's Facebook page 'David Menon Writer' to find out a little more about all of his books, including those he writes when he takes his imagination to the other side of the mirror and writes his 'silver springs' series of novels about the contemporary drama of love and family life. He's also on Twitter as 'David Menon Writer' and Instagram as 'theenglishvisitor'. You'll also find him on Linkedin.

And you can also go to any Amazon site around the world to find out about any of David's books and that's where you'll be able to buy them too!

ONE

The exact skill of being an accomplished killer is in knowing when your victim has actually gone past the point of no return. The moment when you know that they're croaking signifies that they've started on that journey into the next world. The death rattle. The recognizing of that unique sound is a skill acquired through practice and time. The light goes out in their eyes. Your hands are firmly clenched around their throat. Your fingers and thumbs pressed so firmly into their neck that they start to hurt. Their eyes bulging out of their sockets with the sheer terror of what's being done to them. You've proved to yourself one more time that you can kill. It was how it made you feel. It was the satisfaction you got from feeling the strength go from their body. It was the moment when you knew that you held the ultimate power over them and that, this time, you'd discharged it for your own purposes. It was in the act of murder. It was in the turning of the body of a human being into a rag doll.

And this was only the first time that the plan had been executed. But it wasn't going to be the last. The first time was always the hardest. The second time would be easier.

But this wasn't killing just for the sake of it or just for the sake of getting some cheap thrill. This wasn't some bone headed psycho who wanted to know what death looked like. There was real purpose in this killing. This was about exacting revenge on young girls like her who used their poison to make fools out of decent people.

This one had also died quite well. The initial seduction had been easier than could've been imagined. This one had been on the game for a while. She was an experienced hand. She knew what to do with what she had and placed her intentions behind using it to satisfy her clients. She didn't bother about who it was she was giving herself up to and even when she knew this would be her very last time, the poor, frightened little thing had offered little resistance as life was strangled out of her. She'd shown barely a kick or two of fight. Maybe she'd been stoned or high on something or other. Or maybe she was just ready to give it all up. She'd led a sordid little excuse for a life, but she'd nevertheless done enough damage in her twisted place of morality, and it was right that she was stopped.

She was a heavy girl this one. Pregnant maybe? It wouldn't be past her given the circumstances she wrapped herself in. This kind of slut wouldn't know a precaution if it leapt up and slapped her across the face. Getting her next fix to feed her drug habit would be more important. Most of these girls charged less for letting their client fuck them without a condom. And that was attractive to a certain kind of blue- collar working man who had to be careful about hiding a cash withdrawal for his activities from a wife who checked their bank statement. They risked taking disease into the marital bed but then again if they weren't getting their rocks off at home then what did it matter?

An anonymous trip to the special clinic would sort out any infection. A course of penicillin would put that right. Unless it was something way more serious, but they wouldn't get that because they still believed that AIDS was a gay disease. Ignorant cretins.

The distant rumble of the trams going up and down the promenade could be heard as the body was dragged round the back of a derelict looking boarded up terraced house in the shadow of the Blackpool Town football ground. It was now time to take out the syringe and find the vein from which the sample of blood could be extracted. Because the killing would have no real purpose unless the blood was taken. This was tainted blood. It was contaminated. It was the blood of wanton killers.

But it was going to be very useful.

With tonight's mission well and truly accomplished it was now time to dump the body over the wall and then go home and wait.

TWO

DI Layla Khan had come a long way and not just within the police force. It was getting on for twenty years since she'd literally risked life and limb to escape the clutches of her family in Derby who were determined to marry her off to a much older man from a village in the mountains above Islamabad in Pakistan and who didn't speak any English. For days on end her parents had locked her in her room after she'd refused to go to the airport and get on a plane to Pakistan with them. She'd known full well what their agenda had been. They would've given her to the husband they'd chosen, and he would've kept her for the rest of her life as a baby making slave. There would've been no way out. It would've been the full stop on whatever she wanted to do because she would no longer have a say. Her husband and his family would've decided the content of the air she breathed if they thought they could go that far.

But Layla had other ideas. She was proud to call herself a Pakistani Brit. She was proud of her heritage and yet she felt more British than Pakistani. And why wouldn't she? She'd been born and bred in the UK and mixed with people from all kinds of different backgrounds. She didn't tell her parents that. They'd have hated it if they'd known she was actively mixing with people they wouldn't approve of, and that meant anyone who didn't interpret the word of Islam in the same way they did. No potential influence from outside their closeted world could be tolerated. Of course, it was all so different for her brothers who'd all been allowed to mix with whoever they damn well chose and when her younger brother Wahid brought his white girlfriend Sadie home it had been no problem. But Layla was a girl. That meant she had to be 'protected' and there was no room for discussion. No talk of the education that Layla had been determined to pursue. Her O levels had been coming up at the time. She'd intended to take them no matter what her parents said. She was a British girl. She was going to have her future and she was going to determine it herself but how could she do that from a prison cell within her own family home? There were courses she could take later. As soon as she turned sixteen, she'd have the law on her side and others on the outside who could help her. She was sure of that. Someone out there would be able to help her break free and stand on her own two feet. Because she could do that. She didn't need anyone to hold her hand permanently through life. The day she'd managed to get out and her parents had shouted and screamed at her as she ran down the street and through the labyrinth of terraced houses that made up the Normanton area of Derby, she knew she could rely on nobody but herself. That's when she'd begun her journey to where she stood in life today and she hadn't looked back even when both her parents died, and her older brother had cut her off entirely from the rest of her family. Recently her sisters and sisters-in-law had been making overtures towards her and she'd responded tentatively. They'd had positive conversations. But she was wary. They wanted her to be fully rehabilitated into the family but that meant she would have to go to Hadj. But if she did that then she'd be right back at square one and rendered under the control of everything she'd run away from. Besides, she had her long-term boyfriend Steve to consider, and he loved her for who she was and not what he wanted to make her into.

So after all these years of soul searching after wrenching herself away from her family traditions and being looked at as having 'dishonoured' them, and after all the work she'd put in to making something of her life, running away to Blackpool because that would be the last place they'd come and look for her, getting a flat, getting a job in a local hotel, finishing off her exams and joining the Lancashire constabulary, dealing with all the feelings of guilt about having a sexual relationship with Steve until she reached the point when she could truly lie back and enjoy it, after all that the last thing she was going to do was to accept the pig ignorance of a thinly veiled racist scumbag like her new deputy DS Keith Drake. Layla was sitting behind her desk and Drake was standing in front of it. He went to sit down.

'Excuse me?' said Layla. 'I don't remember asking you to sit down so stay standing'.

It took Drake all his time to answer her through his tightly clenched teeth. 'Ma'am'.

'So, let's look at the facts here, Detective Sergeant Drake' Layla continued. She didn't make a habit of using her power to belittle people but in this case, it just had to be done. She could barely look at him. He had hair like he'd combed it ten years ago and thought that would do. He hadn't even bothered to do up his tie. It was loose with the top two buttons of his shirt undone. He showed no respect to the fact that she was his boss. Well, that was going to change. 'You were ordered to arrest Jamie Langham for the alleged assault on pensioner Ken Jones but instead you went to the home of Danny Kirkwood and made such an impression that it's a wonder he hasn't filed a complaint. Care to explain yourself?'

'Is there any point, ma'am?'

'I beg your pardon?'

Drake smirked. 'You've already made up your mind'.

'Then prove me wrong'.

Drake stayed silent.

'You can't prove me wrong, can you DS Drake?'

'It depends on what you think that I think you may be wrong about, ma'am'.

Layla stood up angrily. 'You just wouldn't accept that Jamie Langham was guilty of the assault on Ken Jones and that Danny Kirkwood had nothing whatsoever to do with it. And that's because in that tiny little excuse for a mind of yours you'd made Danny Kirkwood guilty just because he was black. Jamie Langham comes from a nice, cozy middle class white family in St. Annes so of course he couldn't possibly be guilty even though the evidence against him was overwhelming. But Danny Kirkwood was from a not so advantaged black family on the Grange Park estate who just happened to be in the wrong place at the wrong time and that meant that he was guilty to you'.

'You can't blame me for thinking that Kirkwood was the assailant, ma'am. He looked it as soon as we turned our attention on him'.

'Oh, you mean he looked it because he was black? You're unbelievable'.

'Oh, I've no time for this politically correct nonsense' said Drake who turned and made for the door.

'Stay where you are!' Layla demanded. 'Take one more step and I'll see to it that your career ends today'.

Drake paused. She could probably make good on her threat, and he knew it. How had life come to this? His balls had been cut off by all the women in his life including his own daughter who only treated him with any kind of civility when she wanted money. He turned back and faced her.

'You wouldn't do that to any other DI' Layla charged. She was fuming. 'I won't allow you to make me the exception just because they're all white middle-aged men and I'm a brown skinned Muslim woman'.

'Are you threatening me, ma'am?'

'Yes. And I'm also promising you that I mean what I say. Now, when you searched the home of Danny Kirkwood did you find anything incriminating?'

'No, ma'am'.

'And what happened when you eventually decided to obey my

order and search Langham's family home?'

'We found the watch and the wedding ring that had been taken from Ken Jones when he was attacked, ma'am'.

'Which proves my point. You made a judgment on the basis of the colour of someone's skin. I won't tolerate that in my officers. We charge people on the basis of evidence, DI Drake. This is not the fifties or South Yorkshire at any time you care to mention. We do not consider someone guilty on racial grounds,'.

'Another concession to the fascism of political correctness'.

'You just can't accept that you were wrong, can you?'

'Alright, I was wrong'.

'Keith, work with me and we could really make an impression on the crime figures for this town. Work against me or undermine me again in any way and I'll finish you. Do we understand each other?'

Drake hated having to acquiesce, but he didn't feel like he had much choice. He couldn't really afford to do anything else now that his ex-wife was starting to play silly buggers over access to the kids. He had to stay around in Blackpool, and he couldn't afford to lose his job however much working with DI Khan here was going to irritate him. There she was, sat there, a piece of some racial quota that public services no doubt had to live by. It was what made descent white people like himself support the EDL. They felt like they'd lost control of their own country.

'Yes, ma'am'.

'I hope you mean that, DS Drake. I really do'.

After she'd finished with Drake she went outside for some air and a cigarette. She'd stayed true to her Muslim traditions and never touched a drop of alcohol, but she'd never been able to kick the smoking habit. She looked up and around. She and her colleagues in the Blackpool police were settling in well to their swanky new offices that were convenient for the Tesco superstore at Mereside. Whilst she puffed away, she checked her phone for messages. She smiled at her screensaver. It was a head and shoulders of her partner Steve giving a thumbs up and with the scarf of his beloved Fleetwood Town FC wrapped round his neck. He'd made her a fully paid- up member of the 'cod army' almost as soon as they'd met. He owned and ran a garage just off Devonshire Road that did car servicing and repairs. He was fit. She fancied him as much today as she had done the day that she met him. His hair was going grey, and he was starting to lose it on top a bit, but it made no difference to those eyes or that smile. She knew he was getting broody. He wasn't bothered about marriage, but he'd hinted a couple of times lately that he'd like them to at least talk about starting a family. But Layla was torn. It wasn't that she didn't want kids and it certainly wasn't that she didn't want kids with Steve. She wanted nothing more than to have his kids. She didn't really know why she was hesitating. Perhaps it would work itself out. She hoped so because she really couldn't bear to lose him.

The leader of Greater Fylde council was hosting a meeting of fellow local government heads from all across the country, at the Winter Gardens, which served as Blackpool's premier conference venue in the absence of anything having been purposely built for such a role since the century before last. Lesley Hammond had taken over from her Tory predecessor when the Tories had been roundly rejected by the town's voters. But Labour hadn't gained enough seats to win a majority. So, they'd gone into a coalition with Lesley's group of independents and one of the prices of that was to give Lesley the top job of leader of the council. It hadn't gone down well with the older Labour councilors, including most of the women who didn't hold with 'all this pushing women to the top all the time' and besides it was Harry's 'turn' to 'have a go' at being leader and it would spoil his

75th birthday celebrations if it was taken away from him, as well as being another blow to add to the fact that he'd 'really not been well'. Lesley wasn't cold to all of that. Local politics were a very different game from the national one. But she didn't know what any of the perspective of some Labour party councilors had to do with providing what the people of the town needed, especially when it came to the poorest and the most disadvantaged. The younger councilors did. The older ones very definitely didn't. But almost immediately since becoming leader, Lesley had gained a reputation as a 'no nonsense' politician with an often sarcastic, sledgehammer wit who took no prisoners, especially when it came to journalists. A year into the job and she was widely regarded as doing well for the town. She'd also gained the cross- party respect of those at the meeting today and whilst initially she'd had to argue passionately with her Tory counterparts from the more well off shire parts of the country, particularly the home counties of the south, she was now sensing that some of those former sworn enemies were at least in private coming round to see her point that cuts and more cuts would only lead to a deterioration of poverty levels and more and more people slipping through an ever more stretched net. She also insisted that local circumstances have to be taken into account when central government funds are allocated because the problems faced by her administration in Blackpool for instance weren't entirely in tune with those faced in somewhere like Windsor and Maidenhead. She sought to further emphasise these points in her opening speech to the meeting.

'... every Friday night Blackpool North station is awash with people from right across the northwest, mostly young but not all of them so, who've arrived with a bin bag of clothes and fifty quid in their pockets. They head to the part of town where B and B can be had for a tenner. They'll get so out of their heads in the town's bars and clubs that they'll struggle to remember their way back to the B and B. Some of them will barely be able to remember even their own name and half of them won't make it back to the station to catch the train back to wherever they came from. They'll join all the other refugees from within our own shores who think that the end of the yellow brick road is the seaside. Because everything looks better at the seaside. Whatever problems you've got will simply disappear into the malt vinegar haze hanging over every fish and chip shop. But those problems won't disappear. Our streets are not paved with gold for those running from a bad home. But that's the illusion of what a seaside town like ours can perceivably offer in the minds of the really needy. They and all of their problems end up having to be dealt with by my council, and we do it out of a sense of compassion and duty whilst at the same time trying to improve the town for the sake of all our family holidaymakers and for those who live and work here. But none of these extra burdens that we have to finance in comparison to other places are taken into account by central government and unless they are then I fear what will ultimately happen to those who come to us, at the seaside, in desperate need … '

Listening intently to Hammond's speech and noting the varying tone of the audience's response to what she said was Joshua Walker, lead writer with the Blackpool Evening News. Halfway through the morning a coffee break was called and that's when Walker grabbed Hammond and took her off into a quiet corner for a little chat about respective agendas.

'I take it my speech will receive a positive response in the pages of your newspaper, Joshua' said Lesley who added a small smirk at the end of her question. She liked Joshua. He was sympathetic to the political left of which Lesley considered herself a part. She sipped her black coffee and was going to dunk her digestive biscuit into it but then thought better of it. It would only break and splash coffee all over her shirt sleeve. Even closet socialists can have standards. 'We've got to hammer the message home to the government as much as we can'.

'I don't think you'll be displeased with my coverage' Walker replied. He thought he must look so damn scruffy compared to her. Lesley Hammond didn't scale the heights of fashion but was always turned out in a decent suit, inexpensive but decent, with a skirt usually just above the knee and an open necked shirt. She wore some make-up but didn't overdo it. Just enough to accentuate those high cheekbones and bring out the brightness of her crystal blue eyes. Walker rarely wore a tie and when he did it was always loose. He only possessed one suit which he tended to keep for special occasions like funerals or the occasional christening. The rest of the time it was jackets and trousers.

'Good. So, what else is it you want? I take it you haven't come to ask me if I had a good holiday in Cornwall with my family which I did incidentally'.

'I'm very pleased for you,' said Walker. 'But you know why we need to talk'.

Lesley knew exactly what Walker was getting at. 'Yes'.

'So, are you going to help me bring Daniel Lewis down once and for all?'

'Joshua, I was elected by my constituents to represent them on the council. Then I was voted in as council leader. My job is to run this town on behalf of the people'.

'Meaning?'

'Meaning I wasn't elected to use my offices to bring down Blackpool's biggest gangster'.

'The very worst kind of gangster. One who looks oh so respectable on the outside'.

'Yes, I know, Joshua, I have met him'.

'I know you want to help me'.

'Course I want to help you' Lesley retorted with the irritation that comes from knowing that the person you're arguing with is right. 'Daniel Lewis is a despicable human being who the police have been trying to nail for years. They haven't succeeded. What makes you think you would either with or without my help?'

'Because of the motivation you have for making a difference in this town and the way Lewis interferes with that' Walker emphasized. 'You can't keep letting that happen, Lesley'.

'But I could end up potentially putting my entire family at risk, Josh! What if he was to try and get at my two sons or my husband? No, this is a job for the police, Josh, really it is'.

'But they've failed' Walker countered. 'And Daniel Lewis is waiting to get his hands on every vulnerable teenager he can find. Now what if you were the mother of one of those kids? What would you say if you knew that someone in power had known about the darker side of Lewis all along and didn't do anything about it?'

'That was a bloody cheap shot, Walker'.

'Sad but true'.

Lesley knew that she had no moral argument with which to come back at Walker with and she'd been seriously considering whether or not to work with him since he'd asked her several weeks before. Daniel Lewis certainly wasn't a very nice man. He was suspected of giving back handers to someone in the council in return for getting everything passed that needed council approval, but Lesley hadn't yet been able to find out exactly who this money went to. She was intent on running a 'clean' council and she wanted to know. Walker was one of the best investigative journalists in the country and if he said that he could get Daniel Lewis, and not just for bribing council officials, then he probably could. And it was true that Daniel Lewis had got away with being the King of the underworld in Blackpool for far too long. The town needed liberating from him.

'Can we work with the police to protect my family?' she

asked.

'I can approach them' said Walker, not sure of his footing on this particular aspect of things. 'I'm sure we could work something out given the circumstances,'.

'Then if that can be the case, I'm prepared to talk with you further' said Lesley who thought she might regret promising Walker anything but if it meant that Daniel Lewis could be wiped off the face of Blackpool then it would all be for the good. 'But there's also another thing'

'And what's that?' Walker asked.

'Will helping you harm any of my councilors? Bearing in mind my coalition only has a majority of four. In the process of what you want us to do, will I find things out about them that I'd rather not have known?'

Walker grinned. 'What do you think they've been getting up to?'

'Don't tease me, Josh. That's not how I want us working together to work out'.

'Agreed' said Walker. 'But agree to work with me unequivocally and then I'll answer your question. This is where you have to start trusting me, Lesley'.

DAVID MENON

THREE

Angela Lewis was preparing for her interview with local radio station Radio Fylde. She and her husband Daniel were prominent members of the local community and Angela was also gaining quite a reputation in her own right as a media commentator on the raising of children. She had particular views on the subject. She was well known for her opposition to what she called the creeping state interference in the rights of parents to raise their children as they saw fit. She was dedicated to it. She had four children of her own and they'd been brought up in what had been deemed to be a strict, authoritarian old-fashioned manner. When there were guests in the house her children had to remain silent until or unless they were spoken to, and they must not initiate any conversation with a guest. It wasn't the kind of warm, loving household she'd always wanted to raise her children in and even her own parents didn't approve. But when she married Daniel, she'd promised to respect him as the man of the house, and she'd learned very early on in the marriage that he was going to hold her to that.

She also knew that there was a much darker side to her husband's business dealings, but she'd made a success of turning a blind eye to it throughout their marriage. She couldn't develop a conscience about things she didn't know about and why ask questions if you perhaps wouldn't like the answer.

Her husband Daniel had built up his construction business into one of the largest in the northwest and had been made CEO of the holding company that was the Blackpool Enterprise and Development Group. He was a working- class boy made good which was part of her initial attraction to him. His parents still lived in the same council house he'd grown up in. He refused to move them even though he could well afford to because he liked to drive his children round there to impress upon them how far he'd come and how far they'd go back if they didn't tow his line and do as they were told.

His group were bidding for a major contract to redevelop the town centre. Though he needed to portray at least the appearance of political neutrality, it was bloody difficult when there were all those ridiculous socialists on the town council with whom he was completely at odds in every way. And those damn independents. But that was what Angela saw as her job as his wife. Her job as his wife was to support his endeavours at the expense of her own sometimes but with the kind of fundamental belief that comes from a committed and faithful union. At least, that's what he told her. And it's what she told herself when the doubts started to boil over. She'd made that commitment. She'd made that promise before God. She'd done it to please her parents. They'd been desperate to get her married off to someone who would provide the kind of firm support and security that would make her forget the stupid, immature affair she'd had with Vanessa. Angela often thought back to that wonderful summer when being with Vanessa had been the only thing that made any sense to her. But then her parents had found them in bed one day and the next thing she knew they were marrying her off to Daniel. She sometimes wondered where Vanessa got to. And if she was really honest, she'd say that sometimes meant every single day.

She sat in her small office way up in the loft conversion of the family home in Poulton just a few miles inland from Blackpool but a million miles away from the atmosphere of the town. Her children were forbidden from going into Blackpool. At weekends especially the town was full of the most undesirable types who paraded their lost virtue across the pubs and clubs that offered such cheap alcohol they may as well give it away. Angela didn't drink. She suspected that her husband Daniel did but that was probably because of the social aspect of his business life. They never kept alcohol in the house, and she'd be horrified if any of her children consumed it. She'd always been forthright in her views and was often invited onto one of those Sunday morning TV programmes where they discuss life and morality. One thing led to another, and she'd now been on several such programmes plus radio, and she'd written articles for the Daily Mail and Daily Express.

Her husband Daniel was glad of his wife's newfound notoriety because it diverted attention away from suspicions about his more dubious activities.

Her mobile phone rang and the voice on the other end announced herself as the producer of the morning show. She was then put through to the studio and all the usual introductions were made with Ebony the radio show host.

'So, Angela,' said Ebony. 'We're talking to people up and down the Fylde today who hold what could be said were more extreme views than the rest of us on a variety of issues and … '

'… hang on' Angela interrupted. 'Extreme views?'

'Well, you've got to admit that your views on the issue of parenting are pretty extreme positions to take, Angela'

'No, I don't accept that' said Angela, firmly. Her feathers were well and truly ruffled. She detested being labelled as extreme just because she wanted to bring firm and tough discipline back into the privilege of parenting.

'Well, you couldn't say they were mainstream?'

'Only because of the moral delinquency we have to live under these days' Angela countered. 'The boundaries have become so wide they may as well not be there at all'.

'But don't you think that's because they reflect a more modern and more enlightened majority opinion?' Ebony suggested. She'd been caught all through their conversation by the moral lecturing tone in Angela's voice. It made her feel like if she confessed to having had a duvet day watching DVD box sets or had licked the bowl dry when her mother was mixing the ingredients for a cake, it would be tantamount to a complete moral delinquency in Angela's eyes.

'I think that if people have a negative view of the stance that I take then that really is a matter for them and not for me to lose sleep over'.

'Okay, well Angela, you have four children, three daughters and one son. Is that right?'

'Yes,' she answered, proudly. 'That's right'.

'And they're aged 19, 17, 16, and 15?'

'Yes?'

'Your daughters are the oldest three and they all attend or attended the local comprehensive school but your son, the fifteen-year- old is at boarding school in the Ribble valley. Why did you send him away and not your daughters?'

'Because my son needs to be prepared for a professional career whereas my daughters need to learn how to be attentive wives and mothers, so a basic educational grounding is all that's needed'.

Ebony the radio host was utterly astonished. 'Angela, that's not far away from the perspective of the Taliban or Islamic state. Don't you see that?'

'I think that to compare me, a committed Christian, with those terrorist animals, is a gross insult'.

'I asked if you saw the connection?'

'No, I most certainly do not'.

'Oh, come on, Angela? You don't value the education of girls?'

'I didn't say I didn't value it, but I did say that the emphasis for girls should be on preparing them to be wives and mothers in support of husbands who go out and establish their careers. It's only when their children grow older, as mine have done, that you can return to the outside world as I've done in some sort of voluntary or campaigning capacity, as I've done. The problems with delinquency and so on in our society began when women were given this odious thing called choice'.

'You're really saying that gender equality is the cause of everything that's wrong in society?'

'In large part I think it is, yes. My husband and I believe in more traditional values'.

'Okay' said Ebony who'd already heard enough from this stupid, sanctimonious cow but there was still some way to go with the interview. She hated the sound of Angela's voice. It was like listening to a chain saw going through a plank of wood. 'Do you and your husband use corporal punishment on your children?'

'Yes, we do' said Angela who then realised that she'd been led into a trap. But there was nothing she could do about it now. She just had to stick with it.

'Can you give us an example?'

Angela took a deep breath. 'My son had returned home from school with a bad report and so my husband took him upstairs and gave him a good beating'.

'And you don't think there's anything wrong with that?'

'What's wrong is that you're questioning our methods of raising our children'.

'Was your son physically injured as a result of this beating?'

'That's absolutely none of your business'.

'Angela, I'm sure you know the law and it says that reasonable chastisement may be used by a parent when disciplining their child or else you could be subject to up to five years in prison'.

'Course I'm aware of the law and I would like to see it changed'.

'You want a law that allows parents to beat their children?'

'I want a law that allows parents to raise their children as they see fit without any interference from the state'.

'And how often does your husband take his belt off to your son?'

'None of your business'.

'And does he use his belt on your daughters too?'

'None of your business'.

'Angela, if I got into an argument with you in a bar and I hit you then that would be called assault. So, what's the difference between that and your husband beating your children?'

'The difference is that they're children and need to learn' Angela insisted. 'But the other thing to remember when looking at the attacks that are made against me and my family is the part they are playing in the alarming rise in attacks on all devout and committed Christians in our country. It seems to me these days that one can practise any faith and your beliefs will be protected but not if you're a declared Christian'.

'So, you're saying that people might criticise you not for beating your children but just because you're committed Christians?'

'That's exactly what I'm saying. We're seeing examples of it everywhere these days I'm sorry to say'.

'Angela, if someone disagrees with me on something I don't say it's because I'm a black woman. I say it's because they simply have a different perspective to mine'.

'Well as a Christian in this society, which is increasingly hostile to our beliefs, I can't afford the luxury of that comfortable view'.

'Do you really believe it's that bad?'

'The evidence is all there'.

'So, if someone disagrees with you it's not because they have a different view it's simply because they're being anti-Christian?'

'Correct'.

Ebony thought the woman was talking complete crap in trying to conjure up some kind of nationwide conspiracy against Christians just because people disagreed with her. She also had no time for people who beat their kids no matter what the religious affiliation of the family. It was just wrong as far as she was concerned just like it was wrong to bring everything back to being about race. She'd known racism. She'd grown up in Leeds and had only moved to Blackpool to take up the job with Radio Fylde. It didn't take her long to realise that she stood out as a black woman along the Fylde coast though. It was a very white environment, although it was slowly becoming less so, and it didn't make her feel uncomfortable and it certainly didn't make her think that everyone must be a racist. To think that would've been absurd and also insulting to all her white friends.

'Do you think your children love you, Angela?'

'I've no reason to doubt that considering I'm their mother'.

'Well thank you for your time today, Angela'.

Daniel Lewis had always been taught by his mother that a crisply ironed shirt could cover a multitude of other potential sins when it came to his appearance. If your collars were stiff and the right cufflinks were worn, then a man would always be taken seriously. It was as if she'd looked into his future and seen what was ahead. He wiped a bead of sweat from his forehead with the end of his finger. It was well into the summer holiday season, and he was standing in a conference room one floor above the world- famous ballroom in the Blackpool Tower building along with the heads of the other two consortiums bidding for the town centre redevelopment contract. They'd come to make their pitch in front of the local council and other local interested parties plus members of the press. Daniel was up first. He took his place on the podium in front of a giant model of what his consortium's bid would look like. He was determined that people would understand just how much he was prepared to do to bring real development to the town. He wanted to raise the level of sophistication or, more appropriately, he wanted to bring sophistication to the town centre instead of every entertainment outlet appealing to the lowest common denominators.

He could see the leader of Greater Fylde council, Lesley Hammond, sitting there a couple of metres away with a look on her face that spoke so clearly of the animosity between the two of them. She'd no doubt prefer anyone except Daniel to get the council contract, but Daniel had one or two tricks up his sleeve to try and persuade the whole council to find in favour of his consortium's bid. Lesley Hammond herself was proving to be damnably untouchable. There were no skeletons in her closet especially now she'd smashed the myth that every independent councillor was really a closet Tory. She was happily married to one of the town's paramedics. Two sons completed the nice, happy family unit. Daniel had instructed his people to dig as deep as they could, and deeper, but each time they came up with nothing. There were of course other more permanent measures he could take to deal with the threat posed by Councillor Hammond, but he wanted to leave the door open to that particular course of action for the time being.

He'd been brought up to believe that only his opinion mattered and that others had to pay him due respect. He'd grown up in a solidly working- class Tory household and his parents had absolutely doted on him to the point where he didn't pay anyone else any respect. It didn't work the other way round. Others had to bow to what he believed, and he was like a dog with a bone until they did. If it meant undermining other people, then so be it. He'd been known as a bully at school because of the terror he'd been known to unleash on those who'd dared to disagree with him. He'd been highly skilful at manipulating others into believing he was right, and that his victim was the one with the real issues. Normally he picked on someone who he could see was more intelligent than he was because he couldn't have that. He had to be top dog in every way and more importantly he had to be seen and acknowledged as being top dog. It had stood him well in business. He'd pressured one competitor so badly that the man had ended up committing suicide at which Daniel had gone straight round to the man's grief- stricken wife and got her to sign the papers giving him full control of her late husband's building firm. Then he'd bought it from her at less than half its value whilst she was still in mourning. Fleecing people whenever he could to get what he wanted came as second nature to him. His parents probably wouldn't approve of every aspect of the way he lived his life and conducted himself in business. But then again, they lived their life through him so much that they'd believe any old shit he told them.

Then there was his own family. He'd chosen such an obedient wet blanket of a wife in Angela precisely because she was such an obedient wet blanket. She never questioned him. He could write his own blueprint for what family life meant. Their eldest daughter Melissa was now washed and dried up at nineteen. She'd outlived her usefulness in one way but he'd put her in charge of looking after his finances. She could no longer be used to facilitate his business negotiations because she was too old and past it. His associates liked them young and virginal, even if that part of the transaction had to be faked and they didn't like them when they started to look like women. She should find someone stupid enough to marry her and move out, so she'd no longer be a drain on the household finances. But the ungrateful little bitch didn't seem to be taking the hint. If any businessman worth his salt did a feasibility study into the costs of having children, then they wouldn't have any. The costs over the first fifteen to twenty years were insane, especially when you had four of the little cash draining bleeders. That's why he put his daughters out to work for the family business as soon as he could. He had to recoup some of what he'd spent on having them. There had to be some use for them and now Melissa was employed in his company office looking after those company accounts that he let her have access to.

After Melissa came Verity who at seventeen was proving to be mightily useful. But she also had a shelf life, and she was rapidly reaching the end of it. That only left Deborah who at sixteen was perfectly within the age range but she was dog ugly. She had a birth mark right across her cheek and that had rendered her absolutely useless. Nobody wanted to fuck a young girl with all that redness on her face. Not even the desperate ones. Although she tried. Oh yes, she tried. It was so pathetic and pitiful. She wanted to be chosen, Daddy. She could help you, Daddy. No, you bloody couldn't, you ugly little runt.

Then there was his son Samuel upon whose shoulders he'd place everything one day.

Daniel completed his presentational bid and had become quite animated when extolling the virtues of his consortium's intentions. They wanted to 'change the face of Blackpool' just behind the Golden Mile and give the town a hotel and convention centre that would 'equal and surpass' those in larger towns and cities. He'd delivered what he'd considered to be almost a clarion call to arms of all those who believed in a better future for Blackpool. When he'd finished after taking up all of his allocated ten minutes plus a few moments more, it was open to the press to ask him questions.

'Joshua Walker, Blackpool Evening News' said Josh after he'd stood up and been handed a microphone by one of the event organisers. The look of displeasure on the face of Daniel Lewis pleased Josh no end. They were well known to each other. Walker had recently tried to expose corruption and bribery in Daniel Lewis's firm but in the end hadn't been able to prove anything. It had made Lewis very angry, but it wasn't over yet.

Lewis couldn't risk going after Walker because it would look too obvious, but he knew that Walker would be just waiting for another angle from which to approach it.

'I'd like to ask you this, Mr. Lewis? Have you ever beaten your children with a thick leather belt even though it's against the law?'

The carving knife had been sharpened with such excitable relish that it could probably slice through the finest silk without actually touching it. But that didn't stop Daniel from carrying on the job at the table. He stood there with a look of intensity that grew deeper with every turn of the blade against the sharpener. His wife Angela and his three daughters were all sat round the table in complete silence. They knew better than to pierce the air with their voice unless they were spoken to first. The sharp point at the end of the knife had been at the throat of all of them at one time or another. It had indented the skin just below their chin, forcing their head up and back so he could look into their terror filled eyes. It had even drawn the odd spot of blood for which his daughters were sent straight to bed with no supper because it was all their fault that they now had tiny spots of blood on their clothes.

He finally finished sharpening the knife and a chill went down the spines of them all. He'd come home in that mood they recognised. He'd been quiet, almost silent and they knew that meant there was something seriously wrong.

He placed the knife firmly where the leg of the chicken could be separated from the breast and began to cut. There had better not be any pink pieces of flesh otherwise their part-time housekeeper Katja who was from Latvia would be getting her P45. Katja was the only member of the household who wouldn't let him beat her into obedience. He'd tried it once and she'd hit him back so ferociously that the bruise on his face had remained there for weeks. He couldn't risk letting her go. She might talk.

He had to keep her sweet. However, as he sliced the meat and distributed it to their plates, he could see that it had been perfectly cooked. So, she was saved from just an outburst of his fury.

He saw to it that his wife Angela plus Melissa and Verity all had some and told them to help themselves to vegetables and gravy and start eating. When Deborah realised that he wasn't serving up anything for her she also realised that she must be the one who was heading for punishment. But why? What had she done? She felt sick as the terror overwhelmed her. Neither her mother nor either of her sisters made any comment about her lack of food as they tucked into their own.

'Somebody has been talking' said Daniel in a quiet but firm voice. He'd been humiliated at the bidding meeting that day. None of the journalists had wanted to talk about his consortium's bid. They'd only wanted to question him about how he raises his children. 'Somebody has been talking to the wrong people about our private family affairs and it has to stop'.

'It wasn't me, Daddy' Deborah whimpered in a barely audible stuttering voice.

Daniel closed his eyes and placed two fingers on the bridge of his nose. 'Oh Deborah, Deborah, don't lie to me. It must've been you because you're jealous over never being chosen like your sisters. But you know why that is,'

Deborah started to cry. 'It wasn't me, Daddy, I swear it wasn't'.

Daniel swung round and walloped her across the face. Her stunned silence gave him the opportunity to wallop her on the other side too and by now she was almost hysterical with tears. He grabbed her by the hair and pulled her off her chair. She struggled and screamed as he dragged her round the table towards the door. She tried to make eye contact with her mother and her sisters, but they were purposely avoiding her. Still dragging her by her hair he pulled her upstairs and literally threw her into her room. He ignored her cries of pain and locked the door. Then he went back downstairs and resumed his place at the table.

'So?' he asked cheerfully as if what had just happened had all been a mirage and the howls of distress from Deborah upstairs couldn't be heard. 'Tell me what you've all been doing with your day? And Verity? I need you to be ready to leave here about eight'.

Verity smiled obediently and said 'Okay, Daddy'.

Charlie heard the footsteps along the landing and then the knock on his door. He was sat up in bed reading and could've done without the interruption.

'Charlie! Charlie, love, it's me, your mother!'

Who else could it be but his mother? It had only ever been the two of them. He knew his father. He knew that his mother had been head over heels in love with him, but he'd never wanted to be the kind of settled down family man that she'd always needed. Charlie hadn't heard from his father in weeks. The pub, his father's mates or his latest girlfriend had always taken precedence over Charlie who'd grown used to the constant disappointment. But it had now started to turn his soul and his father was going to have to pay for having abandoned him.

'Come in' said Charlie begrudgingly.

His mother Tricia appeared round the door still in the short red dress she'd been wearing when she went out last night. Her shoulder length hair was dyed blond, and she smiled at him as if the roles were reversed.

'Is that you just in, Mum?'

'Oh, don't say it like that, Charlie' she entreated as she walked into his room and plonked herself down on the edge of his bed. 'I am allowed some fun'.

'Yes, but not when it means we have to go cap in hand to Grandma for food in the middle of the week because you've spent what little we have on a new dress to wear at the weekend'.

'Okay' said his mother, sounding indignant. 'I get a dressing down from my own son. As if I couldn't get any lower'.

'Mum, for God's sake! I can smell the alcohol on you from here. You must've been in a right state last night'.

'I ... had a few' she admitted.

'How many?'

'I don't know'.

'How many?'

'Look I lost count after the second bottle of wine, but Charlie please don't be mad at me'.

'I'm not mad at you, Mum. I'm disgusted. I'm disgusted at the way you behave. Every dress or skirt you buy you take the hem up so that men don't have to use much imagination'.

'Hey, I met a really nice guy last night called Richard'.

'And?'

'He's got a really good job doing something with computers for the water board or whatever it's called these days,'

'And?'

'He said that he hadn't met a woman like me for years'.

'And?'

'He was married and only out for a few drinks with the lads,'.

'I knew that would be the punch line'.

'Oh, give me a break! Look, are you ashamed of me or something?'

'Well, if you must know then yes, I am'.

Tricia recoiled slightly. 'Look son, I know I left you on your own last night ... '

'... and I'm used to it'.

'But you had my mobile number' she pleaded. 'And you could've called your grandma'.

'I did. She was at a concert at our Chloe and Abigail's school. They were going out for a meal after that. I didn't feel like I wanted to intrude even though Grandma said she'd pay for the taxi and the meal. Good job because I don't have any money'.

'Oh yes, your perfect cousins from my perfect sister's marriage to her perfect bank manager husband. Yawn, yawn fucking yawn'.

'So where did it go wrong for you, Mum? Why did it work out for Aunty Rosie and not for you?'

'Because some are born lucky, and some aren't'.

'Oh crap! Because some manage to hold onto their dignity, and some don't!'

Tricia had had enough of this dressing down from her son. She'd gone way past wanting him to respect her, but she was trying to draw the line at the outright contempt he treated her to whenever he had the opportunity. He hadn't always been like it. They used to be close at one time but that seemed like a very dim and distant memory now.

'Look Charlie I don't have to be at work until twelve. Come downstairs and I'll make us some breakfast. I know we've got bread and eggs. I could do them scrambled?'

'Okay. I am pretty hungry'.

'Are you going over to Muhammad's later?'

'Yes'.

'Why couldn't you go over there last night?'

'Because it was Friday night and after prayers that means it's a family night in their house'.

'I see' said Tricia putting on a brave face. 'There's another kick in the teeth'.

'It's not all about you, Mum'

'I'll see you downstairs in ten minutes, Charlie' said Tricia as she made for the door and then stopped. 'Look son, I fell in with a drug dealer and the result was you. I could've given you away, but I didn't. I wanted you, Charlie. You're the best thing I've done with my sorry little life. And if I'm not good enough then I'm sorry but I can't change who I am'.

She closed the door behind her, and Charlie lay in his bed wishing his mother had given him away. He didn't feel anything for her anymore, let alone love.

FOUR

'You know I'd walk a million miles for your Chicken Jalfrezi, Ahmed' said Layla, playfully. She could be a flirt. She admitted that. She and her boyfriend Steve were having dinner at one of their favourite Indian restaurants, the Zest of India, down on Squires Gate Lane, South Shore. They were frequent patrons and had been put at a prominent table in the window. They were more than familiar with all the staff, including the manager Ahmed, whose smile always lit up whenever Layla walked in. The way it was run was typical of almost all Indian restaurants. Indian owned but staffed by Bangladeshis.

'Nice one' said Ahmed who displayed all his top teeth when he smiled and dipped his eyes slightly when a compliment was paid him. It was a curiously reassuring habit of his and one of the things you notice about people you see often. He had a youthful, handsome looking face with big, dark eyes and was probably the kind of man who would preserve his looks and wouldn't look any older right the way through until his at least his fifties, if then. He'd been standing back whilst two of his waiters served the food but once they were done, he stepped forward again. Layla was eagerly waiting to tuck into her beloved Jalfrezi, and Steve had also gone for his usual which was a fairly hot Bangladeshi dish called a Lamb Mona Hari. Pilau rice and a couple of garlic naan breads completed the feast just waiting to be consumed by the two eager curry fans. 'Are you alright for drinks?'

Layla still had half a bottle of water to consume. Steve was on the Cobra beers, but he already had almost a full one to get through so Layla politely declined Ahmed's enquiry for the time being.

'I'll let you enjoy your food then' said Ahmed with his usual beaming smile. 'I'll see you later'.

'It's a good job I'm not a jealous kind of guy' said Steve, smiling as he tore off a piece of his garlic naan bread to dip into the Mona Hari sauce of his dish. Just the sauce was like food heaven to him.

'I don't know what you mean' said Layla in feigned innocence.

'You've got them all wrapped round your little finger in here,' said Steve. 'I just come along for the show'.

'Well at least you get a free ticket' said Layla, laughing.

'He's just put his prices up'.

'Now Steve, don't turn into one of those Northern men who moan about the cost of everything and the value of nothing'.

'No chance. I've seen enough of that with my dad and our Trevor. I'll never get like those two, don't you worry'.

Steve's mother had recently celebrated her sixtieth birthday and his father had taken her to Rome because she'd always wanted to go. Apparently, he'd done nothing but moan and complain about the cost of everything whilst they were there and had continued after they'd got back. His Mum had burst into tears at one point and told his father that they should never have gone and that he'd ruined the whole thing for her with his miserable attitude. On hearing that, Steve had wanted to punch his stupid, insensitive louse of a father. It wasn't as if his parents couldn't afford it. They had a fair bit stashed away, but his father hated spending any of it on what he called 'indulgences'. He hated going to restaurants. He didn't see the point of going out to eat when there was food in the house. That had been another one of his gripes about Rome. All that pasta and nothing proper to eat. Whenever Steve's Mum did manage to drag his father for a meal out it was always to their local pub, and he always ordered steak and kidney pudding and chips. He'd done it for years and Steve was determined never to turn into his father like his older brother Trevor had sadly done.

'I'm relieved to hear it' said Layla who never had any doubt in the first place. Steve was nothing like his father or brother. Thank God. She looked at him and breathed in deeply. She loved him so much. He looked great tonight in his plain white t-shirt and faded blue jeans. She followed his fury arms up to where the tattoos on his upper arms were just visible below the short sleeves of his t-shirt. She'd be able to follow the line of each design with her fingertip when they got to bed later.

'Steve, we are okay, aren't we?'

Steve was puzzled by the question. 'Okay? Course we're okay. Why do you ask?'

'Well, I know you want to think about starting a family and I've asked if we can wait'.

'And I'm okay with that. Layla, I understand, you know I do. You've just been promoted, and you need to get some cases under your belt. I get all of that. And we're both young. It doesn't matter if we put it off for a while'.

'That's what I heard you say before'.

'So why are you doubting me now?'

'When I remember how much you want kids and I'm letting my career stand in your way'.

'Layla, I've got all I need in you' said Steve. He took hold of her hand. 'I've never felt more complete than during the time I've been with you. You get me more than any other woman I've ever met and yes, I want kids and I want them with you. But I never want us to have them because you feel under pressure. You do understand that?'

'Yeah, I do,' said Layla. 'And I want kids too'.

'I know,' said Steve. 'But when the time is right for both of us,'.

'I just didn't want you to feel like you were missing out'.

'How could I feel that when I'm with a woman like you?'

'You know what I mean'.

'I do,' said Steve. 'And when you feel ready to start thinking about having a family, we'll talk about it. Now in the meantime keep getting stuck into that Jalfrezi before I stick my fork in and steal it'.

'You wouldn't dare'.

'Try me'.

Iain Kempton was so in need of a holiday. He took his eyes off his computer and leaned back in his chair. He rubbed the bridge of his nose with his forefingers. Only three weeks to go and then he and his husband Gavin would be jetting off to Gran Canaria for a fortnight. He really couldn't wait. Gavin had been working hard in his job as the manager of the council leaders' office and they both needed a break. Iain was a social worker and a rather senior one at that which meant that as government cuts started to really bite into social provision his workload just kept getting bigger and bigger. It was just before eight in the morning but he had to come in early every day now just so he could at least try to keep on top of his emails if nothing else. He wished he hadn't had that last vodka last night though. He really shouldn't drink on a school night, but he'd felt like a cup of tea just wouldn't do what he needed it to. Why couldn't he be stronger and just resist? Still, only three days to go until the weekend. Thank fuck.

He was planning magnificent hangovers for both Saturday and Sunday morning.

He looked up and saw his manager Wendy waddling her way through the large open plan office that Iain and the other social workers shared with all the administration staff. Always immaculately turned out in long skirt and expensive looking blouse, hair and make-up done perfectly, she was clutching her mobile phone in one hand and a carton of cottage cheese in the other. He wondered what the hell she was doing with that. Did she really think it would make people believe she ate healthily? She probably used it as a dip to go with her KFC more like. She was really piling it on. The poor cunt could barely keep a conversation going sometimes as she walked along because she had so little breath and her tits had definitely seen better days. But she was sad. She'd never got over losing the love of her life to another woman years ago and she'd recently bumped into him again. He was still happily married to the bitch who'd taken him off her, they had two 'great' teenage kids and he was enjoying life. Wendy on the other hand spent most Friday and Saturday nights getting pissed alone at home and when she ran out of wine, she ordered a taxi to go and get her a couple more bottles. Iain had tried to warn her about her drinking and her weight gain, but she'd almost given up on herself. She said that she now saw her life as a problem without a solution and she lived in a world of romantic impossibility. She could see no future for herself and could never imagine being happy again. Iain had wanted so much to help her, but he didn't know what to do. He couldn't wave a magic wand and bring her a man to sweep her off her feet. The man would need to have strong muscles to do that anyway. She always wore giant dangly earrings that a small dog could probably jump through once it had got past her half a dozen chins. Iain didn't believe that just because someone was overweight it meant they were unworthy to be loved. He didn't believe that for one second and he only wanted her to lose weight for her health. Like any friend he just wanted her to have a good life. And one thing he was glad that he had in his favour when it came to Wendy was that he was gay, and she liked gay men. She didn't like straight men and immediately went on the defensive whenever she met one although any fool could see that it went back to the bloke who'd dumped her. She'd been lucky though. Two straight male members of staff had accused her of bullying on two separate occasions but each time, like all clever bullies, she'd managed to wriggle her way out of it even though Iain and everyone else knew she was as guilty as sin because they knew full well how she operated in that bitter and twisted side of hers that she couldn't always keep at bay. He was convinced she'd come a cropper one day. Even a fat cat only has nine lives.

'Good morning, darling!' Wendy greeted as she approached Iain's desk.

'Good morning, Wendy' Iain replied between clenched teeth. How many times had he told her that he didn't like being called 'darling' That was a term of endearment reserved only for his mother and for his husband. Everybody has their little foibles, and this was his. But would the fat cow ever listen?

'Iain, could I see you for a minute, please?' Wendy commanded in a husky whispering voice. 'In my office, lovely'.

'Sounds like you haven't given up the fags yet, Wendy?' said Iain as he stood up and followed her.

'No' she smiled. 'And you haven't because you married yours'.

'A bit early for funnies, love' said Iain as he walked into Wendy's office after her and closed the door behind him. He sat down in front of her desk. She manoevred her way slightly awkwardly round her desk and sat down in her large black leather swivel chair. Iain heard it creak as it took her weight. She then composed herself by using a large flannel that she kept in her desk to wipe away the light beads of sweat that had appeared on her face. Then she blew her nose and was ready.

'Now, I'm giving you this case because I know you'll be able to cut through any bullshit the family decide to throw around it' Wendy announced as she handed him a large file that had been sitting on her desk.

'Sounds intriguing?' said Iain as he took the file from her and briefly scanned the first page.

'You might not think so when you get into it' said Wendy. 'Are you familiar with the Lewis family over in Poulton?'

'Isn't the mother the one who wants it to be made legal for parents to be able to beat their children?'

'That's her,' said Wendy. 'Lovely sounding woman. Probably gets into a foul mood if she can't find a puppy to run over and kill on any given day. Anyway, she let it slip over the radio the other day about a specific incident involving the beating of her son Samuel. That has now been backed up by an anonymous phone call to us. We don't have any choice but to investigate'.

'Too right,' said Iain. 'Do we or the police have any idea about who the anonymous caller was?'

'I'm afraid not' Wendy replied. 'Just that it was female and sounded adult. So can I leave it in your capable hands?'

'Yes,' said Iain, relishing the opportunity to get his teeth into something difficult. 'You most certainly can'.

'But tread carefully' Wendy warned. 'There have been whispers about child abuse in the family before, but all previous investigations have ended in a blaze of their accusations that we, social services, were picking on them because they're devout Christians. But it's a smoke screen'.

'A means of preventing us getting to the truth'.

'Precisely. They've got very powerful connections and they can bring stones raining down on our department just to ruin the reputation of otherwise blemish free members of staff'.

'Well,' said Iain, licking his lips eagerly. Everything had been so bloody routine lately. This was like God sending him down something with which he could end up making a real difference. 'They haven't come up against me yet, have they?'

Wendy smiled. 'I was hoping you'd look at it that way'.

When Katja had originally arrived in Blackpool from the Latvian capital city of Riga she hadn't quite known what to make of it. During the years of Soviet occupation of her country a lot of what had been placed in front of the population as popular entertainment had been nothing more than Soviet propaganda that was cheap and nasty with the emphasis on both the cheap and the nasty. She liked the English expression 'cheap and nasty'. She'd used it a lot since she came to Blackpool and despite all she saw in the newspapers about 'immigrants go home' and all the stuff she heard on radio phone-ins and TV debates about there being too many Eastern Europeans in the country, even after Brexit, she'd soon found that she could speak better English than most of those who said that she and her fellow eastern Europeans were taking their jobs. And in Blackpool if you called everybody 'love' then you usually had them eating out of the palm of your hand especially the older ones although some of them could be difficult. They seemed to think it was your fault that they couldn't hear what you were saying rather than the fact that they were going deaf. Some of the workmen who came into the café where she worked thought they had a chance. They probably worked on the assumption that girls like Katja would be so desperate to stay in the UK that they'd marry any old ugly specimen. But she wasn't planning to stay anyway. She planned to perfect her English, earn some proper cash and then she'd be off back home again.

Like many of her fellow Latvians she'd fallen in immediately with the community of her compatriots, thanks to friend of friend contacts she'd been in contact with before she left home, and she'd found herself a flat to share just up from Blackpool North station at the top end of Talbot Road. Her two flatmates, a girl called Marika who worked with her in the café behind the tower and a guy called Igor who spent all day labouring on a building site, were also Latvians and their shared geographical distance from their mother country had bred into them a camaraderie that all three of them cherished. They'd become very close friends and were all grateful that they hadn't come to the UK as the victims of human traffickers who'd brought them over to be part of some slave labour hell hole. They knew it had happened to some of their fellow Latvians, and other Eastern Europeans, and they thanked God every day that they'd each come here of their own free will and not because they'd been desperate enough to pay money to some evil criminals. They did it their own way. They booked their tickets back home for holidays on the budget airline out of Liverpool well in advance so that they'd get the cheapest fares. Some of their friends took the coach back to save even more money but it took almost three days each way and that meant six days out of your time back home.

All three of them had an additional job. Once Katja finished her early shift at the café she caught the bus from round the corner out to Poulton where she cleaned the house and cooked the evening meal for the Lewis family. Her flatmate Marika worked behind the bar of a pub just off the promenade, and Igor put his well- toned body to use as an exotic dancer, mainly in gay clubs and on hen nights. He wasn't gay at all, but he played up to his attractiveness to gay men and he also rather liked the attention of excited, drunken women who wanted to get their hands on his large manhood. They all worked hard. That was the point. They paid their taxes. They wanted nothing more from the country that had given them such opportunity than to make their own unique contribution. They were eager to give as well as to take.

But somehow things had gone a lot deeper than that for

Katja. Her job at the Lewis house was causing her a lot of distress. She'd never known a man as evil as Daniel Lewis in the way he treated his children. He truly was evil. She saw it in his eyes. Her father had once told her of the time when the KGB had tortured the life out of his brother when they suspected him of being a proactive Latvian nationalist in the old days of the Soviet occupation. He said he'd never forget the look in the eyes of the three agents who rang the door of his parents' house one night and dumped the body of his brother when they opened it. The description of that look that her father had told her about was the same as what she saw in the eyes of Daniel Lewis. He was a psychopath. He didn't value any life other than his own.

She was just lying on her bed having a bit of a snooze when she heard the buzzer sound and Igor speaking into the intercom to see who was wanting one of them outside the main door downstairs. Then he knocked on Katja's door and Igor popped his head round.

'Katja, its Melissa. Do you want me to tell her you're out?'

Katja didn't know whether to laugh or cry. 'No, let her up. Thanks'.

'I'll be in the living room if you need me'.

'Thanks, Igor, but I'll be okay'.

In the moments before Melissa appeared Katja wondered what she was going to do. When she came to the UK, she hadn't bargained on falling in love with someone like Melissa Lewis, eldest daughter of the evil Daniel. When she was growing up, she'd always felt like she could be at least bisexual. She used to sometimes get the same kind of feelings from looking at girls as she did at boys and whilst there were places to go in Riga where she could meet other women like her, it wasn't as easy to be anything other than straight in Latvia. But here in Blackpool and other places in the UK she'd been to like Manchester, people seemed to be very open about their feelings. There were pride marches all over the place where the police actually joined in instead of trying to break it up like they did in many places in Eastern Europe and, of course, Russia. Society in the UK is very different to how it is in Latvia, especially when it comes to matters of sexuality. She much preferred the UK for that openness and that visibility where people didn't have to be scared. But one day she was going back to Latvia, and it would all be so different again.

She sat up with a pillow behind her back and crossed her legs over at her ankles. Melissa came in and Katja was immediately struck by her beauty just like she'd been the first time she'd met her at the Lewis house. She thought she'd been quite circumspect that night but then Melissa offered her a lift back into town once she was done, and on the way, she told Katja that she was a lesbian and that she'd noticed the way Katja had been looking at her. She also told her that she felt the same way too. She came back to Katja's flat, and they made out. Melissa had to watch the time because she wasn't allowed to be late back. But the love making they'd indulged themselves in had been enough to make them understand their attraction for each other. Katja had only slept with a couple of women before and though she kept her fingernails short she was still sensitive and delicate with the way she brought Melissa to an orgasm and then licked up every last drop. It had been enough to send Melissa into a lustful frenzy before turning Katja onto her back and finding all those places that made her love doing it to women. Everything a woman had from her lips down through her breasts to the inside of her thighs and that ultimate place of pleasure between her legs were like a magical wonderland to Melissa. She didn't hate men although she could've had every reason to after all the years of her father pimping her out to business associates who he wanted to conclude deals with or enemies he wanted to 'get something on'. She'd been with over forty men in those circumstances and now her sister Verity was taking her turn as the family sex worker. She didn't hate men. But she hated her father and one day she was going to make sure he got his for all the pain he'd caused. What had always made it worse was that her mother had always just stood by and watched. She never did anything to stop him. That made her as bad as him as far as Melissa was concerned. She never spoke about any of this to her sisters or her brother. Such was the way within the family that confidences could be broken as a matter of preserving your own survival. Just like it had been in Nazi Germany or other totalitarian states. That's why her father was no better than any other dictator in promoting a lack of trust amongst inhabitants so as to avoid any of them disclosing any secrets.

'I waited half an hour for you' said Melissa, referring to the previous evening when they'd arranged to meet in town to go for drinks and some dinner. 'I was crushed when you didn't show up'. She was standing at the end of Katja's bed looking down at her in the half light. Katja had her curtains drawn and the sun was beginning to go down outside. 'Why didn't you pick up the phone when I called or answer at least one of my texts? I felt such a fool standing there surrounded by happy people going their various ways'.

'I'm sorry'.

'Sorry? You're sorry? Do you know how easily you can break my heart?'

Katja looked up at her. Her long black hair was smooth and shiny, and she was wearing a white short-sleeved shirt over pink jeans, and white pumps. Her face was the usual porcelain white, and her large eyes and red covered lips were all giving Katja that familiar feeling. Her physical desire for Melissa was strong but she didn't know if she could deal with all the drama that goes with her. She felt sorry for her having to deal with her evil brute of a father and everything he put her and the rest of her family through. God knows what he'd do if he found out about their relationship. It just didn't bear thinking about. She held out her hands and Melissa picked them up and kissed them all over.

Then she placed one on the side of Katja's face and gave her that look that never failed.

'Do you want to take your clothes off and get into bed with me?' Katja asked.

'I thought you'd never ask'.

After they'd made love and were able to rest their mutual lust for a while, they snuggled up together with their arms around each other, face to face.

'Girl, please don't hurt me again like you did last night,' said Melissa. 'I don't think I could take it if you did'.

'I meant it when I said I was sorry, Melissa'.

'I know, I know'.

'No, I don't think you do' said Katja.

'What? Are you saying you don't think we are meant to be together? Are you saying that you are going to break my heart?'

'No, no, no, Melissa. Now listen because this is how I really feel. I want to be with you. I want to be with you more than anything. But I need to know that you want to be with me for all the right reasons,'.

'What do you mean?'

'Melissa, I want you to want to be with me because you love me and not because you can use me to get out of your horrible home situation'.

'Katja, I'd never use you like that'.

'But you see what I mean? I have to protect myself in case you go off with someone else after you're able to leave home for me'.

Melissa started to cry and stroked the side of Katja's face. She'd sometimes wondered if being a lesbian was some kind of subconscious reaction to everything her father had put her through. But over time she'd become convinced that it definitely was not such a reaction. She was a lesbian because she'd been born that way and she never wanted to go back to being anything else. She had to make Katja understand that because the girl held the key to whether or not she was going to be happy.

'Katja, I've been through so much because of my father but he didn't make me a lesbian. He and all his friends didn't make me want to reject men in that way for the rest of my life. Katja, girl, I want to be with you because I love you and you have to believe that. You really have to because it's true. I'm not going to let my father fuck up the rest of my life like he's fucked it up so far by falling for the first woman who gives me any real sense of worth or just because she shows me a way to get out'.

'You're really sure of that?'

'One hundred and ten percent. I feel so lucky that the universe has brought us both together in this way. I need you, Katja. I love you and I need you and it has nothing whatsoever to do with anything my father did to me. You have to believe me, Katja. Please say that you do'.

'I do' said Katja, tearfully. 'You're a nightmare, Melissa, a total nightmare. But a good one and I do love you and I do believe what you say'.

'Good' said Melissa. 'Because I've got a plan and it now includes you. I can't say anything about it at the moment, but we'll soon be living our lives a long way from here and there won't be a thing my father can do about it'.

FIVE

DS Keith Drake was driving, and DI Layla Khan was in the passenger seat. It would've been a short two minute ride from the old police station at Bonny Street to the crime scene they'd just been called out to, but from the new police HQ it was a lot further, and they'd managed to get stuck behind one of the horse and carriages that plied their trade up and down the promenade for the sake of tourists who didn't have anything better to do with their money. They managed to turn off the Promenade at Manchester Square and head down Lytham Road towards one of the dead-end side streets that went off to the left. The delay only served to increase the tension of the barely disguised antagonism between Khan and Drake, and nothing much was made in the way of conversation or even small talk. But Layla also noticed a bit of a smell about Drake. Not a form of body odour as such but the kind of clinging aroma that suggested to Layla that he may have slept last night in the clothes he was wearing today. What was that all about? She lowered the window on her side and hoped that would send him a message to turn up for work in clean clothes in the future. Otherwise, she'd have to have a word and she can't have been the only one who'd noticed.

'There's one body, ma'am' said Sergeant Luke Morris, scene of crime officer once they'd arrived. 'Looks like a teenage girl'.

'And on the game, I expect?' Drake threw in.

'I can't say for sure, sir at this point' Morris answered. 'But this is an area that is known to be used by prostitutes and their clients'.

'So that's a yes then,' said Drake.

'It's an educated guess, sir' said Morris who hadn't taken at all to this prat of a detective who seemed to think he knew it all. 'That's as far as I'm going in the absence of any facts on this unfortunate young woman'.

Drake sighed wearily as if he was addressing the same audience on the same theories for the millionth time. 'Look, she'll be a little scrubber from Leyland or Burnley or some other such hole who thought that Blackpool was mecca and who came here to try and get herself a piece of the big time but instead she ended up falling fowl of her pimp and paid the ultimate price. Sad and all that for a moment or two but at least it's one less for social services to worry about. Her parents, if she's got any, won't miss her unless they were getting benefits for her and if they were then it won't be in their interest to declare her missing because it'll mean them losing some of the cash that keeps them in fags and booze'.

'DS Drake, would you keep your squalid opinions to yourself until we've had time to investigate, please' said Layla, sternly. She'd already had a belly full of him and it was only ten o'clock in the morning on the first day of a murder investigation. But she wouldn't tolerate any kind of class distinction when it came to investigating crime. It was up there with racism and sexism and homophobia. She just wouldn't allow it. Even if Drake turned out to be right in his assumptions.

'I'm merely stating the obvious according to my professional experience, ma'am'.

'Oh well let's just pack up and go home then' said Layla, irritated by the pious tone in his voice. 'Let's not bother being police officers and investigate the murder of this teenager who may be about the same age as your daughter Kirsty'.

'But ma'am, with all due respect ... '

'... well that makes a nice change, DS Drake'.

'We know what the outcome of the investigation into this girl's background will be, ma'am. And the apple doesn't fall far from the tree. Her patch was probably round here'.

'Oh, and is this where you pick up your tricks, DS Drake?' asked Layla lightly as if she was asking him where he bought his winter coat. Out of the corner of her eye she would swear she could see Sergeant Morris trying not to laugh.

'I have never paid for sex in my life' he stated, indignantly.

'Now that does surprise me' said Layla who was aware that she might be going a bit too far but what the fuck. The tosser deserved it and more. 'But perhaps you should. It might even out your temper a little because you're clearly not getting any at the moment'.

Drake was seething. 'If I'd as much as hinted to a female officer that she needed a good shag I'd have been reprimanded'.

'Yes, well you're not a woman and you didn't say it, so you won't be reprimanded' said Layla who loved acting like a lad when the 'lad' in question clearly didn't see how she was taking the piss. 'You don't like a taste of your own medicine, do you Keith?'

'And is that what this is all about?'

'You could say,' said Layla. 'You men have been getting away with it for centuries. We're just getting our own back for a while'.

'And you've got an answer for everything'.

'Yes, it's called being the boss'.

'Excuse me, ma'am?' said Sergeant Morris who'd had quite enough of this little floor show. 'If I could just carry on before getting back to my other duties?'

'Yes, of course, I'm sorry Sergeant Morris. What else can you tell us?'

'The pathologist thinks she's been there for several days. She was found by a tram driver who lives just round the corner on Bloomfield Road and who was taking his dog for a walk before he went in to start his early shift'.

'A tram driver?' Drake questioned. 'You mean ordinary decent people live here amongst all the dregs of society?

'DS Drake' Layla cautioned. 'If you don't mind'. She then turned to Sergeant Morris. 'Well thank you, Sergeant Morris. We'll let you get on now'.

'Thank you, ma'am'.

Layla and Drake walked over to where the scene had been cordoned off with the usual police tape. The short street consisted of a dozen terraced houses on each side, some of which had formerly been small hotels and others had been family homes since they were constructed probably a century ago. Now they'd all been converted into flats. At the dead end of the street a brick wall around five or so metres high separated the street from the large car parking space attached to Blackpool Town football club. The body had been dumped behind a clump of young trees that lined more or less the whole length of the wall. In front of the trees were half a dozen large high rubbish containers for use by all the flat dwellers and the stench was a little distracting.

DI Khan and DS Drake bent down and went under the crime scene tapes. Layla glanced back to the other end of the street where Lytham Road provided the only access. She could see buses and vans going past frequently as well as cars. It was one of the main roads south out of the town and there were heaps of takeaway food outlets in the immediate area too, including a chippy right on the corner. So, did anybody see anything? It was probably late at night or early in the morning when the body was dumped, and nobody liked to take much notice of each other in neighbourhoods like this. The population was transient and low paid. They wouldn't think it was in their interests to get involved with strange goings on. Take the cash they got from working in the chip shop or the amusement arcade and think about where they're going to go for the winter. But it isn't winter yet and there might just be someone who may have seen something. She looked up and around at all the windows. Some of them were open and timid eyes were watching and looking.

'Keith, get uniform to do a thorough door to door going six blocks up and six blocks down' said Layla who then caught another whiff of the smell there was on him today. She deliberately coughed to clear her throat of it. 'I want to know if anyone saw anything over the last few days, however trivial they think it might be and I want to know when these bins are emptied. It might give us an idea as to how long the victim has been here. And see if we can get CCTV of the football ground car park. Even if the killer didn't use that as an access point to the end of this street, it might've picked up something useful'.

'Me and the wife went to see Rod Stewart there last year' Keith stated almost wistfully as he followed Layla's eyes towards the football ground.

'Yes, I remember'.

'He was fantastic. I'll always remember it'.

'Are you okay, Keith?'

'Yes' Keith answered curtly.

'I was just asking out of concern, that's all'.

'Well, I'm okay so don't bother being concerned,' said Drake. Then he added 'Ma'am'.

Drake then used his mobile to carry out his boss's orders whilst Layla herself stood and contemplated further for a moment about what they might be up against with this case. Then when Drake had finished, they both went inside the white tent that had been erected over the body of the victim and began talking to the pathologist, Ross Carter. Carter was in his late twenties and relatively new to the game. Because of his rugged good looks, wavy dark brown hair and that permanent just got of bed stubble on his face, he was the lust magnet for all the ladies, and the men who were that way inclined, of the various Blackpool law enforcement agencies that he came into contact with. Despite himself, Keith actually quite liked Ross and liked being around him. He had this bizarre idea that some of the ladies who Ross attracted wherever he went might give up on their main target and focus on him instead. He'd never admit it, but God knows he needed help in that direction now that he was single again. He didn't like being on his own. He wasn't used to it. He was scared of trying to function as a single man because he'd never had to. He'd met his wife Ellen when they were both fifteen. They'd lost their virginity to each other and there'd never been any other lovers for either of them. And now, almost twenty years and two kids later Ellen wanted out. He could tell that DI Khan suspected that things weren't good with him in some way. It was as clear as mud from what she said before. She wasn't stupid. He'd give her that much at least.

'So, how's Blackpool's law enforcement pin up boy?' Layla greeted as she walked up to Ross Carter and resisted the temptation to pinch his bum.

'Fine, thank you newly promoted DI Khan' said Ross, smiling. 'Congratulations'.

'Thank you. And how are things in Montreal?'

Ross looked away but kept his smile. 'They're good, thank you'.

'When are you going over again?'

'October' Ross answered.

Layla thought there was a slight air of mystery hanging around this hot looking man, a slight air of things not quite ringing altogether true. He'd told Layla just what he'd told everybody else in that his girlfriend was Canadian and lived in Montreal. Nobody had ever seen her or even a picture of her and he'd once admitted to Layla that the UK immigration authorities had turned down their initial application for her to come over and join him in the UK because they didn't believe that their relationship was genuine. Then he claimed that he only went over there two or three times a year because of finances. But Layla had never met a poor pathologist and she knew that tickets could be bought to Montreal for four or five hundred quid which would be nothing on his salary, especially as he only rented here in Blackpool and hadn't yet got himself on the property ladder. There was no reason to believe that he wasn't telling the whole truth but the copper in Layla sensed there was more to Ross Carter's back story than met the eye of his friends around Blackpool. It didn't take anything away from the fact however that the man was as fit as bloody fuck.

'So, what's there to tell us about here, Ross?' asked Layla. She let her lips rest slightly open like she always did when she was talking to him. She'd never taste the goods though even if he did offer it to her on a plate. Lust was one thing, but she loved her Steve too much and would never cheat on him.

'A young girl in her middle teens I suspect' Ross explained. He wiped some sweat from his forehead with the back of his hand. It was one of those hot, humid kind of August days when everyone longed for the lowering of temperatures that always seemed to come with the switching on of the illuminations in September. 'I'll know more when I get the body back to the lab, but it looks to me like she'd been dead for at least twenty-four hours and probably longer. I'd say at first look about three, maybe four days.

'And just look at the way she's been dumped like that' said Layla sadly as she looked down at the body that was awaiting transportation to Ross Carter's lab. 'So young, so much potential and now all flushed out and gone'.

'I know, it's sickening' Ross agreed.

'Any sign of sexual activity?'

'It looks like she'd had sexual intercourse in recent days, yes' said Carter. 'No surprise there but there is something else about her that puzzles me'.

'In what way and why?' asked Drake.

'She was carrying the usual props of the working girl' Ross went on without a hint of judgement in his voice. That's why Layla took him seriously. 'Cigarettes, lighter, perfume, chewing gum, tissues, wet wipes, a wad of cash and a hairbrush. Everything their line of work dictated'.

'So, somebody is knocking off prostitutes' said Layla in a deadpan voice. 'That's not exactly new in the world of crime fighting, Ross'.

'No, but like I say, there is something a little unusual about this one,' said Ross. 'There's a fresh syringe mark against the carotid artery in her neck'.

'So, she was a drug addict,' said Drake. 'Again, nothing new there'.

'That's not where drug addicts inject themselves' said Ross a little impatiently and without looking at Drake because he couldn't stand him. He detested the way he set himself up as some kind of Jeremy Clarkson with a line in offensive talk. All Ross saw was a desperate man trying to make himself stand out in the crowd. Maybe he didn't get enough attention when he was a kid. 'Not in their necks. Their arms or maybe even their legs but not their necks. Now our victim here had been injecting in her arm and there are numerous marks to prove it'.

'Heroin?' Layla suggested more as a loud thought than an actual question.

'Most likely but I'll confirm that after I get her blood tested,' said Ross. 'But the marks on her arms suggest she's been an addict for a while'.

'She could be on methadone?' said Drake. 'That doesn't have to be injected and it's given out to those who are trying to come off heroin'.

'That's right' Ross confirmed. He was astonished that Drake

had actually uttered something sensible. 'And it's yet something else I'll check when we get back to the lab. Now the method of killing is strangulation. There are finger and hand marks round her neck. So, I don't believe at this stage that she was injected with anything as part of the murder'.

'So, what do you think the syringe mark on her neck is all about?' asked Layla.

'I think that a syringe was used to take a sample of her blood after she'd died'.

'Why?' asked Drake.

'Well, that's where I hand over to you detectives to find out,' said Ross. 'But I think the killer took a sample of her blood after they'd killed her. It wouldn't be before because she'd have struggled too much'.

'So, you're saying we could have some kind of vampire on our hands here?' Drake questioned incredulously.

'I'm saying that you need to work out why someone would take a sample of their victims' blood and what they plan to do with it'.

Layla looked down at the victim and felt a shiver go down her spine.

Muhammad was Charlie's best mate from school and his house was like a second home to him. Muhammad had been his best mate since they'd started infants' school together and his house was like a glimpse into a parallel universe where Charlie could witness what a real family looked like. Charlie's Mum and Dad were committed to their kids and the family life they built around them. Muhammad and his two sisters would know nothing of the pain that comes from not knowing where your mother was going to get your next meal from or when you have to hide behind the sofa because there are debt collectors banging on the door. His mother had either drunkenly or angrily told him a thousand times where she got her total lack of a grip on life from. She blamed it entirely on her parents who she said for some reason didn't love her as much as they loved her sister Rosie and that she had to fight for their attention. His Grandma and Granddad had told him that it simply wasn't true. They'd told of a little girl who was never satisfied, who was desperately hard to please and who was so highly strung that she made them want to tear their hair out at times because she could truly cause a row in an empty house. His Grandma blamed her for the fact that her father dropped dead from a massive heart attack just a week short of his sixtieth birthday. Charlie used to think his grandma in particular was too hard on his mother. But now he'd just run out of breaks to give her. It had gone way beyond that now and for him and his mother Charlie just couldn't see a way back.

'I wanted to ask you, mate?' said Charlie. He was lying on his back on the floor of Muhammad's bedroom with his hands crossed behind the back of his head and his feet crossed at his ankles. 'Are you going to that talk at the mosque on Friday by that guy from Iraq?'

'No, mate' said Muhammad who was sitting cross legged on his bed playing with his x-box machine. He stopped and turned to his friend. 'And neither should you'.

'What do you mean?'

'Come on, mate, I know you're tempted,' said Muhammad. 'You want to embrace what you think Islam is all about. But it's not about what that guy is offering, believe me and you don't have to do it in order to thank my family for making you a part of us'.

'I'm not doing that'.

'You are mate. I can see it'.

'But what if he's speaking the truth?'

'Charlie, I know the man. I've read his stuff. It's got nothing to do with who I am as a Muslim and that goes for all of my family. He's going after the impressionable. He's preaching a message of complete intolerance of anything that isn't fundamentalist Muslim and that's not where I or any member of my family is. So, my advice as your best mate, and a practicing Muslim, is not to go anywhere near that meeting'.

SIX

Iain Kempton decided to make an early start to drive out to the boarding school where Samuel Lewis was a student. He'd looked over all the previous accounts when allegations of physical abuse had been leveled against Samuel's father Daniel Lewis and knew that if he was going to get anywhere and finally uncover the truth, he'd need to be particularly careful and thorough in the way he went about everything. Angela Lewis had already hit the air waves in the last twenty-four hours since it had been 'leaked' to the press that another investigation was going to take place and protested at 'the way they were being treated' with Angela Lewis displaying more than enough crocodile tears at their hastily arranged press conference in which they'd accused social services of hounding them for reasons of the current political correctness that is hounding devout Christians. But all that social services had done was to respond to the anonymous tip off about Samuel in the usual way they would whatever the religious creed of the family involved and according to standard procedures. Iain's job as a social worker was to protect vulnerable children in society and it didn't matter one bit to him what the family background was. If someone was guilty, then they were guilty. End of.

He went over the rules in his head for the thousandth time.

If parents are suspected of beating their children with a belt or cane, then they would be reported to 'social care' which is the name of the department where Iain works. If it was a teacher then it would be reported to the child protection officer in the school and then a social worker, like Iain, would call and a social assessment would be made. This was known as an initial assessment. This was when the police could get involved, because only they can prosecute the parents, or remove the children on a child protection order. If it doesn't need to go that far at this initial stage, then a child in need plan can be instigated and the child placed on a child protection plan.

If on the other hand no evidence of abuse can be found, then no further action is taken but the case remains on the system. This is what happened with the Lewis family last time Daniel Lewis was accused of beating their son Samuel. Most parents would deny it happening, but this would make no difference if there was other evidence or if there is a disclosure from the child that the abuse is taking place. And the rule of thumb is that the child is always believed.

But in this case, it wasn't the child who'd talked. Or at least they didn't think it was. When they listened to the recording of the call that had come through it was a woman's voice. Could it have been one of the boy's three sisters in which case they very definitely wouldn't have wanted to be identified? Could it have been the boy's mother Angela Lewis? She'd have had even less reason to be identified unless she was playing some kind of two-handed game where she supports her husband in public whilst trying to bring his reign of terror within the family to an end in private. The one who is guilty is often protesting their innocence from the inside, and Iain knew from much of his own experience that there were mothers out there who protect their husbands from being revealed as a child abuser by behaving as if it isn't happening and by claiming that the child is actually lying. He'd got so frustrated with so many of them. Were they that desperate to hold onto a man that they were prepared to see their children abused? What did that say about them as individual women? He'd always been glad of procedures that prevented him from venting the strength of his own feelings, but they couldn't control the truth of what he kept inside his own head. Those who stand by whilst others are abused were equally as culpable. He'd often tried to put this simple truth across to colleagues in departmental meetings, but he'd always been drowned out by voices calling for more 'compassion and understanding'. Fine, but where does that come in to trying to fix a child whose father had physically abused them whilst their mother had stood by and done nothing? He was trying not to judge the whole thing before he had all the facts or even spoken to Samuel but there was a part of him that couldn't help it. He may be a social worker, but he was still human. So much shit was wrapped up in the word 'professional'. So many progressive truths were buried in it.

It was a fairly direct route over to the picturesque spot in the heart of the Ribble Valley where the boarding school that Samuel Lewis attended was situated. When he got there, he wasn't surprised that it was all very true blue Tory round these parts. He could almost see the top of the aspiration ladder on every flowering bulb in every front garden. It reminded him of the places along the Fylde coast that don't like to be associated with being next to Blackpool like St Annes, Wrea Green or Staining. This was where people didn't give a damn about equality or social justice just as long as their council tax bills were kept low. They'd made it and they didn't see why they should ever have to contribute to wider society. Iain and his husband Gavin had a semi-detached in a street just off Highfield Road in South Shore. Both had come from ordinary working-class backgrounds but Iain in particular detested people thinking that just because he and Gavin lived in a nice house it meant that they'd forgotten about and didn't care anymore about those who don't. It angered him because it was such a lazy assumption to make, and it judged them by their accusers own low and very shallow standards. They did want to see a better society for everyone else. That's why Iain was a social worker and Gavin worked for the Labour party.

The 'King George Boarding school for Boys' was quite an imposing building halfway up the hill as the road led out of Clitheroe town centre. Iain counted three storeys in the L-shaped building, and it looked like it was surrounded by playing fields and facilities that would be the envy of most comprehensives. Iain thought that if he and Gavin ever had children there would be no way they'd send them to a boarding school. Not only did the concept clash with their social ethos, but neither of them wanted to have children and then send them away to be educated and brought up by someone else. Neither did he agree with affluent parents being able to buy their children a better future than those who couldn't afford it. He just didn't agree with the whole concept of private education.

The large wrought iron gates were wide open, and he drove through and then looked around for a place to park. There were places right in the middle of the corner created by the L-shape. He pressed down on the accelerator and swept into one of them. He turned off the ignition and picked up his files that had been lying on the passenger seat beside him. Then it was off to look into the damage done within another dysfunctional family.

Iain ran up the three steps and through the front door of the school to be greeted by a middle- aged woman in a blue velvet skirt. She was also wearing a white open necked blouse with a large 1970s style collar and a red cardigan that wasn't buttoned up. Her blond hair was tied up producing a small ponytail at the back of her head, and her glasses were perched halfway down her nose. She looked flustered, almost as if she was in shock.

'Are you Iain Kempton?' she blurted out once they were close.

'Yes, I am, and ...'

'... from social services in Blackpool?'

Iain breathed in deeply. 'That's right. And you are?'

'I'm Vivian Blackstone' she replied. 'I'm the deputy head of the school. The head, Charles Kent, is in London on business,'

'Right' said Iain who was always surprised at how seemingly upper- class people either think they don't have to tell you anything or they flood you with information you probably don't really need and couldn't give a fuck about. But what Iain really wanted to know was why everybody he could see around him, including this Vivian Blackstone were looking as if the world had come to an end.

'I'm here to see Samuel Lewis' said Iain, tentatively. Something was wrong. Something was seriously wrong here. 'He's a student of yours. We did have an appointment?'

'Yes, but I'm afraid you're rather too late' Vivian announced.

'Too late? What do you mean?'

'Please come with me into the office' said Vivian as she led Iain through a door to the side of reception and into a small corridor. Her office was the first on the left and she closed the door once they were both inside.

'So what's the problem here?'

'I'm sorry to have to tell you but Samuel Lewis is dead' she said in a faltering voice. She took off her glasses and wiped her eyes with a paper tissue. But she was trying to show a little restraint. She didn't want people to know quite how much pain she really was in. 'I don't quite know what to make of it yet as I'm sure you can understand but we've just found him a few minutes ago. She shook her head sadly. 'I'm sorry ... but he was such a lovely boy. His family will be devastated'.

DI Khan had inherited a team that included her old friend DC Philippa Beresford. Back in the day they would go out on the town and talk about all kinds of stuff, especially after Philippa's divorce from her husband Andy. She'd come close to suffering a meltdown then and had taken to the age- old method of self-medication using alcohol. But the second whack in the gut had come when Philippa lost custody of her son Alastair who'd made it clear to the family court that he wanted to live with his father and not his mother. Layla had been there for her, sometimes rescuing her from drunken nights in pubs when she could barely remember her own name, but always being the friend that she needed. She'd steered her back onto the straight and narrow and away from the danger of losing her job. But Philippa had clearly decided since Layla's promotion, to distance herself from her old mate like many of the others had done and apparently forget about all the times that Layla had been there for her. Layla began to smile as she walked towards Philippa's desk but then stopped short when she saw Philippa giving DS Keith Drake a key. What was all that about? She decided to ask her after Drake had walked away.

'Do I have to tell you, ma'am?' Philippa questioned defensively. 'Because I don't think I do'.

God thought Layla. Her friend in human resources had been right. He'd said that even some of her oldest friends would change towards her once she got the promotion badge. It's not the promotion that changes the promoted. They may gain added responsibilities, but they remain the same person inside. It's those around them who change their attitude towards them because of the promotion.

'You're right of course' said Layla after taking a deep breath and being on the receiving end of a stern look from Philippa that she'd never experienced from her before. 'It's absolutely none of my business. Look Philippa, have I done something to offend you?'

'No'.

'Because if I have then I'd like to know so I can put it right'.

'Well with all due respect, ma'am, I think you must be the one with the problem because as far as I'm concerned everything is just fine'.

Like fucking hell, thought Layla. She just didn't have the guts to admit that she'd turned her back on their friendship now that Layla was the boss. Well, if that's the way she wanted it.

'Well, I was just asking as your friend, Philippa, but don't worry, I won't trouble you with that clearly outdated concept again. I'll see you at the meeting in fifteen minutes'

Layla walked away towards her office and immediately regretted having let her guard down and saying all that to Philippa. Talk about unprofessional. She thought about ringing her partner Steve but then decided against it. He had a lot on at the garage and wouldn't want to be interrupted by his daft Doris of a girlfriend every time she thought the world was against her. The land had shifted at work but the dust will settle soon. And if it didn't and there remained a brick wall between her and some of her key staff then she'd have to think of other ways to break it down.

Just over a quarter of an hour later she sat down at the conference room table where the rest of her team had already gathered.

'So, ladies and gentlemen' she began and holding up the e-pic of the murder victim in front of her. 'As you already know, according to the initial report from the pathologist Ross Carter the victim who was strangled, was on heroin, though despite the obvious signs all the way up both her arms, we're waiting for the toxicology report to confirm this. It also looks like she was working as a prostitute from the initial examination of her body and from the belongings she was carrying. Again, according to

Carter she'd been dead for at least a couple of days but there's nothing matching this description on the missing persons list or on any of our other systems. What does that say about the life of this young girl that she hasn't been missed by someone?'

'You say teenager, ma'am?' said DC Philippa Beresford. 'Can we be any more specific than that?'

'We're looking at mid-teens, approximately fourteen through to sixteen'.

'She should've been at school,' said Philippa. 'She's about the same age as my son Alastair. He takes his exams next year. There's so much bloody filth in this town. I tell you, if it wasn't for Alastair growing up here, I'd move. I'd go to Manchester, London, Spain, Australia, anywhere'.

'I think you'll find that all of those places have their dark side, Philippa,' said Khan. 'But let's move on. I'll be reaching out to partners like social services on all associated matters and I need you all to get in touch with your snouts, even those you may not have been in contact with for months, and especially those who dwell inside or on the fringes of the sex industry in this town. I'm also stepping up patrols of the areas known to be where these girls work, and I want us all down there talking to them. I want to know who's been hanging around lately in terms of punters who they maybe haven't seen before and who were perhaps a little stranger than normal'.

'Won't they all scatter to the four winds if we all go down there, ma'am?' suggested Beresford. 'It won't exactly mean safety in numbers with all of us down there. They'll blame us for putting off potential clients.'.

'I'm not after the girls for whatever they're doing, Philippa,' said Layla. 'Not this time. We'll go in two by two, different parts of those streets behind the town centre, subtle, discreet. We won't overwhelm the place and end up cramping their earning style. I'll brief in the usual way before we go down there. I want to catch a killer or killers'

'Ma'am'.

'Ma'am?' asked DC Justin Barnes, the newest member of the squad and someone that Layla did get along with and continued to do so. His attitude hadn't changed with her promotion at all. He was a grown up. 'Did we get an answer on the HIV status for our victim?'

'Well, we know what the answer will be' said DS Drake. 'She was a prostitute at the very bottom end of the market'.

Layla chose to ignore Drake despite all the sniggers at his pronunciation of the word 'bottom' like he was some kind of North Pier variety act from the seventies. 'Yes, Justin, our victim was HIV positive'.

'Well, you'd be able to enlighten us on what that means, Justin' said Drake, still looking down at the papers in his hand and making a deliberate effort not to look up and catch the eye of Barnes.

'I beg your pardon?' Barnes questioned.

'Sir. I beg your pardon, sir'.

Justin screwed up his face in disgust and snarled 'I beg your pardon, sir'.

'Well, if I wanted to push shit up a hill, I'd use a wheelbarrow, but you obviously take a different view'.

Layla was beginning to boil with anger at Drake. He was pushing her into a reaction. He was shaking the cage deliberately and Justin Barnes was being used in his little game. But Justin shouldn't have to get caught up in all the shit Drake was throwing at Layla.

Barnes threw a look at Drake that would've killed him with one blow. He spoke clearly and slowly, making it more of a snarl.

'That is disgusting. Sir. And let me educate you. Sir. Just because someone is gay doesn't mean that they're HIV positive. Sir. I'm gay and I'm not HIV positive. Sir'.

'Well, that's only because you've been lucky so far'.

'DI Drake, that's enough!' Layla commanded, unable to contain herself any longer.

'I was just having some fun' Drake pleaded. 'DC Barnes should learn not to be so touchy and sensitive'.

'That's what all bullies say about their victims and DC Barnes doesn't have to do any such thing'

'Oh yes, I forgot' said Drake in a quiet voice. 'We mustn't upset the minorities'

Layla called a break in the meeting for fifteen minutes so that everybody, especially herself, could cool down. She went outside and lit a cigarette.

'I thought I'd find you out here' said DC Justin Barnes. He stood beside her.

'I can't do this, Justin' said Layla, her eyes looking straight ahead and moist with the threat of tears.

'Don't be ridiculous'

'You saw them in there, Justin' Layla reasoned. 'They, and especially Drake, are never going to let up on me and it's so fucking unfair because they wouldn't do it if I was a white, middle- aged bald- headed twat with a fat stomach and a competence level of less than flaming zero'.

'So, you've met my ex- boyfriend?'

Layla smiled. 'Don't make me laugh, Justin. I'm seriously thinking of jacking it all in'.

'Layla, DI Drake wouldn't know how to get himself a

promotion if his life depended on it and you are not going to let an inferior like him destroy your career'.

'Nice speech. Wish I could believe it right now'.

'And certainly not at the outset of what could prove to be a very delicate investigation' Justin went on. 'How would that look, Layla? It would do terminal damage to your career, and you can't throw it all away after everything you've been through to get to where you are, and you know I'm not just talking about your time in the police'.

Layla stood and thought for a moment. Justin was absolutely right but it was hard. She was letting her emotions get the better of her and it was casting a shadow over her judgement. But Justin had given her the kick up the backside she'd needed. Was she really going to let a tool like Drake destroy everything she'd achieved?

She threw her cigarette end down onto the ground and stubbed it out under her shoe. 'We'd best get back in there'.

'That's more like it'.

'How come a good- looking guy with a big heart like you can't find the great man that you deserve?'

Layla knew that Justin was twenty-seven and single. He'd had relationships but she couldn't understand why nobody had snapped him up and kept hold of him.

'Someday my prince will come' he chirped. He had started seeing someone, but he was having to keep it a secret until his new man sorted out one or two little complications in his life. But he'd promised Justin that he would and that they would be able to come out as a couple. And Justin couldn't wait. 'But look, right now, you need to go in there and show those losers just who is the boss round here'.

'Okay, boss' said Layla, smiling appreciatively. She was so

grateful for her friend. He was one of the best. She kissed him on the cheek. 'Thanks, Justin'.

'Anytime' he replied. 'And at least you know that by sticking up for you I'm not trying to get into your knickers'.

Layla walked back into the conference room, followed by Justin. The rest of the team were all there, but they were talking amongst themselves. She started to slowly hand clap and one by one that got their attention and the room fell silent.

'DS Drake?'

'Ma'am?'

'How long have you been a Detective Sergeant?'

'Six years, ma'am'.

'And how long had I been a DS before I worked like a dog and got my promotion?'

Drake knew the point she was about to make but he couldn't get out of it. 'Two and a half years I believe, ma'am'.

Layla slammed the table with her hand. 'Good, so please do well to remember that and show me the respect I deserve or there's the door! And that goes for the rest of you too. Start doing what you get your paycheck for every month. You are police officers. You're detectives, and I won't tolerate any further spite motivated distractions from the job we're all here to do. Do I make myself clear?'

There was a general murmur of agreement from around the table. It wasn't as unanimous and fulsome as it could've been, except from Justin, but it was enough for Layla to keep moving and maybe she will have done some good for herself and her position in the long run.

'Good' said Layla. 'Because this is not going to be a

straightforward case, as if any of them are. The difference here is that the killer has taken a sample of the victims' blood as some kind of souvenir. Why would the killer do that? We know that the victim was HIV positive. But did the killer know that? Are we looking for someone with medical abilities to be able to carry out this kind of procedure? Or is it someone who is used to using a syringe because they're a drug addict or a diabetic even? Whatever the reason the potential is that we've got some kind of psychopath stalking one of the most vulnerable groups in this seaside holiday town of ours and committing their crimes almost within spitting distance of the Golden Mile. They're taking the piss but now I'm in charge, they've picked on the wrong one. Now, DC Barnes and DC Beresford, I want you to make a start on all the usual suspects and go through the sex offenders list for the Fylde coast and verify individual whereabouts for the last week. It may not be where we find our killer but at least we can eliminate people and not waste any more time on them. And DS Drake, find out where someone would go for treatment in this town if they're HIV positive and all about what kind of treatments are available for them. You never know, you might find some enlightened thought that will illuminate those very dark corners of your mind'.

Drake glared at her. 'Ma'am'.

'People, whoever this psychopathic killer is I want them found before they can turn themselves into a serial killer. And I want justice for this so far anonymous victim'.

SEVEN

DI Khan was about to wrap up her team meeting in the conference room and go downstairs to make a statement to the press when she received a call telling her about the death of Samuel Lewis. She knew who he was. She knew the family he came from. She knew they'd recently been placed under investigation for the physical abuse of Samuel and possibly their other children too. But her unspoken questions about what it had to do with the murder she was investigating were answered when the Inspector from the local CID told her that press clippings of the murdered Blackpool teenage prostitute had been found pinned to the wall of Samuel's room at the boarding school.

'He died as a result of a heroin overdose' DI Khan revealed to her team who were still gathered in the conference room. 'The local CID are not treating it as suspicious, at least until their initial enquiries have been carried out. They believe at this stage that it was suicide. There was no sign of any physical struggle either on the body or in the room but what I'm wondering is why he had those clippings pinned to his wall?'

'Well, he may have taken his own life simply because he couldn't stand the thought of being the one to expose his family demons, ma'am?' suggested DC Barnes. 'But nevertheless, he wanted to leave us a clue that the murder of the prostitute may be linked in some way to his father's underworld dealings. Plus, it could also be why he was using heroin in the first place if his family is as fucked up as all the allegations of physical abuse suggest? He was due to be interviewed about that this morning by a social worker from Blackpool social services, a man by the name of Iain Kempton'.

'I know Iain Kempton' said Layla, a light going on inside her head about the no nonsense straight talking social worker who she'd enjoyed working with before. 'I'll call him and arrange to meet. We'll see what he can tell us but so far DC Barnes what you've suggested is giving me a lot of food for thought'.

'Or he could've just been a client of the prostitute himself, of course' said Barnes.

'Dirty little bastard,' said DS Drake.

'It would be interesting to see if he had any family visitors in the days leading up to his death and what his phone records look like prior to his death too' said DC Barnes, ignoring his superior officer. 'See if anyone was putting him under any kind of pressure'.

'Can I leave that with you, Justin?' said Khan.

'Sure thing, ma'am'.

'Okay. Now, any other theories as to why Samuel Lewis had seemingly taken an interest in the murder of this young girl before killing himself?'

'I think it's unlikely that he killed her, ma'am' Barnes continued. 'I mean, what would his motive be? He was only fifteen and at the time of the killings he was in school anyway. How could he have sneaked out and somehow made the sixty odd mile round trip to kill a prostitute? He'd have needed help at least with the transportation so we'd also be looking for an older accomplice'.

'I don't think that would be impossible' said DC Philippa Beresford.

'Neither do I' said Barnes. 'But my instinct tells me it isn't plausible because of all the planning it would take'.

'But if he could get enough drugs into the school with which to kill himself then surely anything is possible?'

'Well look, if there is a connection with our investigation then it isn't going to be obvious' said Khan. 'So, we have to keep our eyes and our minds open. But in the meantime, there's a killer or killers on the loose out there and it's our job to find them. DS Drake? You can come and face the ladies and gentlemen of the press with me'.

'Keep your enemies close, eh?' DS Drake chided.

'You'd better believe it,' said Khan. 'Until I think I can trust you'.

The number of the press pack that were waiting in the downstairs meeting room at the Blackpool police HQ weren't filling the place out, which relieved Khan, but the duty sergeant on the desk said the flow of arrivals had notably increased in the last ten minutes since the impact of the news about Samuel Lewis. That irked Khan somewhat. Course there was media interest before in the killing of a teenage prostitute but now that a nice upper- class boy from one of the most prominent families in the area had decided to kill himself it had attracted the attention of the regional and national media. Layla shook her head. There was still a class hierarchy when it came to the reporting of death. The richer you were the more likely it was that your demise would be covered.

The e-pic of the still unidentified murder victim was pinned to the wall in front of which Khan sat at a desk alongside DS Keith Drake. She got the introduction formalities over and done with quickly, much to Drake's immense relief who hated these things at the best of times. Then she got down to business by explaining everything about their investigation so far. Which wasn't much. Nobody had come forward to identify the victim. Drake allowed himself to silently wonder about the poor wretch. Assuming that she had come from the bottom of the heap she must've had the sense to appreciate that there was a whole world out there that was far better than the one around her. Her mistake had come in not getting any further than Blackpool and a life of being paid to open her legs. She wouldn't have been able to use education to set herself free because she'd probably never been taught the value of it because nobody in her family knew what that meant. He did actually feel sorry for her. She'd almost been doomed as soon as she'd been born like so many others he came across in his line of work.

'Ladies and gentlemen, we urgently need to identify the body of our victim here who'd been dead for approximately three to four days before she was found. Why hasn't she been missed? Is she even from this area? We've put her picture out on all the local, regional and national news channels and absolutely nothing has come back. But this girl is someone's daughter, sister, perhaps even mother. So, I'm asking for the help of our friends in the media to encourage the parents, or whoever was looking after her, to come forward and please identify her. We need to build up a picture of her life to use in the pursuit of a killer who took a sample of her blood. Why did they do that? What could they possibly gain from it? I know the killer has been nicknamed 'the vampire' because of the taking of the victim's blood but we do need to get very serious about this. A young life has been taken. I want to know why and by whom. This killer must be stopped'.

Josh Walker from the Blackpool Evening News immediately fired the first question. 'Are you sure it's only once that the vampire has struck?'

'At this moment we're investigating the murder of this so far unidentified teenage girl as the only victim we know about thus far who has been murdered in these circumstances' Layla responded. She recognized Josh Walker immediately. She'd met him several times in the line of duty. 'And what I want to reiterate strongly is that we also need to identify her as a first step'.

'Why do you think the killer took a sample of blood from his victim?' Josh Walker pursued. 'To call the killer a vampire isn't such a far fetching of the truth, is it?'

'The taking of a sample of blood is a highly disturbing element to this murder but the sooner we find the killer the sooner we'll know why it was done' Khan responded calmly.

'Do you think her parents or whoever was looking after her may have had something to do with her murder which is why they're not coming forward to identify her?' Walker continued.

'That is a possibility, yes' said Khan. 'But I keep an open mind whilst our enquiries continue, and we remain short of any actual leads'.

'So, you've no leads to go on at the moment?'

'We're conducting our enquiries' said Khan by way of admitting what she really didn't want to. 'When we do have something further to go on, we'll hold another press conference and share whatever information we can with you. In the meantime, I once again ask you to help us identify our victim here. Thank you once again for coming today. It's very much appreciated'.

'Why do you think Samuel Lewis had press clippings of the murder victim pinned to his wall?' Walker asked in a raised voice to ensure he had the last word. 'I'm talking of course about his reported suicide from a heroin overdose earlier this morning. I mean, doesn't that strike you as being rather odd?'

Khan paused and sighed. Word gets out quickly and she'd deliberately left the death of Samuel Lewis out of the press conference because she didn't want the two things to be connected at this stage.

'Yes, Josh, it does seem that way, but we are of course in contact with our colleagues at Burnley CID to see if anything is picked up that might connect the death of Samuel Lewis with our murder victim, but nothing has yet surfaced so anything proposed would be pure speculation at this time'.

Khan then conducted a couple of one- to- one interviews, first with BBC Northwest tonight, one with Granada reports, plus a couple more short spots with two of the national papers who were there. Then Josh Walker came up and asked if he could have a private word. She took him to one side in the corner of the meeting room and they sat down.

'Congratulations on your promotion, DI Khan,' said Josh.

'Thank you, Josh,' said Khan. She exchanged business cards with him whilst DS Drake watched from a long enough distance not to hear clearly everything that was being said but close enough to hear some of the gist. DC Barnes was already back at his desk working. 'Anytime we can help each other out'.

'Well, here's something for starters' said Josh in a quiet almost conspiratorial voice. 'And it's why I wanted to talk to you. He'll be found to be involved in it all somehow, you know?'

'Who will be found to be involved in what, Josh?' asked Khan, straining to hear him above the din of all the other journalists leaving. They never go quietly.

'You'll be able to connect the murder of this teenager to Daniel Lewis in some way' Walker went on. 'He may not have committed it with his own fair hands, but you'll find his hand in there somewhere'.

'Why are you so sure?'

'I'm close, DI Khan'.

'Close to what?'

'Close to exposing Lewis for the evil fraud that he is. I've been working on this for a very long time DI Khan, and I just need a little more to be able to prove my case conclusively. And when the time comes, I'll give you the heads up and hand over to you all the evidence I've been able to gather, because believe me it will be dynamite involving corruption, the local council, not to mention his family affairs. It will be one massive gold star on your professional CV, DI Khan but in return, will you keep me posted re this murder investigation?'

'I think you have yourself a deal, Mr. Walker' said Khan who nevertheless was wondering why he was being so generous to her. But then this wasn't London, or Manchester or some other big city where the local media and the police set themselves up almost in competition with each other. This was Britain's premier holiday resort according to all the town's publicity. The crimes were still as big though and she'd rather have someone like Walker in her corner than out there somewhere batting against her. 'But be clear about one thing. I will not leak anything to you that may threaten our investigation. Is that clear?'

'Absolutely' said Walker. 'And on that basis, you can count on me being in touch'.

'Just something before you go'?

'Yes?'

'If you're right and Daniel Lewis is involved in the murder of this teenager then how do you explain why the killer took a sample of her blood?'

Walker smirked. 'You mean you don't believe in vampires?'

'Unlike large sections of the media and those who read about such things in novels, I'm afraid I don't, no'.

'Well, it is something I'm still trying to work out' Walker admitted. 'And if I find the answer, I'll let you know. Lewis is in trouble for other reasons though'.

'Oh?'

'Word is he's got financial problems and that basically if he doesn't get the contract to rebuild the town centre he could go under. That could make him desperate and even more dangerous than before'.

'And losing his son to suicide won't make any difference to his concentration on his business affairs. Is that what you're saying?'

'Yes,' said Walker.

'But are you sure there is a connection between the murdered teenager that goes right back to Daniel Lewis?'

'DI Khan, I'd stake my life on it'.

DI Khan and her team aborted their mission to talk to the lower end of Blackpool's working girl community after realizing early on that it wasn't going to bring them anything of a breakthrough. They all went back to the HQ to file their paperwork and summarize the lack of progress made during the evening. None of the girls had seemed to be interested in trying to identify and catch a potential serial killer who may strike again at any moment, even though they themselves could be the next victim. What was more important to them was whether or not they were going to be left alone to ply their trade and earn enough for their next fix. And in the process of trying to help a community that didn't want to be helped, they'd come across some bloody sad specimens who should've been working the counter at Boots or the post office but for a twist of fate that hadn't gone in their favour. Khan pitied them all. Maybe they'd been good kids born to bad parents or parents who just didn't know what to do. They shouldn't have had their aspirations clipped by the circumstances they'd been born into. Or maybe that meant that they'd never had any aspirations at all.

'It all comes down to using your head and not your heart and making better choices' said DS Keith Drake in his high- handed pontificating manner that alienated him from so many people around him. He didn't much care about that in his current mood. He didn't know if even he believed any of the shit he came out with. He just sprouted out the words and waited to see where they fell, and he wasn't much in the mood these days for caring about reactions. He was more thoughtful than some of the stuff he came out with, but he sometimes wondered why he should bother. He'd received a letter that day from his wife's solicitors. As part of the financial settlement of their divorce which Keith still didn't want, his wife Ellen would leave him without the proverbial pot to piss in. She'd be alright. She'd carry on living in the marital home which was a block up from North promenade at Gynn Square and which he'd entirely paid for from his police salary. Whilst he would have to find a bedsit somewhere. And he didn't even want to get bloody divorced! He'd searched his soul over and over again, usually with the aid of a bottle of Bushmills, but he couldn't come up with a reason why it had all gone so horribly wrong between them. She'd said some really nasty things to him. He wondered what the hell had got into her. She'd never been like it before? Keith wondered if it was all his fault. Had he exasperated her and driven her to behaving in such a previously uncharacteristic way?

'Is that your message from this evening's trip out, DS Drake?' asked Khan, wearily.

'Let's just say it's some kind of truth that I'm trying to hold onto through difficult days' Drake went on. 'And I won't be elaborating. Goodnight, all'.

'I'll be off too, ma'am' said DC Barnes. 'I'll see you tomorrow'.

'Okay, Justin, and thanks again. Enjoy what's left of the evening'.

'Thanks, ma'am' said Barnes who was already in the middle of texting his new lover to say he was on his way home if he could get away.

DC Philippa Beresford was the only one left standing when the rest had all gone. She seemed to be hanging around as if she wanted to talk about something.

'Are you okay there, Philippa?' Khan asked.

'Well, I wouldn't mind a chat to be honest. But I know it's late'.

'Oh don't worry about that' said Khan who was glad of the obvious overture that her old friend Philippa was making. 'I tell you what, make us both a brew and bring it into my office. I'm parched'.

Beresford made them both a mug of tea and took it in to Khan who gestured for Beresford to take a seat in front of her desk.

'So, what's on your mind?' Khan ventured.

'I've been much less than fair to you, Layla' Beresford began.

'Okay?'

'I let myself get carried away with the attitude that's been stirred up against you' admitted Beresford. 'I went against all the years of friendship we'd enjoyed and I'm sorry'.

'Well, that's an impressive start, I must say,' said Khan. 'And good on you for being so candid with me. I did hope you'd come round in the end, and you have'.

'And I mean it'.

'I know'.

'You do deserve this promotion, Layla, and I won't let them gang up on you again,' said Beresford. 'And I'll tell Drake to wind his fat neck in'.

'Yeah. What is it between you two? I see you whispering and exchanging keys when you think nobody has noticed? Spill, girlfriend'.

Beresford laughed. 'Well, it's nothing like you're implying by that look on your face! He and Ellen have split up as you know. She's thrown him out and I've rented him my spare room'.

'I see' said Khan who didn't know if she liked the sound of Drake sharing with Beresford or not. He certainly had issues as far as Khan was concerned and she wouldn't want anything to ruin things if her friendship with Beresford could get back to how it used to be. She didn't want to start getting paranoid and believing that everything she said to Beresford would go straight back to Drake. No, she believed that Beresford was being genuine. She didn't want to believe otherwise.

'You're looking doubtful'.

'Well, I didn't think you were that close'.

'We're not' said Beresford, shifting in her seat. 'But he needed somewhere to go. It's been tough on him. He's really hurt at the way Ellen has behaved. She's been heartless, I mean really cruel. She's said all kinds of horrible things to him, and it's really given him a kick inside, you know. He'd never admit it though and if you pried, you'd never get it out of him'.

'Well, he's lucky he's got you to talk to,' said Khan. 'If things have been that bad'.

'The thing is too,' said Beresford. 'Well, I needed the money'.

Khan threw her head back. 'Oh God Philippa not again'. She bailed Beresford out the last time she'd got into financial dire straits. Hadn't she learned anything? 'And look, there's just the two of us here so it's Layla'.

'You know how utterly hopeless I am with money, Layla,' said Beresford. 'And I'll always be grateful to you for getting me out of trouble before. But I couldn't ask you again. Do you see that? My pride just wouldn't let me. So that's when I came up with the idea of offering Keith the spare room for four hundred a month plus a share of the bills. It just seemed like a good way to get my finances back on track. I told Andy and he was okay about it'.

'How is Andy these days? And Alastair?'

Beresford's marriage to Andy, her ex, had broken down partly because of Philippa's reckless spending that had led to bailiffs knocking on the door at one stage. He left her shortly after that and their teenage son Alastair opted to go with him. That had broken Philippa's heart, but she accepted that Alastair was better off with his father, and it wasn't just the money problems that had come between her and Andy. Philippa had also had a problem with fidelity. She'd had at least a couple of affairs that Khan knew about but there'd been a fair few more than that. In her defence Beresford had always maintained that with the other men it was only about sex and that Andy was the only man she actually loved. So why had she looked elsewhere? It was just, by her own admission, that she was a spoilt brat who couldn't keep her knickers on if a man paid her the right attention. But Andy had eventually reached the point where he'd had enough, and he now had a house up at Cleveleys in the same road as his parents so that they could look after Alastair when he was at work. He was a specialist nurse in the oncology department of Blackpool Victoria Hospital.

'Alastair seems happy enough and that's the main thing as far as both me and Andy are concerned. He comes to me a couple of times a week. I don't know if Andy is seeing anyone. I hope that if he is then she's making him happier than I ever could'.

'Oh Philippa. You still love him, don't you?'

'Only with all of my heart' Beresford admitted, tearfully. 'But it's no good. He just doesn't feel the same way about me anymore. It's my own fault, Layla. I fucked things up for us'

'Well don't go falling into bed with Keith Drake as a way of restoring your feelings'.

'Layla! Give me some credit. I don't fancy Keith one little bit. Not even a smidge when it's late and we've both had a lot to drink'.

Layla couldn't help smiling at the thought of Beresford and Drake being legless and trying to avoid getting fresh with each other. 'Well, it's none of my business anyway. Just watch yourself, that's all'.

'Oh, it's a bit late for that,' said Philippa.

'What do you mean?'

'Oh I … I just meant with the divorce and losing custody of Alastair, that's all. And I am sorry for being such a bloody cow with you'.

'Don't be,' said Layla. 'I'm just glad things are back to normal between us'

'Me too'.

EIGHT

'What do you mean by a growing attachment?' Iain Kempton asked as if he didn't know what she was driving at.

He'd driven back over to the boarding school near Clitheroe to speak with Vivian Blackstone, deputy head, about her newly deceased student and what his time had been like at the school. The atmosphere at the school was extremely tense. There were still a fair number of police officers around, every student and staff member were in the process of being interviewed, and the Head of the school was still in London trying to placate a group of Chinese businessmen who'd been planning to send their sons to the school whilst they were living in the UK and who'd been put off by the dramatic events of recent days. Iain thought the Head had his priorities entirely wrong and that he should be back at the school helping Vivian who was clearly showing the strain of having to deal with parents, the press, and the police. But Iain wanted to know from her what kind of pressures Samuel had been under from his family if she'd noticed any. It was when she started to hint at the boy's sexuality that he realized he was going to get from her more than he'd bargained for.

'I mean he was involved in a homosexual relationship

with another student, Ben Cartwright. We try to discourage those kind of things of course. We're known for what you might call traditional values which is why the parents of our students choose us, but also the emotional fallout from same-sex relationships between boys that young can be pretty intense and it's the last thing we need to have to deal with in the school. Young love and all that. But we're dealing with a lot of young men who've reached the age when their burgeoning sexuality starts to make its presence felt. Some of them go out into the local areas and start looking for girls in the normal, sorry, I didn't mean to use that word but I'm sure you get my gist anyway, way. Others, like Samuel and Ben, look for something rather different'.

'Love is the same whatever the gender, Vivian'.

'Yes, I know, and I agree, but it's my clumsy use of words again, sorry'.

Iain smiled. 'It's okay'.

'Samuel and Ben hit it off right from the start and became best friends the first term they were both here. Then I noticed that something deeper was happening. Ben has been utterly distraught since Samuel's death. He's had to go home and seek treatment from his local doctor. I have to say that his parents have been a great deal more understanding about things than Samuel's have. Daniel and Angela Lewis blame me, the school, Ben Cartwright, anyone they can poke a stick at for their son's predicament'.

'So, am I getting the feeling that you quietly encouraged the relationship between Samuel and Ben?'

Vivian breathed in deeply and placed her hand over her mouth for a moment. Iain could see that she was clearly shaken by something other than just the suicide of Samuel Lewis.

'I accepted that it was happening, and I didn't do anything

to stop it' Vivian answered in that oblique way that infuriates straight talkers like Iain. He found there was always an agenda behind people not talking straight. They were usually hiding something that might not put them in a great light, or they may be protecting a guilty party in some way. He didn't know which of those two particular holes Vivian would fall into.

'So, you let it flourish?'

'I don't want to incriminate myself from a legal perspective, Iain,' said Vivian. 'I'm well aware that they were both underage and that Samuel's parents were dead against the very idea'.

'And Ben Cartwright's parents weren't opposed to their relationship?'

'No, they weren't. They saw it as him developing into the person he was meant to be'.

'Very enlightened,' said Iain. He didn't quite know what to make of her law- abiding citizen spin on things although he thought that she meant well, and her heart was in the right place. If she had turned a blind eye to Samuel and Ben's love affair, which she apparently seemed to have done, then it was a human reaction to the realities of life that Iain would applaud her for. To look at her right there and then he would never have expected such open- eyed liberalism from her, especially when she ran a place like this. She was dressed once again in the crisp no creases visible attire of the professional woman of a certain age. There was no ring on that finger he noticed, and he wondered if she'd ever been married or had children. And she did have that very haggard look all over her face. Her eyes were deep set and shadowed. She looked like she'd been awake all night. 'I wish there were more like Ben Cartwright's parents. But coming back to the whole issue of them being underage, that would not be a concern of mine and discretion would need to be applied. Vivian, if Ben had been a teacher at the school and several years older than Samuel then there would've been no negotiation on it at all and the older man would've been charged under the full weight of the law. But as they were both underage it means that it would've been treated very differently by us at social services and by the police'.

'Well, I suppose it is better than the boys going out and getting local girls pregnant' said Vivian with a drip of false laughter. 'I let Samuel know that I was there if he ever needed to talk about his feelings and what was going on'.

'And did you have the same conversation with Ben?'

'Yes, of course' said Vivian. 'But as I said before Ben has parents who will support him and love him no matter what. Samuel on the other hand was in an altogether different situation. He couldn't talk to his parents about anything, especially not personal things'.

'Did they know about his sexuality and his relationship with Ben?'

'Oh yes' said Vivian. 'Only recently but they were absolutely furious. They called me everything from a pig to a goat. It was all my fault apparently. That's when they called him home for the weekend and when he came back …'

Vivian's voice began to falter, and Iain could clearly see the tears welling in her eyes. 'Vivian? What's wrong?'

'He was covered in bruises and marks that had been left by his father's belt' she recalled, staring out of the window and letting the tears flow freely down her cheeks. 'He'd been beaten so badly he could barely stand up. I wanted to call the police, but he begged me not to. He said that his father would only take it out on his sisters if I did and especially the one with the birthmark on her face who his father considered ugly and unworthy. But I had to do something. I couldn't just let it pass. Iain, it was me who made the anonymous phone call to you at social services. I had to get somebody in to do something. I didn't think it would ever result in this'.

Vivian broke down and sobbed. Iain stood up and went round to comfort her. He put his arms round her and held her as tight as he thought was appropriate, but her cries were coming from deep down inside her. This really had affected her very deeply.

'And is that the first time you noticed the bruises and marks on Samuel's body?'

'No' she said, softly. 'There were half a dozen other occasions and all of those too had been when he'd come back to school from being at home'.

'So why didn't you report it those other times?'

Vivian just didn't know what to say and settled for just shaking her head. Iain knew he wasn't going to get any more out of her about reporting the abuse, so he went for a different line.

'Vivian, how did Samuel get the drugs in here?'

'I don't know!' she insisted between more sobbing. 'Just like I don't know why he had the clippings of that murdered girl in Blackpool. All I know is that he was the kindest, sweetest boy whose life was beaten out of him by his father whilst his mother did nothing at all to stop it. If anybody has got some explaining to do over this, it's both of them'.

There was a single track leading out of Blackpool South station that took the oldest trains that the franchise operator could just about get away with using, on a trawl along the Fylde coast to Preston and then up into the hills of East Lancashire. DI Keith Drake had been a bit of a train spotter in his youth, and it annoyed him the way some communities had to put up with a less than acceptable service because they weren't situated along high profile lines between major cities. Though broadly a supporter of the Conservative party he would have to admit that on some issues he was more to the left and did indeed support bringing Britain's railways back into public ownership.

The body had been spotted by someone sitting on a train that had pulled into the station a couple of hours before. It had been full of holiday makers desperate to get to their bed and breakfast lodgings and then out onto the promenade. It was turning into a rather warm and sunny summer in the meteorological sense and bookings across the town's hotels were all said to be up, reflecting the loads that were being brought in on the trains. None of the passengers on this particular arrival however had expected to see the kind of real-life example of what they may see later in the Blackpool Tower dungeon as the train came into the station and they gathered together their family size bottles of coke and endless bags of crisps.

'Let me help you, ma'am' said DS Drake as he held out his hand to help DI Khan step across a pile of bricks that was all that was scattered across the single track that led in and out of Blackpool South station. It was just before the track lurched to the right and headed towards the Pleasure Beach. The crime scene was about half a mile south from where the first body had been found and just before a road bridge over the train line which marked the Lytham Road boundary between inner town and outer suburb.

'How gallant of you, DS Drake,' said Khan. She was trying to be a little more sympathetic towards Drake after what DC Philippa Beresford had told her about the nature of his marriage breakdown. She was trying anyway. The odd, pleasant remark exchanged is a start. 'Thank you'.

'I have my moments, ma'am'.

She looked around. The street they were in ran parallel to the Blackpool South station platform. There was just one platform because it was the end of the line, and the trains just came in and went back again. The area wasn't what you'd call salubrious.

It was the continuation of inner town bedsit land, and it didn't look like the landlords of these properties did much to look after the outward appearance of them. Or maybe it was the tenants who didn't give a damn about how the properties were treated. So, the landlords didn't either. So long as they got their rent payments via the DWP they were happy because Khan imagined that most of the tenants would be made up of people who'd been in prison, drug addicts, drug dealers posing as drug addicts, people who've had mental breakdowns, the formerly homeless, people who are down on their luck and have nowhere else to go. A lot of them were washed up into this part of central Blackpool. And still only one block back from all the happy, smiley people on the Promenade.

'You wouldn't choose to live round here, would you' Khan remarked.

'Everything on Lytham Road up to here, where the bridge goes over the railway line, is still part of the inner town as it were so it looks pretty shabby' said Drake, agreeing with his boss. That was a first. 'Then on the other side of the bridge the housing gets altogether nicer and the more salubrious south shore end of town begins'.

'That bridge is like the Berlin Wall'.

'That's a good way of putting it, ma'am'.

The pathologist Ross Carter was waiting for them under the white tent. The body had been found in a small area between the back of the first house and the railway line. It was also just a couple of steps down from the main road that the street itself ran off. Khan looked at Ross Carter and once again had to keep her lustful feelings in check. Men like Carter make it bloody hard for a woman though.

'Same method of execution here which is strangulation' Carter announced. 'And signs of drug abuse going up her left arm, but she can't have been taking it for long because there aren't that many marks'.

'And are there any signs that this is due to our neighbourhood vampire having been up to his tricks again?' asked Drake with a wry smile.

Carter stared at him coldly for a moment. He didn't think this was the time for Drake's attempt at humour. 'Yes,' he confirmed. 'There's a fresh syringe mark on her carotid artery in her neck. Just like the other one. And this one is fairly fresh. I don't think she's been here for longer than a few hours, maybe twenty-four at the most'.

'How old, Ross?' Khan asked.

'Younger than the one last week'.

'Younger?' Drake questioned. 'So how old are we talking about here?'

Carter kneeled down and pulled back the sheet that had been covering the body. 'As you can see, she looks younger than last week's victim. I'd say maybe twelve or thirteen. There are signs of recent sexual activity'.

'What kind of dirty, twisted bastard goes with a child like this?'

'One who may also have killed her, Keith' said Khan, looking down pitifully at the mangled hair and now worthless face. Then in stunned revulsion she said 'Wait a minute. She's in some kind of school uniform'. She knelt down to take a closer look. 'I recognize it. It's one of the local schools on South Shore. I think Steve's niece goes to it. But the badges indicating the school's identity seemed to have been torn off'.

'It makes no difference which school it was, ma'am,' said Drake. 'She was catering for a particular end of the market. The sickest end if you ask me'.

'For once we absolutely agree, Keith,' said Khan. She stood up and turned back to Carter. 'Anything else, Ross?'

'Yeah' he replied, holding some kind of garment in his hands.

'That looks like a cardigan to me,' said Khan. Her heart was breaking as they discussed the victim lying on the ground with her eyes closed and her young body covered in mud and soil.

'Well, it was half on and half off her body' Carter told them. 'It had obviously been ripped and torn during a struggle. But interestingly there's something here that might really help you in identifying her'.

Just inside the neck of the cardigan was the usual label telling people not to mix different colours in their wash and not to exceed 40 degrees for this particular garment otherwise it might shrink etc etc. Then just underneath was another label that looked like it had been stitched on by hand. With a felt tip or marker type pen had been written 'This belongs to Beverley Cooper class 4B'.

When they first got to the Cooper house on the St Annes Road estate it looked like any other of the row upon row of semi-detached council housing that dominated the dozen or so streets and roads that made up the estate. Khan noticed that the hedgerow at the front was high, way above the downstairs windows, and when she and DS Drake went through the gate, they entered a world of overgrown lawn that was scattered with various bits and pieces of litter amongst all the drying dog and cat shit. The two windows, one either side of the front door looked like they hadn't been cleaned in a while and the net curtains on the inside of them may possibly have been white at some stage. It took Khan's mind back to when she was a child. Her parents had arrived in the UK from Pakistan without much to their name, but they were proud, and they'd have never let their garden get into this state or their curtains look like dirty old rags. They did a lot with what they had, and the appearance of a well- kept home and family had meant everything to her mother. Khan and her siblings were always well dressed and their shoes always cleaned and polished. They did their homework on time, and they didn't complain about it. Khan's parents had a strong commitment to make life for their family so much better than they'd ever known it. That's why she couldn't understand why, when it came to her and her two sisters, her parents reverted to tradition that meant that girls had no say in their future, despite the British education that had opened up their minds. It had broken Khan's heart. Surely all the sacrifices her family had made hadn't all been for the sake of her brothers. She looked up briefly at the heavens. Her parents were both long dead, but she hoped that despite everything they were looking down and were proud of her. It was a long shot, she knew, considering that the last words they said to her were that they wished she was dead. But maybe with the peace and wisdom of the other side which has to come if the pain and ignorance of this world are to ever make any sense, they could somehow find it in their hearts to

She knocked on the door and when it was opened, they were greeted by a middle-aged woman with shoulder length dyed black hair. She was wearing mascara around her eyes which took temporary attention away from the wrinkles that on further inspection made her face look like it had been trampled over by a crow's foot. She was wearing torn blue jeans, a purple- coloured knitted polo neck sweater with a fairly loose, wide neck and the whole ensemble was completed by red shoes that consisted of two brick like blocks with the leather holding the foot down on them with a buckle. Not exactly the kind of platform shoes that Stevie Nicks would wear on stage but a much less sophisticated imitation. Drake was amazed at how she could possibly walk in them, but she seemed to be doing okay.

'How do you want me?' she asked in as broad a Blackpool accent as he'd ever heard.

'I beg your pardon?' Khan questioned.

'Well, the last lot of press folk wanted me in various positions looking harassed and drawn. They didn't want me to get washed or anything. They wanted me to look drab. And well, you do as you're told, don't you, when someone is handing you a fat cheque for your story and I'm going to do this house up top to flaming bottom and make all of the toffee- nosed ones round here sit up and take flaming notice. Anyway, I'm sorry, loves, but if you're after one of them exclusives I've already sold it'.

Both Khan and Drake were temporarily lost for words. Then Drake broke the purgatory.

'Weren't you told that two police officers would be coming to see you? I understand from my colleagues that you were?' Earlier that day, after the identification of the body had been made and her mother had been in to confirm it, she'd dismissed the idea of having a family liaison officer assigned to her on the grounds that were a family who likes to 'do things my own way'. Clearly, as far as Drake could see, that meant making as much money out of her daughter's murder as possible.

'Look, all sorts have been turning up at all hours so you can't blame me for getting confused. Anyway, have you found him?'

'Who, Mrs. Cooper?'

'The pervert who did this to our Beverley?'

'Could we come in and talk about it, Mrs. Cooper?' asked Khan. 'I think that would be best'.

In the hallway of the Cooper home were seven vacuum cleaners lined up like soldiers. They were the old- fashioned stand-up kind with a foot pedal at the back so that the handle with the bag attached could be lowered. Khan wondered what all that was about, and she exchanged questioning looks with Drake but what was really getting to her was the smell in the place. It was like cat's piss. The carpet was thread bare and filthy. The paint was peeling off the walls and the skirting boards looked like they were used to break the teeth of wild animals. They were led into the living room with its two leather sofas, both of which were torn in several places and had indeterminable stains on them, and then there was the smell. Khan wondered if they'd ever heard of litter trays in this house. It smelt as if the whole house was used as one.

Khan and Drake sat down with a good deal of trepidation coming from a fear of what they might be sitting on, and the only cat visible that could be contributing to the smell was a small grey one of indeterminable breed. The poor little thing only had three legs and, much as it tried, it just couldn't jump onto the coffee table despite all its desperate attempts.

'I'd like to say how very sorry we are for your loss, Mrs. Cooper' Khan began, trying not to laugh as she caught the cat jumping up at the coffee table but failing miserably, out of the corner of her eye. 'Now I know that you were Beverley's stepmother … '

'… but I loved her as much as if I'd given birth to her myself' Maggie Cooper emphasized with just enough emotion to make it sound real without bursting into tears. She'd perfected that particular art quite well when it came to discussing her stepdaughter.

'Well, that's not why we're here, Mrs. Cooper,' said Khan.

'So why are you here? Is it to harass my son Troy? He's up in court next Wednesday for causing GBH and I still haven't got him a shirt and tie, so he'll probably have to borrow one from his brother but look, he's innocent. Well, I mean, he isn't innocent, he did brake that bottle, and that barman did end up in hospital and that but my lad was provoked. Why don't you people take that into account? It bothers me, it really does. My lad could go down and he's a good kid really'.

'Mrs. Cooper, we're here to talk about Beverley and to try

and get a picture of what she was like' said Khan, trying to keep the exasperation out of her voice. This woman was utterly grotesque. 'We understand you married her father Mike when Beverley was two. Is that correct?'

'Yes,' said Maggie, her voice calmer than before. 'I also had my son Troy who was seven at the time. Then I had two more with Mike and then two more, one each with the two losers I've hooked up with since Mike left. Neither of whom stuck around'.

'What happened to Beverley's birth mother?'

'I haven't got a flaming clue,' said Maggie. 'She'd pissed off long before I came along'.

'And you say that Beverley's father walked out?'

'He walked out on us five years ago and I haven't seen him since'.

'So potentially he doesn't know that his daughter is dead?'

'Well, I haven't told him because I don't know where he is,'.

'Do you have contact details for the men with whom you had these last two relationships, Mrs. Cooper?' asked Drake. He was so glad that women like Maggie Cooper existed. They proved all his points about what's wrong with society. She hasn't got a flaming clue. It made him wonder how the fuck she'd made it down the birth canal.

'I'll do my best to find them' she answered. 'It hasn't been that long since the last one legged it. About three months I think'.

'Was there anything about Beverley's recent behaviour that might suggest to you that she was in trouble of some kind?' asked Khan.

'She came and go as she pleased really' Maggie replied. 'I've never been one for laying down the law with my kids. But they've always known I'm there for them'.

'So, you weren't aware if she was having difficulty with any particular individual?'

'No' said Maggie. 'I wasn't at all, no'.

'Mrs. Cooper, did you ever wonder where Beverley was when she was out at all hours of the night?'

Maggie hesitated. This was where they were going to get her. They'd accuse her of child neglect or some other shit like that and it wasn't fair when Beverley wasn't even her child. It was true that she loved her as if she was her own, but she'd been dumped on her by her errant father. Where the fuck was he? He should be crawling out from wherever he's been these past few years and helping her to face the music. Bloody typical of all the men she met. Never flaming well there when they were really needed. She'd tried to steer her own sons onto a more responsible path. She had thought that by giving them their freedom at an early age they'd respond with a sense of responsibility. But Troy was already in trouble, and it probably wouldn't be long before the others followed suit. She wished her Mam was still alive. She'd know what to do with them all.

'I'm sorry but … well no I didn't'.

'Mrs. Cooper, there are some fairly delicate matters we need to discuss' said Khan. Was this woman unfortunate, careless, or just plain stupid? It was probably a mixture of all three.

'You want to ask me if I knew that Beverley was on the game and shooting herself up with heroin?'

'That's just about it, yes'.

Maggie leaned back and sucked up such a deep breath that Khan was thinking she might pass out. 'I knew she was getting money from somewhere, but I didn't question it because she was giving me some of it and to be honest the cash was useful. I was also relieved that she wasn't pregnant. As for the drugs … well yes, I had my suspicions, but I didn't say anything because

I didn't want to make her angry and then run away. Oh, I know what you're thinking. Stupid isn't the word for mothers like me'.

Tricia was sitting at her dressing table in her bedroom applying her make-up in readiness for going out with the girls later. The door was half open and out of the corner of her eye she could see her son Charlie standing there watching her. She didn't like the look he was giving her. In fact, it was giving her the creeps.

'Charlie? What's up, love?'

'Why are you plastering your face with that muck?'

'You mean my make-up?'

'If that's what you call it'.

'What's wrong with you?'

'Nothing's wrong with me except my mother goes out of a night looking like a tart'.

'Hey, now just a minute young man. Don't speak to me like that'.

'Why not?'

'Because I'm your mother and I demand you show me some respect'.

'I will when you show yourself some'.

And with that Charlie sloped off downstairs and threw himself onto the sofa. He picked up the TV listings magazine but after going through it he decided there was nothing he wanted to watch. Besides, he had other plans for the evening. He was going to go online and talk to some other lads who were planning to make the same transition as he was. He couldn't wait to get onto it. So-called Western society had given him nothing. He'd lived a hand to mouth existence from the moment he was born because his father had taken more interest in dealing drugs than in his son and his mother would fork out eighty quid on a skirt for the weekend even though it wouldn't leave enough money in her account to pay the electricity bill when the direct debit came through. Neither of them had given a damn about what he needed. It's true that his mother had given him a roof over his head, but it was precarious to say the least. She was always getting into arrears with the rent even though most of it was covered by housing benefit. It was different somehow when his Granddad was alive. Charlie had felt like he'd had some kind of anchor then. The two of them had been extremely close. Then his Granddad became ill with cancer, and it took him away a couple of years ago. It had been the last straw for Charlie. He felt like he had nobody after that. He wasn't as close to his grandma. He didn't like to think about what his Granddad would say if he knew what he was planning. It was the only dark side of his newly found purpose.

Tricia came downstairs in a defiant mood. She refused to be censored by her own fifteen- year-old son. She was going out to meet the girls and it wouldn't be a wildly expensive night. They'd have bottles of gin, vodka, and Bacardi in their handbags and surreptitiously pour their contents over the course of the night into their legitimately purchased tonics and diet cokes. But that was only until they found enough men to buy them all the full ticket of a drink. Maybe she'd have to drop her knickers in return for some bloke in the back of his car or behind the back of the pub. It wasn't the life she would've chosen but it was the only one she felt she could have. She picked up her handbag and was about to leave without saying anything but decided to pause instead.

'Charlie, I've asked you this about a million times and perhaps you've given me the answer, I don't know, but why has our relationship been reduced to me trying to talk to you and you just insulting me at every opportunity you get?'

Charlie looked at her with complete contempt and said, 'I grew up. You didn't'.

NINE

Khan pinned the e-fit picture of their first victim plus the photograph of Beverley Cooper given to them by her stepmother on to the left- hand side of the white board in the team briefing room. On the right- hand side, she pinned a picture of Samuel Lewis. She then turned to her team who were all gathered and awaiting her briefing.

'Now let's review progress, such as it is which isn't a great deal,' said Khan. 'DC Hughes, what did you find out from the mobile phone records of Samuel Lewis?'

'Well after it was announced that social services would be investigating his father for abuse, he received several calls a day from his mother, some of which lasted forty and even fifty minutes'.

'So, it was his mother who in particular was putting him under pressure?' said DI Drake.

'It looks like it, sir, yes. She was certainly anxious about something which she had to speak to her son at great length about'.

'Right' said Khan. 'Bring her in. I want to know why those phone calls appeared to be so intense and I want to see her reaction when we place the pictures of the murdered girls in front of her'.

'Do you think she could be a suspect, ma'am?' asked DC Philippa Beresford.

'Who knows?' Khan answered. 'I'm not ruling anyone out of anything'.

'Is that what your friend Josh Walker at the Blackpool Evening News has been feeding you, ma'am?' DS Drake intervened.

'Is there something you want to say, DS Drake?'

'I'm merely asking a question, ma'am'.

'Bullshit' said Khan. She knew it had been too good to last. Drake being a decent human being and talking to her with some degree of respect. Maybe it was only going to work between them when it was just the two of them together. But put him in front of an audience and the briefing room turned into a stage. 'You were trying to make a point and my point back to you is that I'm not ruling anything or anyone out of greater involvement than first appears. Is that clear?'

There was a general murmur of agreement around the room and then Khan pinned a picture of Samuel Lewis's lover Ben Cartwright.

'So, what are we saying about these two, ma'am?' DS Drake questioned, in a more reasonable tone than before. 'Are they suspects?'

'No' said Khan. 'Let's not forget that they're roughly the same age as both of our victims and there's absolutely no evidence to implicate either of them'.

'There's even less evidence to suspect Angela Lewis' DS Drake countered.

'I didn't say that I thought Angela Lewis had committed any crime. I simply indicated that I wasn't ruling her out. Ben Cartwright confirms that he and Samuel Lewis were together on each night of the week before that first body was found but Cartwright has no idea why Samuel had taken such an interest in the murder to stick a clipping about it on the wall above the study desk in his room. He apparently seems as puzzled as the rest of us. So, what it comes down to at the moment is that the killer has been able to strike twice, and we haven't been able to stop him. How long have we got before he's able to strike a third time? And were these two victims chosen because of their HIV status? And if that's the case then what's he going to do with the blood he's taken from them?'

'Well taking the blood has surely got to be a large part of his motive, if not the entire part?' said DS Drake. 'He's going to do something with it that suits his purpose for killing these girls in some way or other'.

'I agree with your analysis, DS Drake,' said Khan. 'But how did he know that these two girls were HIV positive? It isn't the kind of information they would volunteer to a potential client'.

'Maybe he's known to these girls, and they're known to him?' DS Drake went on.

'But just because they were HIV positive doesn't mean to say that they themselves knew' reasoned DC Justin Barnes.

'Very true, DC Barnes' said Khan.

'Well, I think we're looking for someone on some kind of moral crusade, ma'am' DC Justin Barnes suggested. 'There was that lunatic in Sweden the other day who took a gun against immigrant children in a school. Our guy here is concentrating on the sex trade to settle whatever score he has with the universe for his sad, little life. Maybe for some reason he can't have sex and there are these girls tantalising him with what they can offer that he can't take up. There could be all kinds of reasons'

'Have you been on a profiler course whilst we weren't looking, DC Barnes?' asked DS Drake.

'No' answered Barnes, flatly and without looking at Drake. 'I thought it was my job'. That was telling the pea brained little fucker. 'But ma'am, I think it has to be remembered that some clients who use the sex trade will go with a girl who's HIV as a kind of Russian roulette. Like firing a handgun at someone when there's only one bullet in the six barrels. The victim has got a one in six chance of death. And some girls will have unprotected sex with a client when the girl knows she's HIV and the client has been too stupid to ask. It's stupid in the extreme, I know, but it does still happen. You talk to anyone on the vice squad, and they'll tell you'.

'No, that's true, Justin' Khan agreed. 'The world is full of sick perverted bastards'

'It used to be full of married men according to that book by Jackie Collins' quipped DC Phillipa Beresford.

Khan smiled. 'I know. I read it. I've read all of hers'. She then turned her attention back to the pictures of the two victims and focused on the one who was yet to be identified. Who was she? Her face was haunting her. The picture had gone nationwide but still nothing. God, it felt so bloody sad. How did she get to Blackpool, or had she always been here, living just under the radar of social services? A girl who was damaged but not enough to warrant their attention. Or was there some other reason why she didn't matter? Because as it stood at the moment her life appeared to have been for no apparent purpose. Khan wanted to give her life at least some dignity but how could she do that if she couldn't find whoever had murdered her?

Arthur Bellow had represented his town centre ward on Blackpool council for almost ten years. He prided himself on knowing the labyrinth of social and low- grade private housing that made up the area and Arthur was happy with the low aspirational nature of the people who lived there because it meant he didn't have to do anything to encourage people to do the best for themselves. He could just sit back and tick all the necessary boxes and knowing that his seat was safe no matter what he did or didn't do. It had been Labour since the pope was an altar boy and he liked being known as a councillor. He liked the kudos that the title gave him. He liked being part of the social circle of councillors. His wife Barbara liked the almost royal treatment she got when she went to get her hair done every Friday morning. He liked the fact that he was looked up to. He didn't like all the modern direction of local government where councillors were expected to take 'cabinet' style responsibility for the various tasks entrusted to it and he was convinced that all the talk of the northern powerhouse and devolution for cities like Manchester and Liverpool would soon hit Blackpool and then they'd have their work cut out for them. Then they really would come under scrutiny, and it would be no good just turning up at every election and smiling before your vote was confirmed with a whopping majority. You'd have to go out and actually campaign. The signs were already there. Two of the newer members of the local party had gone out to knock on doors on a sheltered housing estate in Arthur's ward. Before they'd left the campaign office, he'd told them that he was a friend of all the 'old dears' who lived there and jokingly warned them not to upset all his 'faithful voters' with all their 'modern ways'. When the members got back from the estate, they said that none of his 'faithful voters' had seen him since the last election, and they were all thinking of voting Conservative. His reaction was to look at his potential votes and calculate that even without the estate he was still cruising for an overwhelming win. The two new members accused him of taking his 'faithful voters' for granted and that's how Labour would lose more seats than they already had done to the Conservatives. They were shouted down by Arthur's 'old guard' comrades who'd now become the faction within the Blackpool Labour party that doesn't talk to any new members.

It wasn't easy these days for Arthur to find the time to sneak out and pursue a little pastime of his that had been part of his life for decades. Even without his high profile that came with being a councillor he also had his work with the local church. But they were both on the other side of town and the north/south divide wasn't confined to the whole country. It went right through the heart of Blackpool.

It was what could be described as a 'balmy' evening and Arthur had always loved the drive up past Norbreck castle on the right and the cliffs leading down to the Irish Sea on the left. It was still bright enough to see the trace of the Lake District and the white wind generating energy machines out to sea. It was a familiar landscape to him although he didn't make it up to North Shore very often these days.

He indicated left and after checking that there no trams in the immediate vicinity he crossed the tram line and continued past the old tram station building of Little Bispham with its pillars and brickwork and down towards the promenade.

There were one or two cars out tonight. He parked up and sat for a moment. He loved the thrill of it all, the excitement and the danger. It was like a lottery. You just didn't know what was going to happen. Sometimes nothing happened, sometimes it happened but wasn't worth writing home about, and sometimes it turned out to be one a glorious night in a lifetime that would be forever printed on his memory.

He reached over and pushed open his passenger door as wide as he could. That was the signal that he was open to offers. There were no houses along this part of the Promenade that led into Cleveleys town centre. The houses started half a mile up ahead. The sea was calm and lapping up gently against new style concrete that formed the barrier between land and sea. Arthur had seen it much worse than his. Some of the storms, even in summer, could be fierce. But tonight, it was a quiet night as far as the weather was concerned.

He didn't have to wait long before he spotted him. About six- foot tall, blue denim jacket, black jeans, white t-shirt. What looked from a distance like dark blond hair and a masculine swagger all added up to an instant appeal for Arthur. It was alright for men who liked men these days. Nobody batted an eyelid anymore and there were openly gay members of the local council and right across the national political scene. But back in Arthur's day it wasn't possible to live your own life unless you were prepared to move away to London or even further and cut yourself off from your family. Instead, he met Barbara, they had their three kids and now they have their grandchildren. His true self had disappeared into the conventions of the time.

The guy he'd spotted seemed to loiter when he got as far as Arthur's car. Closer up he did indeed look handsome. It made Arthur wonder what the hell he was doing here. Why would someone who looked like he was in his mid-thirties and was decent looking want to come out and find excitement in this way? He wondered but then he didn't care if his own needs were catered for.

The guy leaned forward against the low wall of the promenade, looking out to sea and with his back to Arthur's car. Arthur got out of his car and closed both his and the passenger door. There were other players around, some were still sitting in their cars, some had their dogs with them, but Arthur stepped forward and in the stillness of the evening air he leaned forward on the low promenade wall, just about four or five metres along from the guy he was targeting.

Or was the guy targeting him?

They looked at each other and smiled. The other guy ran his tongue along his upper lip. Arthur noticed his hands were large, so were his feet, and it made him wonder about the size of his cock. They began to talk. It was a lovely night. The weather has been good lately. The new football season starts next week. The new promenade looks really good. I live just down the road in Bispham.

'I can't accommodate' said Arthur who knew the green lights were flashing and this was his lucky night because this guy really was a handsome bugger. So many men come down here who could never find sex elsewhere. A case of the desperate meeting the needs of the desperate. But this guy looked ordinary. Clean and well turned out. Arthur couldn't quite believe his luck with this one. 'My wife is out for the evening, but we've got our daughter and her kids staying with us for a while'.

'I can accommodate' the stranger revealed. 'Like I say, I live just down the road in Bispham. I've got my own flat'.

'Is it on the ground floor? And if it isn't, is there a lift? Only I've not long had a hip replacement and I can't always manage the stairs very well'

'Well, don't worry,' said the stranger. 'My flat is on the ground floor. I came up here on the tram though, so I'll need a lift?'

'Course' said Arthur as the excitement grew inside him. 'Jump in and you can direct me to your place'.

Iain Kempton was having a seriously bad day when his old friend, DI Layla Khan, accompanied by her DS, Keith Drake, descended on him at work. He made himself and the two of them some coffee and took them into one of the interview rooms they used that had a complete glass front, including the door. This was so everybody else could see what was happening inside and nobody could make any false allegations of assault against a member of staff.

He didn't always like working with the police because he often felt like they would take any opportunity to 'put him in his place' and come across like the 'real' work should be left to the 'big boys' like them. But he felt positively disposed towards this particular meeting because of his personal friendship with Layla Khan – they used to live next door to each other – and he always loved seeing her. He also wanted to help her move forward with her investigations. Not that he had too much to offer her. The trail he'd been following had led to the same place as the one she and her team had been following – nowhere. He told them that social services couldn't identify the first murder victim and that although the family of the second murder victim, Beverley Cooper, were known to social services, they were considered to be low risk and therefore hadn't been visited for some time.

'How were they known to you in the first place?' asked DS Drake.

'Their kids, including Beverley, weren't attending school' Iain replied. 'Maggie Cooper, their mother was pretty useless in trying to encourage them to tell you the truth. But there were never any suspicions of abuse in the family, physically or otherwise'.

'Just another example of useless parenting' said Drake on the verge of going into full throttle moral outrage but deciding to hold back after a warning look from Khan. 'Of which you must see a lot in your line of work'

'You could say that' Iain agreed. 'Some of the cases we deal with really do break your heart. It really doesn't seem fair the amount of bad luck that's thrown at some people'.

'And the other cases?'

'You wish you had a gun and could shoot someone'.

DS Drake smiled in appreciation of Iain's remarks. He didn't think he'd get on with him terribly well, but he didn't seem quite the rabid left leaning do good type that normally populates this profession and that pleasantly surprised Drake. He rubbed the bridge of his nose with the ends of his fingers. Lodging with DC Philippa Beresford had been great in terms of giving him some space to get his thoughts together. But every night the wine came out and the two of them sat there drowning their respective sorrows and waking up in the morning with fuzzy heads. Keith was grateful to Philippa for giving him a roof over his head, but she was like one of his kids around the house. She was always leaving stuff everywhere – piles of clothes, opened letters, newspapers and magazines. CD's left on the side with the cover for them in some other place, the same with DVD's. She didn't seem to have heard of streaming. She certainly didn't keep house like his wife Ellen did and it would make him crazy if he wasn't so desperate for somewhere to stay but perhaps the drastic change in domestic routine would do him some good somehow.

'I need something a lot stronger than this today I can tell you' Iain said after sipping some more of his coffee which was still piping hot.

'Well, I see it's been a good day for the Blackpool lawyers hired by Daniel Lewis' said Khan.

'Only if they make it all the way through' said Iain.

The Lewis family had declared their intention to sue Blackpool social services on the grounds of what they called an 'anti-Christian' campaign of hatred against the family that led to the suicide of their son Samuel. They were also suing Samuel's lover Ben Cartwright for having underage sex with their son and for introducing him to evil and immoral sexual acts. In their press conference, Angela Lewis made no mention of the allegations of parental child abuse that Blackpool social services had been set to question her son about on the day he took his overdose. The autopsy had shown clear evidence of bruising all over Samuel Lewis's body that was consistent with a beating of some kind, but Angela Lewis had blamed that entirely on Ben

Cartwright. She said that Ben must've beaten her son up.

'You don't think these lawyers will actually get anywhere do you, Iain?' Khan wanted to know. 'It's just the Lewis family venting their spleen?'

'Well, the case against the council is flimsy enough. We were only acting on information provided to us and we can't be held responsible for what Samuel Lewis did to himself on the grounds that we were going to talk to him. Same with the case against Ben Cartwright which I don't think has got any chance at all. How can they prove it? Ben Cartwright has absolutely no record of violence and, like I said, according to Vivian Blackstone the bruises only appeared on Samuel's body when he came back to school from being at home'.

'They had broken the law though' DS Drake pointed out. 'That has to be remembered'.

'Yes, but hard as it is to explain to two police officers, it's also about a question of degree when it comes to this particular law being broken,' said Iain. 'Two fifteen- year- olds in what was by all accounts a very loving relationship isn't the same as someone in their fifties going after a fifteen- year-old'.

'Yeah, I get that, I really do,' said Khan. 'Although in those circumstances we would still have to charge them and then hand them over to you, Iain. But going back, as a professional with experience of this kind of thing, do you believe that Samuel Lewis was physically abused by his father according to what you know?'

'Well yes I do,' said Iain. 'The physical evidence from the autopsy and from what Vivian Blackstone told me is all there'.

'But that doesn't prove that his father did it,' said DS Drake.

'But who else was there?' Iain argued. 'His mother? Or some random stranger? I think that his father couldn't accept his son's sexuality and tried to beat it out of him'.

'Okay, but why didn't Vivian Blackstone report the abuse she claims to have seen on Samuel Lewis?'

'That's a question I couldn't get her to answer' said Iain who felt embarrassed at having not been more forceful in getting Vivian Blackstone to answer that one. It was so glaringly obvious.

'She also seems to have taken a particularly personal interest in Samuel Lewis' DS Drake continued. 'Is that usual? I mean, was she like that with any of her other boarding students?'

'I don't know' said Iain who felt even more embarrassed now that he realised what a gaping hole he'd left behind. 'I really don't know'.

Charlie was just about dropping off to sleep when he heard noises outside the front door and his mother's high pitch cackle of a laugh which sounded like silver foil being crunched together. He could also hear a man's voice. She'd pulled. That meant there'd be noises all night until they both passed out thorough drink and then more noises in the morning and then awkward silences when the man tried to step his way round Charlie when they couldn't avoid each other in the kitchen or the living room. Then he'd be off into the daylight never to darken Charlie's Mum's door again. Charlie knew the pattern. He knew how it worked. And he knew the reason it gave him to go to war against this kind of disgusting filth.

He didn't know when exactly it was but sometime in the early hours Charlie heard the turn of his doorknob. It would be enough to terrify him, and it did once but he'd grown used to it now. The number of strangers his mother brought into the house meant that a percentage of them must be sexual deviants in some way. It stood to reason. And here was another one who was about to appreciate just how wrong they could be.

Charlie grabbed the knife that he kept under his pillow for these kind of situations, and leapt out of bed brandishing it in front of a very startled looking man of about forty who was stark bollock naked.

'Hey, hey, don't be like that' the man whispered. 'I saw pictures of you downstairs. I wanted to see if you were up for some fun. Your mother doesn't need to know'.

'I'm underage. Doesn't that make any difference to you? Or is that what you get off on? Picking up women who'll open their legs for anybody just so you can get at their kids?'

'Oh you've got a very vivid and very wrong imagination, son'.

'Don't fucking call me that!'.

'Alright, alright. You just had to say no and that would've been enough'.

'You didn't have the fucking right to ask me in the first place. My mother is probably too far gone to give it to you now, which means you'll have to wait until the morning. So, you thought you'd come and see how tight my arse was? Is that it? Well, I tell you, it's a fucking million times tighter than my mother's vagina because she'll let anything down there which means it gets a lot of attention which means it you probably wouldn't even touch the fucking sides'.

'I'll let you go down on me if you prefer that?'

Charlie lunged forward. 'For crying out loud you haven't listened to a word I've said! Now fuck off you piece of slime'.

The man recoiled holding up his hands in a kind of terrified defence. 'Okay, okay, I got it wrong. I'm sorry. Please don't tell your mother'.

Charlie got back into bed after the man had gone and lay there waiting for his heart to settle back down to a steady beat. It shouldn't be like this. He tried not to cry but it really shouldn't be like this.

TEN

The next morning Charlie got out of bed and went downstairs not expecting to see anyone but sitting at the kitchen table large as life was his nocturnal visitor from the early hours looking flushed and pleased with his stupid self.

'Hello, Charlie'.

'Where's my Mum?' asked Charlie immediately on guard.

'She wanted to cook me bacon and eggs for breakfast. But she didn't have any bacon or any eggs, so she's had to pop out to the shop to get some'.

'You're some kind of twisted fuck'.

'Why? Because I like bacon and eggs for breakfast? Aren't we being a touch over sensitive, Charlie? And you're right. It was like throwing a sausage up the Mersey tunnel with your mother but she's very capable and I got off on it alright. I'm not a fussy man and I take what I can get'.

Charlie clenched his fists. The twat was goading him. He wondered how many of his school mates had to deal with this on a Saturday morning. His Dad should be here and if he was then this kind of shit wouldn't be happening. His Granddad shouldn't have died. He wondered desperately why nobody was ever there for him. Why nobody ever had been.

'Look, let's start again, eh? Forget last night. I'm Bruce'.

Charlie was as tall as his mother's latest shag, and he was just contemplating thumping the bastard with all the anger and resentment he could summon up inside him when his mother came back with a bag of groceries that looked to Charlie like they would be covering more than just breakfast.

'Oh, I'm glad you two have met,' said Tricia. 'Bruce is staying for the weekend, Charlie. Won't that be fun? You'll have someone to talk man talk with'.

Either his mother was stupid, or she just hadn't picked up on the heavy atmosphere in the room. He already knew she was stupid so that must be it. He left them to talk whilst he went into the living room to take his money out of his piggy bank. He would then get showered and dressed and leave them to it. He'd be able to stay at Muhammad's tonight and Muhammad's Mum would feed him up just like proper mother's do. He lifted up the piggy bank, but it was empty. What the fuck? There'd been twenty quid in there last night. He went back into the kitchen. His mother was sitting on Bruce's knee, and they were snogging.

'Mum, what's happened to my money?' Charlie asked.

'Oh, I borrowed it darling to get the groceries with' Tricia confessed, still with her arms round Bruce's neck. 'You don't mind, do you?'

'But there's nothing left and it's the weekend'.

'No, but I'll pay it back when I get paid' said Tricia who was giving him the look that told him not to embarrass her.

'But I wanted to do stuff'.

'Well, we've got a guest now, so you don't need to go off and do whatever stuff you were planning'.

'Yeah' said Bruce. 'I haven't got to be out of here until tomorrow afternoon. Come and sit next to me and we can talk and get to know each other'.

'Go on, Charlie,' said Tricia. 'Bruce works on the oil rigs. He's got lots of stories to tell'.

'I'd rather drink my own piss' said Charlie who then stormed off down the hall and up the stairs with his mother in hot pursuit.

'Charlie! Come back here and apologise now! Do you hear me? How dare you be so rude to our guest! Charlie! I said get down here now!'

DI Layla Khan could think of a million better things to do with her Saturday night but with a serial killer on the loose who has a thirst for his victim's blood she needed to use the hours that could prove to be the most useful in terms of information gathering.

'So, you're sending us all back onto the streets to talk to the working girls again tonight, ma'am?' said DS Keith Drake after he'd knocked on the open door to Khan's office. 'And on a Saturday night too. You must be well in with the top brass for them to have sanctioned the overtime. I suppose that with a second murder victim the girls might now be getting scared enough to talk'.

'Let's hope so' said Khan who decided not to respond to

Drake's jibe about her and the top brass as he called them. She was trying to get the better of her ridiculously terse exchanges with DI Keith Drake for the sake of the work they had to do. She'd been talking about it the previous evening with her boyfriend Steve who told her to respond in kind if he's being pleasant and ignore him when he isn't. So that's what she was going to do. 'He's got to slip up sometime, Keith'.

'He seems to have planned things fairly meticulously so far though, ma'am'.

'So where do you think he is? Where is this vampire killer of ours?'

'Sitting in a room somewhere planning his next murder,' said Keith. 'Working with colleagues who have no idea what he's up to. Stopping off at the supermarket on the way home to buy some fresh pasta for dinner. Making momentary eye contact with strangers who don't know that they're looking back at a wanted killer. He's sitting on a tram next to an elderly couple who are up here for the week from Wolverhampton, and they think he's a 'very nice young man' for giving them directions to the Tower, even though you can't fucking miss it. He believes he's right. He doesn't see any wrong in what he's doing'.

'You scoffed at DC Barnes the other day when he was trying to profile our killer and now, you're doing the same'.

'I wasn't being entirely serious' Drake confessed who found it great sport to wind DC Justin Barnes up now and then. 'But you probably knew that. I think you're tuned into me now'.

Khan didn't know the answer to that one. 'So, where's the link with the Lewis family?'

'If there is one?'

'You don't believe there is?'

'I can see nothing that points to that other than a press clipping on the wall of a young man who took an overdose,' said Drake. 'And we've not been able to find anything that links him with either of our two victims. Our conversation yesterday with the social worker Iain Kempton did put a couple of question marks in my mind though I must admit'.

'Such as?' asked Khan who was liking this side of Keith Drake. He was actually talking like a police officer with a job to do rather than an axe to grind in the back of her neck.

'Vivian Blackstone and her apparent closeness to Samuel Lewis?'

'But she is the school nurse' Khan countered in the way of playing devil's advocate. 'So, if he was appearing to be unwell in any way?'

'But then if she cared that much then why didn't she report the alleged abuse?'

'Well, that'll be question number one when we bring her in,' said Khan. 'But for now, let's entirely focus on our two murdered girls, especially the one who is lying there alone in the morgue without anyone coming to claim any connection with her. That's sad, you know, Keith. That's really sad'.

'It's getting to you?'

'It is to be honest' Khan admitted. She herself had been a runaway girl once. She'd managed to get herself a life that didn't involve any kind of criminal activity and she'd met a wonderful man called Steve. The universe had ended up being kind to her despite all the stuff she'd had to go through to get there. 'It's such a waste, Keith. Life should never have ended for her like that. Nor for Beverley Cooper either but at least someone is claiming her as belonging to them. It's the single most important thing that's driving my motivation to get a result here because I want to restore some dignity to our unidentified victim'.

'I understand that'.

'You do? You mean you're agreeing with me? Are you sure you haven't had a bump to your head?'

'No, ma'am,' said Keith, smiling. 'I might just be trying to make things work between us'

'That works for me, Keith and is much appreciated. Now by the way, I understand you're renting a room off DC Beresford?'

Keith straightened up a little defensively. 'Yes, I am. So?'

'No negatives, Keith'. I'm just glad you've been able to find somewhere to stay whilst you sort things out with Ellen. That is still possible, isn't it?'

'I'm afraid not, ma'am, no'.

'In this context, Keith, it's Layla, and why not?'

'She maintained that she wasn't seeing someone else and that nobody else was involved in her wanting to split up with me'.

'But she was lying?'

'All the way, Layla. I'm sleeping in a colleague's spare room and being asked to virtually rape myself financially whilst another man is sleeping with my wife in the home that I paid for and in our bed. And then they wonder why men in my position these days get so fucking bitter'.

'I'm sorry, Keith. Really, I am'.

'I just wish she hadn't lied through her teeth all the way through'.

'She wanted to spare your feelings?'

'Well, the way she's been acting since then tells me she has absolutely no regard for my feelings at all, Layla'.

'Keith, you had two kids together. Surely there must be something left of what she felt for you?'

'Well, if there is then it's not on display,' said Keith. 'Quite the reverse to be honest. She's been unbelievably cold. And of course, I'm torturing myself now wondering how long it had been going on with this other bloke and how long she was lying to me when I thought we were alright'.

The leader of the Greater Fylde council, Lesley Hammond,

had been taking calls all day from her two sons with regard to the fact that the family dog, Patch, a male black labrador who was eight years old, had gone missing from the front garden of their home in the Highfield area of the town. Her sons were absolutely distraught. Her husband was on a day off and they'd been all over the neighbourhood looking for Patch, but it was as if he'd just vanished out of thin air. Lesley was pretty upset about it herself, and she was desperate to get home and help her sons through the trauma. But before she could call it a day and get back to them, she had one little job to do, and it really couldn't wait. Her office in the town hall on Talbot Square, just opposite the North Pier, was small and what might be described as intimate. There was one tall thin window that opened out onto the back of the town hall which was a street made up of bus stops and pubs and though she liked to have fresh air coming through she sometimes had to close it for the noise. Pictures of her husband and two sons took prominent position on her desk but the only thing that adorned the walls was a large street map of the entire town. She kept meaning to bring in some other pictures just to brighten the place up a bit, but she'd never got round to it.

Councillor Arthur Bellow swaggered into her office with his usual mixture of affected charm and total disrespect and once he was in there and sat down it felt like the office was full. Sometimes his smile was so clearly false that it almost made her want to throw up. He was one of those Labour councillors who were supposed to be part of the coalition that Lesley led but in fact had formed an 'opposition within'. Nothing to do with policy but in their eyes she'd 'stolen' the leaders' position from 'Harry' whose 'turn' it had been. They were the ones who she knew briefed against her to the press and anybody else who'd listen, and they seemed to spend their time cosying up to their Tory councillor friends to the point where Lesley sometimes wanted to tell them to piss off and join the opposition if they were so bloody keen on their company.

'So, what did you want to see me about, Lesley?' asked Arthur, looking everywhere except straight at her and dusting off his trousers with his fingers in the way the comedian Dave Allen used to do. It was always the same when the two of them were together. They tended to regard each other as a bad smell. 'It's Thursday and so the wife is doing steak and kidney pudding. People have come miles for her steak and kidney pudding. She does it with all the trimmings and you can keep all your foreign so-called food once you've tasted her steak and kidney pudding, I can tell you'.

Lesley looked at him pitifully. 'I'll bear it in mind'. She couldn't stand the sight of his sweat- stained shiny face and his combed over white hair. It's a face she could cheerfully slap but judging by the photographs that had fallen luckily into her possession, he'd rather like that.

'So, what do you want to see me about? The full council meeting isn't until tomorrow'.

'At which the four competing bids for the town centre redevelopment will be discussed and decided upon'.

'Correct?'

'One of those bids is from the Daniel Lewis Corporation'.

'Yes?'

'You'll be voting against it'.

'In your dreams' snarled Arthur. 'You may think that as council leader you can dictate to the rest of us what to do but you can't. Some of us are more independently minded and have got the guts to follow our own conscience'.

Lesley could've laughed out loud. The guts to follow his own conscience. That was hilarious judging by what she'd got on him.

'Do you always follow your own conscience, Arthur?'

'You know I do. My voting record speaks for itself and as for voting against the Daniel Lewis Corporation bid it would be a cold day in Hell before I did that'.

'Yes, why do you have such faith in Daniel Lewis, Arthur?'

'Because he's done a lot for this town and unlike some of the so-called comrades, I'm not afraid of embracing private enterprise'.

This time she couldn't help herself. She covered her mouth and did her best to stifle the need to laugh that was consuming her. This crass idiot really didn't have any idea of what was about to hit him.

'Sorry, have I missed something? Is something funny?'

'Forgive me, Arthur' said Lesley with affected sincerity. 'Let me put you out of your misery and in the process, I'll be putting you out of mine too'.

'I don't understand?'

Lesley suddenly felt nervous as she reached into the drawer of her desk and brought out a large brown manila envelope. She'd never relished confrontation although she'd never shirked from stepping up to the plate when she had to. And she really wasn't sure how this was going to go. She couldn't predict and she had no gut feeling telling her one way or the other.

Inside the envelope were a number of photographs that Lesley took out and spread across her desk. Once she'd done, she looked up and saw that the colour had completely drained from Arthur's face. They showed him in various sexual positions with another man and in one of them he was handcuffed to the bed whilst the man was down on him. Arthur knew exactly who and when it was. Just a few nights ago. He'd picked him up from the usual cruising area below the tram station at Little Bispham. He knew he was taking photographs, but he didn't think anything more about it because he was so momentarily in love with the guy who was hot and handsome and nothing like Arthur had ever been able to pull before. He'd got carried away on the idea that this had been all his Christmases and Birthdays rolled into one. He might've known it was too good to be true. What a bloody fool he'd been. What a fucking mess.

'Did ... did he send these to you?' asked Arthur. His mouth was dry, and he could feel himself shaking. In a fleeting moment he'd thought about trying to brazen it out but how could he? It would've made him look even more ridiculous. There was no doubting that it was him in the pictures.

'Never mind how I got them, Arthur,' said Lesley. She'd actually been given them by the Blackpool Evening News journalist Josh Walker with whom she'd agreed to work to bring down the local businessman Daniel Lewis. In the process she'd always known that one or two of her councillors would be caught in the maelstrom, but she'd worked out how she could use their downfall to her distinct advantage. 'But it seems we have ourselves a bit of a situation here'.

'You've set me up'.

'Your words not mine'.

'Are you going to blackmail me or something?'

'Don't be crude' said Lesley who was actually beginning to enjoy herself. Watching him squirm was entertainment in itself. 'But I am going to use the situation to rid the council of a useless waste of space like you'.

'You rotten bitch'.

'Sticks and stones, Arthur. Now here's what's going to happen. You will not support the Daniel Lewis bid and you will take steps to persuade any others who might be inclined to vote for it to not to'.

'You don't know how much you're asking'.

'And furthermore, you will not seek re-selection for your council seat next time round'.

'Damn it, woman! It's my turn to be mayor after the next council elections. My wife has already started buying the frocks!'

'And there's my point with you and all those who think like you!' Lesley raged. 'You think your turn as mayor is more important than providing every less advantaged child in this town with a more equal start in life. You think that your own position comes before fighting government cuts to our budget that will further penalise the poor of this town. And what makes my blood absolutely boil is that you can't seem to get it through your thick skull that there's anything wrong with the attitude you take. And you're supposed to be Labour for crying out loud. Well let me tell you I know for a fact that that there are at least two younger potential candidates in your ward who are desperate to step into your worn- out shoes. And unlike you they want to make a difference in this town for the sake of the people not for the sake of themselves'.

'Oh, you can look down your Guardian reading nose at people like me if you like' Arthur sneered. 'But tell me what you'll do if I don't comply with what you ask'.

'Well first of all it isn't a request. If you don't do as I'm telling you then these pictures will find their way into the local and national press and to your wife'.

'You haven't got the guts'

'Try me'.

'You're an amateur in the games that we grown- ups play with Daniel Lewis'.

'Is that the best insult you can come up with? And whilst you play your sordid little games nothing is improving in this town for the likes of ordinary people because you're too obsessed with doing anything to protect your turn as mayor'.

Arthur shifted around uncomfortably in his seat. She really didn't know the potential consequences of what she was asking. 'Can't we come to some sort of deal?'

'The deal is on the table, Arthur, and it's up to you to either take it or leave it'.

'You know that I'll have to take it'.

'Good. I'm glad we finally understand each other'.

'Daniel Lewis doesn't like to lose'.

'Then he'd better get used to it'.

Arthur shook his head. 'I hope you know what you're doing. Because I fear for you if you don't'.

'What's got into you today, man?' asked Muhammad. He was sitting in the back garden of his Derby home with Charlie. 'You're on an even bigger downer than usual'.

'Sorry'.

'It's alright' said Muhammad who'd always seen his mate as something of a mission. His parents had brought him up to always look out for anyone less fortunate than himself and to open his heart up to them. They said that was one of the true meanings of Islam and it seemed more relevant in this day and age than ever before. And Charlie had become like a brother. 'But it's just that you seem like you're in a darker place than usual today. It's like with those girls we met down the park earlier. You did everything you could to get them to piss off. And they did'.

'They were tarts'

'They were young girls,'.

'They were tarts' said Charlie, grimacing. 'They had everything on show'.

Muhammad smiled at the memory of how the girls looked. 'They looked alright to me'.

'Would you really want to be with someone that cheap?'

'Are you serious?'

'Never more so,' said Charlie. 'Everywhere you look there are girls who are showing you everything and more besides. They tease you and goad you and before you know it, they've made you as dirty and filthy and disgusting as they are'.

'Where are you getting all this from, man?'

'Though my open eyes, man, through my open eyes'.

'Oh, so it's got nothing to do with those meetings you've been going to at the mosque. Charlie, that man is a fucking tool! He preaches a completely perverted view of Islam'.

'He makes a lot of sense to me'.

'Charlie, trust me. He's not your friend. He's using you and all the others who listen to him to further his own twisted agenda. Don't take this the wrong way, man, but he's taking in all the vulnerable ones from bad homes. He's offering you all an easy solution to all your problems. He's not going after all the kids like me from safe, normal backgrounds. It's like all the white lads from homes and families that are a complete mess. Along come the EDL who give them something to pin their frustrations on. Do you see what I'm getting at?'

'But why do you think he's wrong?'

'Because he wants me to turn against my own country!'

'But what has your country ever done for you except wage war against all your Muslim brothers in the Middle East?'

'Look, my grandparents came here from Pakistan with nothing, and they got jobs and made a life here'.

'And what good did it do them?'

'It gave their whole family a future you idiot! I'm a Muslim and I'm proud to be a Muslim. What's happening in the Middle East is terrible but I don't see it as dividing me as a Muslim from Christians or Jews or anybody else. People who think like that are just thugs, man, they just want a fight. ISIS and all the fuckwits like them are just thugs and are not following anything that's written in the Quran, believe me. And I'm so not playing that game'.

'The government wants to take all your rights as a Muslim away from you'.

'No, they don't! Look, you can keep all that extremist shit to yourself because it means nothing to me and if you follow that twisted fuck at the mosque then I worry, as your mate, as your brother, about where you're going to end up'.

ELEVEN

The Blackpool Victoria hospital was an absolute maze of doorways, corridors, and more doorways and corridors that led to all kinds of places and departments that in the normal manner of things you wouldn't want to know about. Chief Superintendent Richard Langton had got to know the geography of the complex pretty well just three years ago when his son had been born premature. He and his wife had married fairly late in life and weren't sure if they would be able to have any children and they were in their mid-forties when little Michael came along although he had to stay in hospital for a few weeks whilst he stabilised. He was now the absolute joy of their lives, a thriving three- year- old who was into everything and stole the show wherever he went. He was a very social child too who already had a lot of little friends, and his parents were glad he was like that rather be all clingy and shy like some only children can be.

But it wasn't the premature baby unit he was visiting today, and he first called on DC Justin Barnes who he found was awake and, with the okay from the doctor looking after him, was happy to talk for a few minutes to his superior officer.

'So how are you feeling, DC Barnes?'

'Pretty groggy, Sir, but I have to say that I think I'll live' Justin answered. His neck was in a brace and his throat was sore giving him a husky note to his voice. He also felt like he'd been picked up and battered senseless against a brick wall. But he thought all that might be too much information for the Chief Superintendent.

'You've sustained some pretty horrendous injuries though' said Chief Superintendent who'd been briefed by the doctor about DC Barnes and his broken arm, broken leg, fractured skull and collar bone.

'Well like I say, Sir, I'll survive'.

'Are you ready to tell me what happened?'

Justin slowly moved his head away from the Chief Superintendent. He hoped he wouldn't have to stay in hospital too long because he would get so sick and tired of the view of those bloody ceiling panels above him. Once he was discharged, he'd still need looking after and he was going to go and stay with his parents. He gathered his thoughts and tried to throw them into shape. It was hard though. The memories were a little sketchy even though the events were only three or four hours ago.

'We'd been down on the streets for almost ninety minutes,

and we were about to call it a night, Sir' he began to explain. 'We hadn't managed to get anything in the way of useful information from any of the girls who were out. I was with DS Drake and we received a call from DI Khan to wind things up and meet her at the bottom of Hornby Road'.

'And DC Beresford was with DI Khan?'

'That's right, sir' said Justin although he wished it had been the other way round. DS Drake had been trying to be his friend all of a sudden lately after being a total shit to him for so long. Justin had found it almost creepy but given the events of a few hours ago it was something he should just deal with. They were grown- ups.

'Go on, DC Barnes'.

'It all happened so fast, but DS Drake and I were walking down Hornby Road when we heard the call for back-up from DI Khan. We started running towards her stated position, but we didn't have visual at that point because they were round the corner from where we were. When we did turn the corner, we saw DI Khan and DC Beresford were holding each other up. DI Khan said the assailant was dressed all in black and wearing a hoodie and what looked like a balaclava over their face. He'd burst through from nowhere and managed to punch them both before disappearing into the back yards of the nearby houses. DS Drake and I set off in pursuit with DS Drake running up to the far end and I started where we were. It was naturally very dark, and the only lighting came from inside the houses, and it was quiet. There are garages lined up at the back of all the houses with space between them for the residents to gain access. We checked in and out, but we couldn't see any sign of anyone. He must've got away. He must know the area and knew exactly where he was going. I'm sorry, sir'.

'Look, don't worry about that now' said Chief Superintendent Langton. 'But how did you then sustain your injuries?'

'I was standing there catching my breath. I was leaning forward with my hands on my knees, and I heard a car accelerating before it came right round the corner and hit me before driving on'.

'So, the car mounted the pavement in some kind of deliberate act to hit you?'

'It certainly looked that way, sir. All things considered I consider myself quite lucky. It could've been a lot worse'.

'You're not kidding'.

'The driver of the car must've been the same suspect who DS Drake and I tried to chase through the neighbourhood but who managed to get to their car and in the process of getting away as quickly as he could he rubbed our noses in it by hitting me. And it wouldn't surprise me if a third body is found of another teenage girl before we've been able to get to him, sir'.

Chief Superintendent Langton made the short journey from the ward where DC Justin Barnes was beginning his recuperation to the neighbouring ward where DC Philippa Beresford had also been receiving medical attention. But she'd just been discharged and gone home so he moved on to where DI Khan was being prepared for discharge a couple of beds away. Her bed was surrounded by a drawn curtain and without throwing his weight around he managed to silently get the message across to medical staff that he needed to have a private conversation with her. She'd been brought in because tonight's assailant had apparently hit her first in the process of trying to get past her and DC Beresford but there were wider implications from tonight's events that he needed to talk to her about. If she wasn't careful the leaves would be falling off her career and Langton felt a responsibility because he'd personally championed her promotion to DI and she wasn't winning many plaudits from this, her first big case.

'I think DC Beresford and I got off lightly, sir' Khan explained as she sat on the edge of her bed. She was still in the clothes she'd been wearing when she came in and Steve was on his way to pick her up. She had a splitting headache and was waiting for the painkillers to kick in. 'It's DC Barnes I'm worried about'.

'It sounds like you'd sprung your assailant though,' said Langton. 'Or were in danger of doing so. That's why he hit out and fled'

'How is DC Barnes, sir? I haven't been able to go and see him yet'.

'He's being remarkably positive considering' Langton answered. 'It really could've been a whole lot worse'.

'I know, sir,' said Khan. 'DS Drake is the only one who was unscathed'.

'So, you're not able to describe the attacker?'

'Sir, he was dressed all in black with a hoodie and a balaclava and we had literally three of four seconds tops to get anything. I really couldn't say any more than average height and build'.

'And we've no registration for the car either'.

That's when Khan saw it written all over Chief Superintendent Langton's face. He wasn't here just to see how she'd been affected by the incident. He'd come to give her a mild, or otherwise, rebuke.

'Look, DI Khan, I know you'd want me to be direct with you and that's exactly how I'm going to be. There are mutterings amongst the top brass'.

'About me?'

'Yes, about you and the way you're conducting this investigation'.

'I take it the mutterings are not positive?'

'And you'd be right. They've been about your leadership skills to start with'.

'And I don't suppose they think I've got any'.

'Layla, I appreciate you're fighting on all sides, not just on your abilities as a police officer but also, and let's put it crudely, because you're a Muslim woman at a time when Islamophobia is rife everywhere, including amongst our own ranks. I'm aware of the whispers and what's said behind your back. I'm aware of the show we make of a multi-cultural force working on behalf of a multi-cultural community. But I'm also aware of the realities faced by those of our officers who come from ethnic minorities'.

'Thank you, sir'.

'But Layla, I championed your promotion because I believed and still do that you can rise above that and wipe the floor with the ignorance of others by showing them what a first- class officer you are'.

'And you think I've let you down?'

'No' said Langton, emphatically. 'But it does seem like you need to get more of a grip'.

'More of a grip?' Khan questioned forcefully and on the verge of blowing her top before remembering that she was standing in front of the Chief Superintendent who'd just been singing her praises. But she still had to have her say. 'Sir, with all due respect this has been like trying to nail fog to the wall right from the beginning. We've done everything by the book, according to procedure, following every guideline, and we've come up with absolutely nothing. Absolutely no substantial leads whatsoever have come out of our enquiries, and nobody has come forward to identify our first victim. We've conducted house-to-house, tonight was our second night on the street with the girls, we've been down the list of known sex offenders and have had to eliminate them one by one because there's no evidence to link them to these crimes. And now that DC Barnes is going to be incapacitated for the foreseeable future that's going to leave a massive hole in my team strength, believe me'.

'I do understand the difficulties, DI Khan'.

'Course you do, sir'.

'Angela Lewis? I understand you want to bring her in. Can you tell me how that will progress the investigation?'

Khan ran her hand through her hair. This was turning out to be the night from hell.

'Sir, the night before Samuel Lewis took a heroin overdose his mobile was inundated with calls from his mother Angela'.

'Well, if he was in some kind of distress then, as his mother, she was no doubt trying to talk to him about it'.

'Granted, but why did Samuel Lewis have that press clipping of our first victim stuck to the wall of his room, sir? ' Khan reasoned. 'Is that why his mother was calling? Does she know why?'

Chief Superintendent Langton had put up with a lot of 'instinctive' fellow coppers in his time and sometimes he wanted to chastise them for the stupid fucking idiots they could sometimes be. Good solid police detective work is based on facts. Convictions can only be made with the support of facts. On the other hand, plenty of crimes have been solved by police officers following their 'instincts' and so he was prepared to give DI Khan the benefit of the doubt. Her instincts were what had caught his eye initially when she started to climb up through the ranks and her example in the solving of previous cases was what had given him his faith. But the pressure was on with regard to this case. Not just to get it solved and cleared up but also with regard to the allegations of her family being the subject of anti-Christian persecution that Angela Lewis was throwing out like rice at a wedding. She'd even got the Chief Constable of Lancashire involved and he'd not been best pleased at having to deal with the mater that he considered people further down the chain of command should've been able to sort out without him having to know anything about it.

'I'll give you as much time as I can, DI Khan,' said Langton. 'But I'll need positive results or at least tangible leads as soon as possible'.

'I understand, sir,' said Khan. 'And I'll be working flat out on it. But the suicide of Samuel Lewis is hanging over the murder of those two girls like the darkest shadow. I intend to find out why, sir, and when I do, I'll be able to unlock this entire case'.

'You just don't get it, man' said Muhammad as he tried to persuade Charlie that the propaganda he'd been absorbing from the visiting preacher at the mosque was not the voice of true Islam. They were on their way to school. He was getting increasingly worried that his friend was being sucked in by the extremist message to cover up the massive gap there'd been in his life so far. He was desperate to get him off this path. He felt like Charlie was slipping away. It scared him. 'I know you feel like this country has let you down and you want to somehow get your own back. But it isn't the country that's let you down, Charlie. It's your Mum and Dad because they were never there for you. You can't blame the whole county for that. Don't you see that, Charlie? Am I fucking getting through or what?'

'It's easy for you to say all that'.

'Why is it?'

'Because you're part of a family that acts like a family'.

'So, you think there are no skeletons in our cupboard? Well, you'd be wrong'.

'Is that why your Mum was crying when I got here earlier?'

'As it happens, yes' said Muhammad. 'She'd had a row with my dad. He can be a bloody awkward bastard at times'

'It's better than having a dad who's never there and couldn't give a shit about you'.

'I know, man, I know. I'm just trying to say that the grass isn't always greener and I'm glad my dad isn't the kind of ultra- traditional Muslim head of the family. You'll know that he doesn't force any dress code on my Mum or my sisters. He's brought us up to be good Muslims but also to be good British citizens and that means rejecting all that extremist shit'.

'Yeah, I know, I've got that for the thousandth time'.

'But even my dad clings on to some of the traditional ways when they clash with the British culture which we've been brought up in' said Muhammad. 'And even when it really hurts our family'.

'How so?'

'My Mum was crying because she and my Aunties have been trying to reach out to my dad's sister who was kicked out of the family by my grandparents years ago because she wouldn't go through with an arranged marriage'.

'You mean she disgraced the family'.

'You really have been listening to that extremist twat, haven't you? Look, my grandparents didn't grow up here. My Dad and his brothers and sisters did. They grew up Muslim, but they also grew up British and my Aunty Layla wanted to make her own choices about who she wanted to marry, and I don't blame her'.

'She should've obeyed her father'.

'Why should she? Why should she be forced into marrying someone she doesn't know and doesn't love? I tell you, if my parents tried to force that on my sisters, I'd fight my parents all the way. We'll all probably marry Muslims, but they'll be people of our own choice and because we're in love with them'.

'You're betraying your faith'.

'How dare you say that to me'.

'It's true! Okay, so tell me why your dad was arguing with your Mum?'

'Because he doesn't think that Aunty Layla should ever be brought back into the family out of respect for the wishes of my grandparents'.

'But you disagree?'

'Course I do. I respect my grandparents, but things have moved on. Aunty Layla is a police officer up in Blackpool. She's done really well for herself and the whole family should be

IN THE SHADOW OF THE TOWER

proud'.

'She's become part of the instrument of oppression against your faith. How can you defend her?'

'I don't defend her because I don't have to. She's done nothing wrong in my eyes. Now shut your fucking head if you're going to come out with all that crap about my Aunty. I mean it, Charlie. I don't want to hear it'.

Charlie went home after his spat with Muhammad. They needed to have a break from each other, but it didn't alter Charlie's view that Muhammad was going soft when it came to his faith. He didn't seem to mind that his sisters walked around wearing short skirts and that neither they nor his mother wore a scarf round their heads. Muhammad should be working with his father to discipline the female members of the family. They should be made to wear the burka. That's what a true Muslim male would be doing to separate the female members of his family from all the Western permissiveness that's all around them. It was only by adhering to the true meaning of Islam that the moral depravity of the western world could be overcome and these filthy, disgusting bitches with everything on show of a weekend could be stopped from contaminating the purity of Muslim girls who should be covered up to stop the lurid thoughts of all the sick minded young white men. Charlie had separated himself from his contemporaries. Every day at school these days he looks around and feels he has absolutely nothing in common with any of them and that they were heading for Hell with their barely disguised everyday comments about Islam and about how it was going to destroy civilisation. Well, he was going to fucking show them. Oh yes, his day would come when glory was only a kill away.

But what Charlie really couldn't get his head around was the disrespect Muhammad was showing his father over the way this Aunty Layla of his had clearly spat on the family honour. Why didn't Muhammad see the need to respect and support his father in keeping her out of the family? From the teaching Charlie had received he could see it as clear as daylight. She'd disobeyed her parents and if there was any justice then she should be punished for it, especially as she'd aligned herself with the enemy of Islam in the British establishment by becoming a police officer for fuck's sake. Why wasn't it grinding into Muhammad's soul like a poison? Why didn't he want to get revenge that would restore the family honour?

He put his key in the front door and could immediately smell the vile mix of cigarettes and alcohol that told him his mother was in somewhere. He found her in the lounge. She was sitting at the table with her back to the door and turned round when he came in. Her face was set. He'd never seen her eyes so cold.

'What's he done?' Charlie demanded.

'What's who done?'

'That prick who was here this morning?'

Tricia closed her eyes and rubbed the bridge of her nose. This wasn't going to be easy. But it had to be done. She lit another cigarette and dragged on it deeply before exhaling slowly and turning back to her son.

'If you're referring to Bruce he's gone'.

'Is he coming back?'

'No is the answer to that and it's your fault he's gone in the first place'.

'What are you blaming me for?'

'You couldn't just let me have a bit of happiness, could you? He'd been here less than a week. Less than a bloody week. I'd been happy for the first time in ages, and you had to go and destroy it with your rudeness and your attitude. Well, this morning he said he'd got second thoughts about staying any longer. He said his time off was too precious to spend it in the company of a teenager who didn't seem difficult but absolutely impossible. So, thank you, Charlie. Thank you for destroying my life one more flaming time'.

'What kind of mother puts that kind of shit on their son?'

'The kind of mother who's got you for a son, that's who!' she barged.

'You should love me and care for me, but you don't give a shit'.

'Oh, get the fucking violin out!' she mocked. 'Poor, pitiful Charlie who's had such a tragic life with such a lousy mother'.

'Yeah, well you got that right!'

Tricia stood up and marched over to him. Her face was almost touching his. 'It's your birthday in a couple of weeks. You'll be sixteen and do you know what I'm getting you for a birthday present?'

'It'll be the first time you've got me anything,' said Charlie. He detested her being so close. Her breath stank and her face was as ugly as Hell. She should be put into a hole in the ground and stoned to death.

'Well, this will be the first and the last' said Tricia in a voice of triumph. 'I don't know how I'm going to get the money together. I'll beg, borrow, or steal it if I have to but I'll get you some cash together and you're to leave this house with the proviso that you never come back here and you never try and contact me again. Do you understand, Charlie?'

'So that's your fucking birthday present? You're throwing me out?'

'Throwing you out? I'm disowning you, Charlie! I'm cutting you out of my life for good and making the best of a bad lot for both of us. We can both get on with our lives. We're toxic for each other, Charlie and once you're sixteen I'm no longer legally responsible for you. I'm counting the fucking days'

'He came into my room that first night he was stayed over'.

'Who did?'

'Who do you think? Bruce did!'

'You're a liar'.

'I'm not a liar!'

'Yes, you are! And if you think that making up lies like that is going to make me change my mind then you can forget it. Two weeks, Charlie. Two weeks and then we're done for good'.

TWELVE

'You look absolutely done in, babe' said Steve as he sat with his girlfriend at the breakfast table.

'And does my bum look big in this?' Khan questioned with a broad smile on her face. 'Do you want to tell me that as well?'

Steve laughed. 'Okay. But you know what I mean'.

'I do' said Khan who linked hands with her lover.

'We didn't get in from the hospital until after two and it's now coming up to eight o'clock' said Steve more earnestly than before. 'That's tough considering what you've got to go through. Couldn't you take the morning off and go in about one?'

'Steve, it's the same for you' Khan reasoned. 'You've got a full day ahead just like me and you've had no more sleep than I have'.

'But I'm not trying to catch a killer or killers in the line of what I do each day'.

'Babe, I'll be alright'.

'I worry about you'.

'There's no need. I'm not going to deliberately place

myself in danger' said Khan who then brushed the shoulder of Steve's car mechanic overalls with the palm of her hand. He had a grey t-shirt on today which meant that nobody would be tempted to treat by his exposed hairy chest like when he didn't wear anything underneath his overalls.

'Alright' said Steve who knew he may as well admit defeat. Layla was a strong woman who knew her own mind. It was one of the things he loved about her. 'But tonight, I'm claiming exclusive rights. We'll share a bath and I'll make your favourite for dinner. Then we'll relax in front of the TV. Do you get me?'

'Oh, I get you, Steve Palmer' said Khan who then moved her lips on his and they snogged for a good few minutes. 'I get you more and more each passing day'.

Khan answered a call on her mobile phone whilst Steve gathered up the breakfast dishes and loaded up the dishwasher. When Khan had finished on the phone she quickly picked up her things and made for the door.

'I've got to go, babe' she said before stopping to kiss Steve. The call had told her that another body had been found and just a short distance from where she and DC Beresford had encountered their assailant last night. How the blazes had the night team who'd been scouring the area missed it until now? I'm looking forward to our quiet night in tonight'.

'Me too. Stay safe on those mean streets, detective!'

Khan laughed. 'Mean streets? This is Blackpool we're talking about'.

'Exactly. So stay safe on those mean streets. There's a lot that a load of candy floss and arcades can hide'.

It had quite slipped Khan's mind that today all the local

schools went back after the summer holidays and therefore the roads were busier than they'd been of late in the hour between eight and nine. Clifton Drive was living up to its reputation as a nightmare during rush hour and Khan cursed because it had been so easy getting through during the holidays. In the years to come she and Steve would be spending the holidays entertaining the kids they were going to have one day. She got that sinking feeling when she turned onto Hornby Road. She'd only been there a few hours before.

'Sergeant Luke Morris' Khan greeted after she'd got out of her car and caught sight of who was waiting for her. 'Fancy seeing you here. You get all the nice jobs'

'So, it would seem, ma'am' replied Morris, cheerfully. 'Is there nobody with you today?'

The call Khan had received alerting her of the situation had come from central control who told her that they hadn't been able to contact DS Keith Drake. Well, he'd get it when she got hold of him and that was for sure. If she could be alive and kicking only hours after their incident the night before then Drake could be because he wasn't even injured.

'No, it looks like I'm handling this one solo for the moment,' said Khan. 'One of my team is off sick anyway after an incident we had last night'.

'Yes, I heard about that,' said Morris. 'It's the talk of the steamy as they say'.

'What?'

'My mother is from Glasgow, ma'am. It's a saying from up there when everybody's talking about a certain situation'.

'Got you,' said Khan. She wouldn't have expected anything else. News travels fast and what happened last night was probably all over the entire Lancashire force by now albeit with the usual embellishments of course. She dreaded what they might be because they'd probably show her in a less positive light than she'd like or that was fair. It went with the rank, especially as a woman. But it struck her as she stood there contemplating that Sergeant Luke Morris might be deserving of a temporary secondment to her murder squad. After all, she was going to feel the gap left by DC Justin Barnes and that meant she could justify asking for Morris to join her team on a temporary basis. From the way he conducted himself she was sure he was on course for a glittering career and maybe she could help him out a little bit with that. She made a mental note to speak to Chief Superintendent Langton. 'So, it looks like it's you and me for now, Sergeant Morris. Talk me through what we've got here'.

'Well, we're expecting the ambulance any moment, ma'am'.

'To take away the body?'

'No, ma'am,' said Morris. 'This one is still alive'.

'What? Are you sure?'

'She's hanging on apparently but yes, she's still with us. But there are other differences with the previous two cases, ma'am'.

'Oh?'

'But I'll let the pathologist explain those to you'.

Khan hoped she wasn't going to be looking at some kind of copycat shit from some piece of trash who thought they could be clever.

'Ah, DI Khan' said the pathologist, Ross Carter.

'You're a sight for sore eyes in the morning'.

'Oh, you make me blush'

'I don't think anybody could make you blush'.

'Oh, you'd be surprised'.

'I'm sure I wouldn't' said Khan eyeing his stubble and noting that it added to his sexual allure. She loved it when Steve didn't shave. She loved rubbing faces with him when his was covered in stubble. She loved it even more when he went down on her and his face was covered in stubble. Oh God, she loved that. But enough of these lustful wanderings. 'Now talk to me'.

'Well, she's still alive but she's unconscious and her vital signs are weak. The quicker that ambulance gets here, and we can get her to hospital the better'.

Khan turned to Sergeant Luke Morris and asked him to use his radio to find out where the ambulance was. He told her that it was only seconds away.

'And what else?'

'We've got an ID' Carter revealed.

'Yes? And? There's obviously something exciting about it so don't keep me waiting, Ross'.

'Her name is Deborah Lewis'.

'Lewis? As in the daughter of Daniel and Angela Lewis?'

'That's it' Carter confirmed. He led her across to where the unconscious body of Deborah Lewis was lying on a stretcher. 'She had ID in her bag and what makes her different is that she must've struggled more forcefully than the other two girls. There's been an attempt at strangulation, but the cause of her unconsciousness is a blow to the side of the head'.

'What the hell was she doing down here?'

'This is certainly turning out to be a murky case for you'.

'You're not kidding'. She looked down at Deborah Lewis's body. 'That's a nasty birthmark she's got on the side of her face. And it's a shame because she's a pretty girl but I bet the superficiality of people today means they never see past that scar'.

'You're probably right,' said Carter. 'Now there's been no attempt made to take any blood from her. So, I'm guessing that means she's not HIV positive and the killer realised that about her'.

'So, he must've known her'

'That or the activity of your patrol last night disturbed him before he'd had a chance to take the blood'.

'So, she could be HIV positive?'

'Well of course she could be, but I won't know that until we're back at the lab. What I can say with some degree of professional certainty is that it doesn't look like she was a drug user because there are no syringe marks either up her arms or anywhere else. But there are marks all over her body showing that she's been systemically beaten'.

The ambulance turned up and as she watched it speed away to Blackpool Victoria hospital with the still unconscious Deborah Lewis, Khan sensed that the development could provide her with the breakthrough she needed once she was able to talk to Deborah and despite the obvious pain that the Lewis family must be going through regardless of who was to blame. But before she did anything else she had to make a call to someone who would find this latest twist in the story useful enough to give her something back in return. The likes of Chief Superintendent Langton wouldn't like her association with Josh Walker of the Blackpool Evening News but stuff him. If Walker could help her get to a result, then she had no qualms about using him in a potentially mutually beneficial relationship.

Marilyn Blunt had been an independent councilor on the Greater Fylde council for over ten years. She'd steered her way quite successfully from retirement as a head teacher at one of the town's comprehensives to a council seat that became available when the previous Tory councilor died. His rather premature death at the age of fifty-eight from a heart attack gave Marilyn Blunt just the break she needed, and his death really couldn't have come at a more convenient time for her and the plans that she and her friends had made for her. His body wasn't even cold before Marilyn was writing campaign leaflets with her own name on them.

But much as Marilyn could stick the knife into the backs of her colleagues without blinking if it meant she got what she wanted, all her actions were about preserving her own position. She did only as much as she needed to as a councilor so that nobody outside her own circles would notice that she was a fucking lazy bitch. Her campaign team had given up trying to get her out on the doorstep doing some proper campaigning as councilors really should do.

The meeting of the council cabinet had ended, and all the other councilors were filing out of the room on the first floor of the town hall on Talbot Square. Lesley watched as Arthur Bellow tried to make eye contact with Marilyn, but she was too busy talking to one of the other members of their little self- serving coterie. Lesley hated the sight of them, but she was delighting in starting to finally get the better of them with information given to her by Josh Walker on the Blackpool Evening News. Arthur Bellow was behaving himself politically after their little talk the other day and now she had a meteorite aimed at the heart and soul of Marilyn Blunt that would sort her out once and for all too.

'Have they managed to find your dog yet, Lesley?' Marilyn asked once the room was empty. With only the two of them in there its size suddenly became more noticeable and it was almost as if their voices were echoing.

'Sadly not, no' Lesley replied. It had been a hell of a week at home since the family dog 'Patch' had disappeared. The black

Labrador was such a part of the family, and it broke her heart to see her boys in such pain. 'It's really affected the boys because he really is their dog. We've had him since they were both toddlers. They don't know what to do with themselves and we're all so worried in case the worst happens, and we never see him again'.

'I can't imagine how bad it must be,' said Marilyn. 'Especially, like you say, for the boys'

'Well anyway, shall we go through to my office?' Lesley suggested. All the false concern from Marilyn was starting to make her feel quite sick. 'It'll be easier to talk there'.

'Will it take long? Only I've got an appointment at the nail salon. It's my niece's own business, you know, up on Dickson Road near Gynn Square. She's doing ever so well. She's got this lovely Dutch girl called Judith working for her now too. She's married to a local lad, and they live up in Cleveleys. She speaks impeccable English'.

'Well let's go down to my office and it'll take however long it takes' said Lesley who wanted to tell the stupid Dame Edna lookalike to shut the fuck up. But instead, she let her follow her down to her office without any words being spoken and once they were inside, she gestured for Marilyn to take a seat before doing so herself. And there they were. Either side of Lesley's desk. She then produced a file from a drawer on the left of her desk and waited a few seconds before continuing.

'So, then Marilyn' she began. 'How's your bank balance looking these days?'

'What?' Marilyn questioned indignantly. 'That's none of your business'.

'Oh, but it is when some of the cash sloshing around in that account of yours is dirty'.

'Now just a minute, lady. You'd better shut your mouth now unless you've got a very good lawyer'.

Lesley had never used much make-up and she couldn't stand the look of these women in their sixties, like Marilyn in front of her, who thought they'd look twenty years younger by slapping it all on. It didn't make them look any younger in Lesley's opinion. It just made them look like overly made- up tarts who were living under the very grand illusion that they were evergreen. She blamed Joan Collins for it. Lesley thought that the veteran so-called actress looked more like a man in drag these days and a total caricature of her incredibly talentless self. She compared the likes of her and Marilyn to some of the women who lived in Lesley's council ward and for whom life had been anything but kind. She watched them struggling with the pain that tore them to pieces inside. She did whatever she could for those women because they were heroes in Lesley's eyes. That's why she made sure the council was investing in services to assist with things like domestic violence and teenagers who were on drugs. That's one of the things Lesley believed was her job as a councilor. Those people needed a champion. They didn't need someone like Marilyn Blunt.

'Oh, I don't need a lawyer, Marilyn,' said Lesley. 'I've got all the proof I need, and it'll be you needing the lawyer unless we can come to an amicable agreement'.

'What the hell are you talking about?'

'Oh, I haven't got time for you to start being cute, Marilyn, so let me spell it out for you loud and clear. For several years now you've had an offshore account on the Isle of Man that you've been feeding rather generously with heaps of regular cash'.

'Don't be absurd'.

'Oh, I've got all the details here, Marilyn,' said Lesley. 'Copies of your statements going back to 2006. Now, when I say you've been feeding your offshore account that's not quite true, is it? It's been fed so handsomely by a trail of cash which goes back to the Daniel Lewis Corporation. And how strange that during all that time your son-in-law has been working in the planning department of this very council and every time an application for something came through from the Daniel Lewis Corporation it was passed. Office blocks that have never be let, luxury apartments that have never been sold, all investments by the Daniel Lewis Corporation to cleanse some of their dirtier cash from some of their more questionable investments. They wouldn't want it known that they were making millions from companies based in the illegally occupied West Bank for instance. And you and your son-in-law have been providing them with the perfect cover. And coming back to your son-in-law he now of course has his own offshore account so he can watch his own considerable pile gain in value. So good to keep it in the family'.

'How did you get hold of this fairy tale?'

'Never mind how I got hold of it, Marilyn. But you're looking seriously worried. In fact, you really look like someone has stepped over your grave'.

'You don't understand'.

'What don't I understand, Marilyn?'

'The potential, no, the certain consequences of your actions' spluttered Marilyn whose façade was clearly slipping fast. 'Can I have a glass of water, please?'

Lesley poured the glass of water and handed it to Marilyn. Her hand was shaking as she took it and brought it to her mouth. 'You're enjoying this aren't you?'

'I admit I'm taking a certain amount of satisfaction from it, yes'.

'You've had it in for me all along'.

'And you haven't had it in for me? There's a line of candidates waiting to fill your shoes who actually want to make a difference to the lives of the people of this town, Marilyn. All you're doing is treading water from election to election and yes, I wanted to stop you and give some of those other people a chance. I just didn't realise that the chance would land in my lap with such dynamite power'.

'You don't know the people of this town' Marilyn scoffed. 'Half of them have never seen a thousand pounds in their sad, stupid lives because they're too bone idle to get off their fat backsides and earn it. And the rest couldn't care less about anyone else as long as they don't have to pay huge amounts of tax. Oh sorry, what people like you call progressive taxation. Look, I only stood as an independent because that was the only way to get elected in my ward'.

'And because you wouldn't know a political principle from a piece of toilet paper' Lesley scoffed. God this woman made her skin crawl.

'That's what so-called conviction politicians like you don't get about local government. We're not here to change the world. We're only here to maintain the status quo in our little bit of it'.

'You're a shameful piece of opportunistic trash. Yes, I'm here to make a difference and yes, I'm here to change lives for the better and yes, I believe in the ticket I stand on and that makes me a far superior person to you, Marilyn. So let me tell you what's going to be happening here. You and your son-in-law are in very serious trouble, or you would be if I passed this information on to the police'.

'You can't be serious?'

'Oh, I am serious. I'm deadly serious in fact. I want to rid the council of parasites like you so that the people can be properly and meaningfully represented. So, this is what we're going to do. You are going to vote in the council exactly as I tell you to which will mean voting against the Daniel Lewis Corporation when the vote comes up for the council to decide on which bid has won the contract for the town centre redevelopment'.

'You really are deluded' Marilyn sneered.

'Well, the alternative is for you to go to prison for fraud'.

'Go on?'

'You will also not seek re-selection in your ward when that comes up. And you will also tell your son-in-law that he will take voluntary redundancy when it is offered to him in the coming months'.

'So, I'll be your bloody lap dog until the next local election?'

'In a manner of speaking, yes'.

'Well, if you think I'm putting up with that'.

'Well like I said, Marilyn, the alternative is for you to go to prison. So, do we have a deal?'

'It doesn't look like you leave me much choice'.

'No it doesn't, does it. But look at it this way. I'm letting you off quite lightly really. I mean, if I did send this file to the police then the ensuing scandal would be an unnecessary diversion from serving the people of this town. And there's been too much of that already from the likes of you. Now I think we're done here. So, if you don't mind'.

Marilyn Blunt stood up and was initially unsteady on her feet. She stepped round to the door and then tearfully said 'It was my turn to be deputy mayor after the next election'.

Lesley looked up at her and said, 'Oh get over it'.

The next morning Lesley Hammond was feeling rather pleased with herself politically. She now had both Arthur Bellow and Marilyn Blunt, two of her weakest links, right where she wanted them and for all the right reasons. The overall goal was to get a team of councilors who were all committed to making the town a better place for everyone and to rid the council of individuals who were carpet bagging the office of elected councilor for their own egotistical reasons.

Her sons had gone back to school, but they were still so worried about the disappearance of the family dog 'Patch'. He'd never run off before. It just wasn't like him. He loved his home. He loved his family. She really didn't know what they were going to do.

She decided to nip out and get a sandwich for lunch and as she walked past the security desk just inside the main door, Alf was on duty at the welcome/security desk.

'How's the misses, Alf?' asked Lesley who knew that Alf's wife Maureen had been getting over an operation to remove a cancerous growth from her lung.

'She's not too bad, thanks. She was quite perky this morning to be honest'.

'And how are you coping?'

'Oh, I'm alright,' said Alf.

'Well, you know where I am if you need a chat'.

'I do and thank you, I appreciate it'.

'No worries' said Lesley, smiling as she made for the door. Then Alf stopped her.

'By the way, Lesley. A parcel has been handed in for you'.

'A parcel?' said Lesley who turned back to Alf's desk. 'For me?'

'Yes. Some young girl handed it to me. I didn't get chance to get her name before she was off again'. He reached below his desk and pulled out the parcel. It was quite heavy and there was a note attached in an envelope.

'Thanks, Alf' said Lesley as she took the envelope and opened it. Inside was a note that read '... hope you enjoy the enclosed steaks and minced meat. The steaks would be perfect for a family barbecue, and you could turn the minced meat into meatballs. I usually prefer beef, but they say it's not a 'Patch' on the real thing ... '

Lesley felt the weight of what she was looking at come crashing down on her. She recoiled and stepped back. The rotten, stinking bastard. She knew this would be the doing of Daniel Lewis. All of a sudden, she felt light- headed. She started to hyper ventilate and thought she was going to faint. Then Alf came round and put his arms round her.

'Lesley? What's wrong?'

'Oh my God, Alf' said Lesley after she'd regained some of her composure but then started to cry. 'What the hell am I going to tell my poor boys?'

THIRTEEN

The NHS health centre on Whitegate Drive in Blackpool was the kind of ultra- modern state-of-the-art facility that still wouldn't please the most implacably opposed individual to the whole idea of universally free medical care at the point of need.

'Still doesn't restore my faith in the NHS' grumbled DS Drake, his face set and determined not to see any good anywhere. 'The whole service is bankrupt'.

'Look around you, Keith' Khan retorted as she spun round in the reception area and pointed at all she found. 'It doesn't look very bankrupt to me'.

'We're only seeing what they want us to see, ma'am. A bit like if we visited North Korea'.

Oh, give me strength, thought Layla. 'Keith, when did you last use the NHS?'

'Well in terms of me personally it's been years since I've been ill' he admitted. 'Ellen always sorts all that out with the kids and largely shuts me out. It's been one of the biggest problems between us to be honest'.

'So, you've no idea what goes on in today's NHS other than what you get from the Daily hate sheets and anecdotes from people who think they know everything about everything but actually don't know anything about anything at all'.

'Well, if you put it that way, ma'am'

'Well, I do so shut the fuck up about it'.

Drake was stunned into silence by his boss's forthright

nature, but he'd come to expect it as part of her way of dealing with the ongoing repairs they were making to their relationship. They had their good days and bad days, but Drake wondered how long it could go on for. One of them would get fed up sooner or later and as far as Drake was concerned it wasn't that he had anything against Khan personally. The problem was that he'd always seen her as a professional rival and now she'd overtaken him. That's what it all came down to.

They were just short of the large grey plastic looking doors that led to the sexual health clinic when Khan stopped and turned to Drake.

'How's DC Beresford?' she asked.

'She's fine, ma'am' said Drake who actually thought that DC Beresford had been swinging the leg a little since the incident on the street the other night when they'd all been out trying to gather some useful information. He thought she could be back at work now, but he wasn't going to drop her in it with the boss. 'She's hoping to be back at work tomorrow'.

The receptionist at the sexual health clinic led them into the consulting room of Dr Kieran Gillespie. Khan thought he was a very modern looking doctor in his light blue polo shirt and jeans, trainers on his feet and short dark hair, boyish good looks and probably in his mid- thirties. She had a friend who fancied her doctor. She used to insist on him listening to her chest even when she went in with a suspected in growing toenail. All the hints she dropped and demure looks she gave him never got her anywhere though. She eventually found out that he was very happily married and intended to stay that way.

'Thank you for taking time to see us, Dr Gillespie' said Khan after she'd sat down in one of the two grey swivel chairs the doctor had brought across from where they'd been parked against the wall. Drake sat in the other. Dr Gillespie sat with his back to his desk facing them. He moved about a lot as he talked. Either he was leaning forward with his elbows on his knees, or he stretched out against the back of his chair and his long legs stuck out in front of him like they were about to take root. His big hands with their long thick fingers were either folded in front of him, or on his lap or folded across the back of his head. He must be able to switch on the big doctor thing when he needed to, thought Khan. The way he was coming across was so laid back he was almost lying on the floor. One other thing that Khan noticed to her great pleasure was that he was speaking with quite a strong and very broad Geordie accent and that had always been one of her favourites. He was probably one of the few working- class boys who'd listened to his teachers and done good.

'Always happy to help wherever I can, officers' said Dr Gillespie. 'I assume it's about the murders you're investigating. I won't say the word 'vampire' because I don't want to insult your intelligence and I expect you're pretty sick and tired of hearing all the wisecracks around it, right?'

Khan smiled. Cute and sensitive. Just like her Steve. 'You'd be right there, doctor, yes'.

'So do you know why he changed his MO for this latest one?' asked Dr Gillespie. 'I mean, I understand he didn't take any blood and the victim is alive but still unconscious?'

'That's right' said Khan who'd been thinking of little else in the hours since Deborah Lewis had been found still alive and in full possession of all her blood. Was it just that the killer had been startled into making a run for it before he'd had the chance to take the blood? Or had this latest attempted murder been the work of a second killer? It had kept her awake half the night. And Deborah Lewis? How the hell had she got mixed up with all this? 'It's interesting, doctor, because we'd been working on the assumption that whoever had murdered the first two victims had known about their HIV status. Otherwise, what would be the point of taking their tainted blood? The killer must have some purpose in taking it'

'But not from the latest victim'.

'No. But if we could get it about why he took it from the first two we might be on to something'.

'That's why we've come to see you, Dr Gillespie,' said Drake. 'To see if you can help us shed some light on where we might look'.

'Assuming you are looking for some kind of medical professional or someone associated with the treatment of HIV?'

'Well, whoever is doing it must have some kind of specialist knowledge'.

'Yes. I agree' said Dr Gillespie. 'I ran the details of the first two victims through our system here and they came back negative'.

'Which means?'

'Which means that neither of them sought treatment here'.

'But where else could they seek diagnosis and possible treatment in Blackpool other than here?' asked Khan. 'Is there anywhere else?'

'Well, yes, there are two possibilities' said Dr Gillespie. 'There's a gay men's sauna downtown on Church Street ... '

'... oh well' said Khan, smiling mischievously. 'DS Drake can check that one out. Alone and with a rather large towel to wrap around himself'.

Dr Gillespie smiled back at her, noting the look of discomfort on DS Drake's face. 'And then there's a charity called The Blackpool HIV Trust'.

'No imagination lost on thinking up the title,' said Drake. 'But I guess the title doesn't really mean much'.

'You mean you've never heard of it?'

Drake blushed. 'Can't say I have, no'.

'Well, it comes up if you do a google search. Anyway, the point here is that they may have touched the system through either of these two ways. Also, the HIV virus can't survive outside the body'.

Drake was a touch confused by this. 'So how do people like

haemophiliacs contract it from what they call contaminated blood?'

'Well, what I was going to go on and say' said Dr Gillespie who was continually amazed at how ignorant people could still be when it came to HIV. Even professionals like police officers didn't seem to know the basics. 'Is that the virus can't survive outside the body unless the blood it has contaminated is specially stored in the way that all donated blood is'

'So, what are you saying, Doctor?' asked Khan.

'I'm saying that it must be being stored somewhere that will preserve it until whoever it is has been able to do with it what they intend. Now in my opinion that means your killer is some kind of medical professional or someone with close access to medical facilities. Now, in all seriousness, the probability of your victims consulting the gay men's sauna is probably small but worth checking out. I do think you should contact the Blackpool HIV Trust because they have been holding mobile HIV testing centres in the parts of town where the working girls operate and offer them a confidential way of getting tested. All the people who work for them are medical professionals and although their service is offered as confidential to their clients, they do obviously take some basic details about who they're dealing with and that includes a photograph. You might think that's strange, but it's sold to them by the trust as a means of matching any future developments with an individual's history'.

'I see,' said Khan. 'Can you tell us how we get in touch with them doctor, please?'

Dr Gillespie turned to his desk and picked up a file which, after turning back again, he handed to Khan. 'It's all in there. The guy in charge of it is a retired doctor called Malcolm Arnott. You'd think he'd be a bit old school but he's actually quite approachable. His number is on the paperwork there. It's not a big charity but they do what they can and if there's anything they can't handle then they usually refer their clients to us whether they listen or not'.

'But doesn't that go against their whole independent ethos?' Khan questioned.

'People have to be treated at some point,' said Dr Gillespie.

'Okay, well we'll need to take statements from yourself and the rest of the staff here regarding your movements over the last seven days' said Khan. 'And we'll need the contact details of anyone who isn't on duty today. DI Drake here will stay behind and take those statements'

Dr Gillespie was slightly taken aback by the sudden apparent sternness in DI Khan but that was probably just her switching back to business mode when necessary. 'Of course. We'll make it as easy as we can for you'.

'If I could set up in a room somewhere that would be good' said Drake who was wondering about having to think about all this protection from sexual diseases stuff if and when he did start dating again. He didn't really know if he wanted a real full-on relationship again, at least not for some time yet until his wounds had at least begun to heal, but he did miss sex.

'Doctor, can I ask you something?' said Khan who'd been lost in her own silent wanderings and the more she thought the more something was starting to come together that might add up to a motive.

'I thought that's why you were here, officer?'

Khan smiled. 'Quite so. I know that there are people out there who are HIV positive and who deliberately infect other people as a means of getting back at fate and whatnot. But is it really that common?'

'Not as much as it was but it does come into play now and then'.

'So, there are people out there who will use their HIV status to get back at someone in some way?'

'Well, yes. Why do you ask?'

'Just something that's crossing my mind'.

The Curry Leaf Indian restaurant on Red Bank Road in Bispham was the other curry house of choice for Khan and Steve. She drove past it at four that afternoon and was suddenly overwhelmed with hunger. She could just picture their garlic chicken on a plate in front of her ready to be devoured. She'd missed lunch and by the time she realised she'd kind of gone past it. But now she had to put the consumption of food on her near agenda. She'd text Steve and tell him not to make any dinner. They'd go to the Curry Leaf. Her treat. It would give him a break from seeing to all their catering arrangements. He was a fantastic cook and he enjoyed it whereas Khan could barely put a meal together and she hated even thinking about food shopping. Steve got it from his Mum who was also a great cook. Whenever she made a cottage pie and knew that Khan was going round she always made extra because she knew that Khan loved it and would always go for second helpings. Khan loved Steve's Mum. They were very close. It was almost as if the universe had sent her Steve's Mum to make up for the fact that her own Mum had disowned her for wanting to make her own choices in life. But whatever the reason as Mum-in-laws go she was an absolute diamond.

She reached the traffic lights at the top of Red Bank Road and turned right along the coast road. She'd always loved the view of the Irish Sea from this part of the North Shore. With only the Blackpool to Fleetwood tramway and short stretch of grass between that and the walking path along the cliff edge it was a clear view. She always found it inspiring and today with everything that was swimming through her head she needed it to speak to her and give her a clue as to how she was going to join up the dots of her thoughts.

She took the first right and parked up in a side street next to the local Methodist church. She then walked back onto the coast road and back in the direction of the junction of Red Bank Road where she crossed over to the tram station and then to the right where a small children's park area had been created with swings, roundabouts, and even a couple of trampolines. There were a couple of families around and then she saw Josh Walker of the Courier sitting on a bench facing the sea.

'If I didn't know any better, I'd be suspecting you of being a paedophile sat there amongst all these kids' said Khan.

'Don't be disgusting'.

'Hey, lighten up. I was only joking'.

'Well just because I'm a single man in my late thirties who isn't gay doesn't mean that I'm a kid fiddler. Alright?'

Josh stood up and started walking along the cliff. Khan followed him. She didn't have time for this. She needed information. A journalist behaving like a normal human being who gets stressed is so not what she needed.

'Look, what's wrong with you?' asked Khan. He did look more put out than usual, to be fair, she thought. She was well used to him with his tie two floors down, his shirt open at the neck, his suit looking like he'd just slept in it and his eyes looking like he hadn't closed them in sleep since the last election. But this was more serious.

'I was sexually abused as a child by my uncle' he revealed.

Khan felt awful. 'Josh, I'm so sorry. I didn't know and even though I didn't know the joke, if you can call it that, was pretty crass anyway'.

Joshua stopped. 'You weren't to know. But I don't talk about it so now I've told you please respect that'.

'I will, Josh. Absolutely I will'.

'Okay' he said, gesturing to a long polished wooden seat that was one of several that were placed along the cliff edge. 'Let's sit over there and talk'.

They sat down on the bench and Khan asked 'So what's this all about? What have you found out about Daniel Lewis? I assume it's all about him?'

'You assume correctly, officer. He's been using some of the youngest and most vulnerable of the working girls in this town as weapons against his business opponents'.

'How do you mean?'

'I mean he offers them these young girls for sex in exchange for supporting his business objectives. Even local councillors have partaken of his generosity. It's the sickest trade'.

'It's revolting, Josh'.

'He had the dog of the leader of Blackpool council turned into steaks'.

DI Khan thought she might be sick. 'What?'

'He thought it would break Councillor Hammond's resolve and determination to deal with him and finish his involvement with more or less every crime in this town. With my help she's found out things about a couple of her councillors and she's used the information against them to make them toe the line and vote against the awarding of the town centre redevelopment plan to Lewis. Anyway, Lewis found out what she'd done to thwart his plans and was none too pleased about it so he had her family dog taken from outside their house and turned into steaks that he delivered to her at the town hall'.

'God in Heaven'.

'Well, I don't believe in him, but I get your gist'.

'She hasn't reported this to us'

'She's probably too scared'.

'Or she's staying quiet for some other reason. Either way, I'm not happy that she hasn't brought the matter to the police'.

'Yes, well I'd talk to her if I was you'.

'Don't you worry, I intend to'.

'But coming back to the evil one himself, he's been using his own daughters, Melissa and Verity, to sleep with his potential business partners'

'But not the other one? Not Deborah?'

'No. Because of the birthmark scar on her face she wasn't considered pretty enough'.

'So, what was she doing out on the streets that night she was nearly killed? She's still unconscious by the way. We haven't been able to talk to her'.

'I think she was trying to prove to Daddy that she was just as good as the other two when it came to doing her bit for the family business. I once reported about a girl who was so screwed up that she killed herself because her Daddy never came to her room at night like he went to the rooms of her two sisters'.

'Some people lead such horrible lives' said Khan. 'It doesn't bear thinking about'.

Walker reached into his over the shoulder bag and produced a thick dossier which he handed to Khan. 'Everything is in there. Dates, places, people'.

'This is very generous, Josh, considering I haven't been able to give you much'.

'Well, it's gone beyond that now, at least it has for me. I want you to destroy the bastard'.

'I wish all journalists were like you instead of the usual thing of holding back what we need to make an arrest so that they'll steal the glory with a front page'.

'Yeah well, have your dig. But we'll be running all this on Friday which is the day the council makes its decision on whether or not to grant the Lewis corporation the contract to redevelop the town centre'.

'And presumably they're not going to get it?'

'Correct. Councillor Hammond will be able to gather enough votes together to make the decision go her way and award it to someone else. That will be the end financially for Lewis. It all sounds so simple when you're talking about bringing an end to local government corruption but of course it won't quite go as smoothly as that'.

Khan couldn't wait to get back to the office and start reading Walker's dossier. She skipped through the pages with her fingers. 'I'll need to pass this to the fraud squad'.

'I thought you would,' said Josh. 'It makes sense. Well, I'm going into hiding until after the arrest of Daniel Lewis and believe me, there's more than enough in there for that to happen pretty soon'.

'I can understand that'.

'Nobody will know where I am including my parents'.

'This stuff must be hot'.

'Oh, you'll burn your fingers' said Josh. 'But there is one more thing I can tell you'.

'Which is?'

'Angela Lewis is not the mother of Samuel Lewis'.

Khan recoiled with surprise. 'Could you say that again, please?'

'She's the mother of Melissa, Verity, and Deborah Lewis but not Samuel'.

'So, who is, was Samuel's mother?'

'That's the answer I've not been able to find, officer. I hope you and your team will have more luck. But keep looking over your shoulder. This is an evil man you're dealing with'.

'And you watch yourself too, my friend'.

'Tell me what it's been like?' Tricia asked. She was watching Charlie packing his things together. He was going to move into his mate Muhammad's house now that his mother was chucking him out. She was drinking a rather large vodka and tonic. It was the only thing she could do to get through.

'I don't know what you mean'.

'Tell me what it's been like to hate me so much for all these years?'

'You wouldn't understand. If you did, then you wouldn't even need to ask me that kind of stupid question'.

'Because you see I've been thinking' said Tricia who was on the edge of inebriation but not quite there yet. She was sitting on the end of Charlie's bed whilst he emptied the room of everything he had. 'You've been so consumed by all this hatred for me that you've just never been able to work out that it wasn't all my fault. Oh, I do admit I haven't always got it right, but I have always been here for you'.

Charlie saw red. 'Been here for me? Fucking been here for me? How can you sit there and talk such rubbish! As soon as I was able to stand and walk for myself and could get something I recognised as food from the fridge you washed your hands of me. Been there for me? What a laugh. I wish Aunty Rosie had been my Mum. She is a Mum to Chloe and Abigail. She's a proper Mum. Whereas you're just a drunken old slag who never gave a damn about me as long as you picked yourself up a fuck for the night'.

'You don't know how lonely I've been since your father walked out!'

'Walked out? He never walked in! He never lived with you or with us. He took one look at you and the tsunami you call a life and ran as fast as he could. I don't blame him anymore. I don't even hate him. But I hate you'.

'What? You don't hate him, but you hate me for sticking around and doing the best I could? You ungrateful little piece of shit'.

'Yeah, that's me. Ungrateful for getting fuck all. You're like Mother Teresa. She gets all those poor kids to get down on their knees and thank God. Thank him? What for? They've got nothing. And nothing is what you've given to me. That Teresa bitch should've got what was due her. You all should've. All of you Christian slags who fucked us all up. You should be buried in the ground until only your head and neck are showing and then you should be stoned to death. Do you hear me? Stoned to death!'

Tricia felt a chill go down her spine at the look of sheer hatred in her son's eyes. Where was all this talk coming from?

'You can't mean that?'

'Too right I mean it. Sharia law would sort slags like you out'.

'You've gone mad'.

'You haven't got a clue what I'm talking about, have you?'

'No, no I don't, but you're scaring the bloody life out of me'.

'Well, I haven't even started yet'.

'What do you mean?'

'You'll soon see. But why should it be anything to do with you? You're throwing me out on my sixteenth birthday. Time to do exactly what I want'.

FOURTEEN

Getting an agreement from the powers that be for Sergeant Luke Morris to join Khan's team on a temporary basis was surprisingly quick and easy despite all the internal bullshit of bureaucracy. Chief Superintendent Langton had agreed straight away and Luke's keenness to join Khan's team, even for a temporary period until DC Justin Barnes was able to return to work, had clearly supported his case. There had been rumblings, especially from the police federation, the police officer's trade union, that she should have put it out to an open recruitment process and invited people to apply. But bullshit to all that. They had a point, but she didn't have the time. There was a killer or killers still out there waiting to be captured.

'Okay, Luke?' she said as she walked into the main office where DS Drake and Sergeant Luke Morris were busy at their desk computers. A sudden bolt of clarity had shot through her brain reminding her of something she'd almost forgotten. 'Now before DC Barnes was so rudely interrupted by our hit and run bastard, he was about to look into someone for me. Now it's going to be your job'.

'Bring it on, ma'am,' said Morris.

'I want you to get everything you can find on a woman

IN THE SHADOW OF THE TOWER

called Vivian Blackstone who is deputy head of the boarding school where Samuel Lewis took his overdose. And I mean I want everything. Where she's from, where she's been, who her friends are, what newspaper she reads, how long she's been teaching and if she had any other career before that. And if you can really get deep into her habits then how often she masturbates'.

That last sentence drew a broad smile from Morris and a raised eyebrow from Drake.

'Oh don't look at me like that, Drake' said Khan. 'You're a man of the world and it's no less than a male officer in my position would say'.

Drake shrugged his shoulders. 'It's a brave new world I suppose, ma'am'.

'It is if you've never masturbated before' Khan quipped. She'd once had to show a girl friend of hers how to masturbate because she genuinely didn't know. The poor cow now lived with about a dozen cats and at thirty-two had never had a lasting boyfriend. 'Any old how, and this is for both of you. It's almost six o'clock and I'm going to call it a night for all of us. Go home and get some rest because I want you both here by eight o'clock in the morning for a full briefing fully functioning and ready to make some real breakthroughs on this case. Something is in there that we're failing to see but our blindness is not going to go on endlessly. DS Drake?'

'Yes, ma'am?'

'Do you know if DC Philippa Beresford will be joining us?'

'I don't, ma'am, no, I'm sorry'.

'It's okay, you're not her keeper. I just wondered if she'd said anything to you, that's all'.

'No. And she hasn't been in contact with you?'

'No, she hasn't. I've tried calling her, but it goes straight to voicemail. Any news on when Malcolm Arnott of the Blackpool HIV trust will be back from his holidays and able to speak to us?'

'Apparently, the day after tomorrow, ma'am,' said Morris.

'Good, that'll give us plenty of time to get at Angela Lewis when we interview her in the morning. Did we find anything out about Arnott?'

'Well, it seems he's been a one for the ladies in his time' Drake explained. 'He left his wife and four children back in the late nineties for his then receptionist. Despite the scandal it caused they stuck it out and he built a practice in Layton that is still thriving now although they are both retired from it. He and Marcia are still together even though it's rumoured he's had a few affairs over the years. But the most interesting thing about him is that he seems to have done well financially for a retired GP'.

'And do we know why that could be?'

'It's rumoured that he's been taking back handers from pharmaceutical companies for several years now to get doctors across the region to order the said company's drugs. He's also a close friend of Daniel Lewis. Arnott has managed to accumulate a property portfolio up and down the Fylde that's currently worth about half a million pounds'

'Nice work if you can get it,' said Morris.

'It certainly is' said Khan. 'And I reckon that Arnott and his HIV trust provided Lewis with shall we say, discreet, treatment for the prostitutes controlled by Lewis. Well, it will sure give us a lot to talk to Mr. Arnott about when he comes back from sunning himself'.

The next morning DS Keith Drake woke up with a start and opened his eyes wide. This was a feeling he hadn't known for years. It was the feeling of waking up with someone beside him and yet feeling even lonelier than if he'd woken up alone. Because waking up alone was what he was getting used to. Waking up alone was what he was beginning to count on as the day began.

From the other side of the room, he could hear someone crying and then he remembered. Was it that second bottle of wine with Philippa last night? Or was it the third that led to those moments of getting closer and closer and the assertions that they were two grown- ups who could take it and then leave it. Just one night when the wall of pain inside them both could come falling down. Drake knew it could turn out to be a bad idea when they shared a house together which was difficult if they wanted to keep it casual. But then as he kissed Philippa and tasted the sheer pleasure of a woman again, he couldn't help himself. They'd undressed each other with ridiculous speed and before he knew it, he was inside her and she was arching her back to enhance the sensation. They'd carried on again when they'd got up to bed. So why was she now crying?

He lifted himself up on his elbows. 'Philippa? Phil? What's wrong?'

Philippa was sat on the floor in the corner of the room, naked and crying her heart out. She didn't answer his question. She just shook her head.

'Philippa, it wasn't that bad, was it?'

'Oh God, Keith, you men and your performance obsessions! Well look, if it had not been for my other worries then I'd have been quite happy with last night. There, isn't that what you wanted to hear?

'Only if it's the truth?'

'Well let me tell you something you don't want to hear but which is the truth. It's the unmistakable, undeniable truth that says we really shouldn't have done that last night'.

Keith scratched his head. 'I don't understand, Philippa. I don't have any regrets. Why should you? We're both free agents. And what did you mean just then about your other worries? What's that all about?'

'I need to tell you something'.

'Tell me what? Do you think I used you, is that it?'

'We used each other, Keith. But we should've used protection'.

'What about the morning after pill?'

'Jesus, are you thick or something?'

'I beg your pardon?'

'Getting pregnant is the least of my bloody worries. Keith, I'm HIV positive! That's why last night should never have happened. And I'm sorry. I'm really, really sorry for potentially making you part of my illness'.

Khan was beginning to wonder what she'd done in a past life to deserve the investigation from hell and the staff from the same department of fiery vengeance. DC Philippa Beresford still wasn't answering her calls and DS Keith Drake was running twenty minutes late and low and behold, he wasn't answering his phone either. She sat in her office and seethed. This wouldn't do. This just wouldn't fucking well do at all.

She was about to call Drake again when he turned up looking for all the world like he'd been dragged through a hedge backwards.

'Oh, so you are in the land of the living? Although by the looks of you that's doubtful'.

'I'm sorry, ma'am' said Drake, looking all around and doing everything he could to avoid looking directly at his boss. 'I overslept and got in here as quickly as I could'.

'DS Drake, that's just not good enough. This is a crucial time in this investigation, and I need to know that if I say eight o'clock that means eight o'clock with no excuses. You're my senior officer and I need to be able to depend on you'.

'Well like I said, I'm sorry, ma'am'.

'And do you mean it?'

'Yes, ma'am. I do mean it. I am sorry'.

Khan took a deep breath. 'Alright, we'll let it go there for today. But don't let it ever happen again'.

'I won't, ma'am, I won't, I promise you'.

'DS Drake, are you alright?'

'Alright? Course I'm alright. I just overslept that's all. Why do you ask?'

'You just look a bit … strange?'

'No, I'm fine. In need of some coffee but other than that I'm okay to do my job, ma'am'.

'Okay. Well, there's been a change of plan with regard to Angela Lewis. We're bringing her in'.

'In the light of the information we've received that she wasn't Samuel Lewis's mother?'

'Precisely' said Khan. The rest of the dossier given to her by the journalist Josh Walker was now in the hands of Chief Inspector Langton for him to hand out to the various other police departments in what was becoming a co-ordinated operation against Daniel Lewis. 'Now let's go and get her. In the car I'll give you the briefing you should've had if you'd turned up on time. You're driving. Can you manage that in this strange state you're in today?'

'Yes, ma'am, I can' he replied testily. He couldn't get Philippa's face out of his head. She'd looked so sad. And what the hell was he going to do now that he could be infected with a killer disease?

'And what about DC Beresford? Is she going to be showing her face today or even perhaps answering my calls?'

Khan noticed a definite darkening of DS Drake's expression at the mention of Philippa Beresford's name. Had something gone on between them?

'I can't answer for DC Beresford, ma'am'.

And it sounded like that was all she was going to get so she decided to shut up. There would be time to get to the bottom of that later. Meanwhile she left a slightly terrified looking Sergeant Luke Morris in charge and headed out to the car with Drake.

'It's going to look rather unseemly to pick Angela Lewis up the day before Samuel Lewis's funeral' Drake remarked after they'd both got into the car.

'Unseemly? This woman lied about Samuel being her son all his life, Keith. She let her husband beat him to within an inch of his life. Save your concern for someone who actually deserves it'.

'Don't you think my family have suffered enough?' demanded an emotional Angela Lewis. She was sitting in the interview room on one side of the table with DI Khan and DS Drake on the other. A uniformed male officer was standing beside the closed door. Angela was holding her arms folded over her stomach and her eyes were red. 'We've lost Samuel after lies were told about my husband's mistreatment of him and now you've brought me in here. It's too much, it really is too much'.

'Who is Samuel's real mother?'

'I'm his mother!'

'No, I asked you who was his real mother?'

'I'm his real mother!'

'No, you're not' said Khan, firmly. 'You're lying and I want to know why. You brought him up as your own and yet he was born to some other woman. I want to know who that was,'.

Angela pursed her lips. 'It's none of your business'.

'So, it is true? Well, you've just admitted it. So why don't you tell us the story beginning with who his real mother is?'

Angela banged her fist on the desk. 'I told you it's none of your damn business!'

'I can well imagine what a touchy subject this is for you, Mrs. Lewis, but I wouldn't ask if I didn't have a reason'.

'You don't have a reason because it's none of your business and I will tell you again and again until it gets through because you're clearly just not listening!'

Khan sat back, stretched out her legs and folded her arms across her chest. 'We've got time, Mrs. Lewis. We've got time enough to wait for it to get through to you that I intend for you to give me an answer to my question'.

'Why are you being like this with me?'

'I'm not being like anything. I'm just doing my job'.

Angela's head was all over the place. Nobody from the police had ever asked about Samuel in this way before and she couldn't work out who had told them unless Samuel's mother herself had told someone but surely even she wouldn't be that stupid and that selfish after all these years? But who else could it have been? The stupid bitch must've finally lost it. Oh God it was all starting to unravel. The whole damn mess was starting to unravel and with it the family were going to be torn apart. She already knew that Daniel was in financial strife. He hadn't told her. He was too bloody proud to tell her. She'd had to hear it from their daughter Melissa who was looking after her father's financial affairs. And this intervention now from the police was what she feared would happen all along. But still she wanted to remain defiant for as long as she could.

'I suppose you're enjoying this, aren't you?'

'Excuse me?' said Khan.

'You, a Muslim, thinking she's got an upper hand over me, an honest and practising Christian. A successful Christian from a successful Christian family. And that's the kind you hate the most'

Khan sat up straight and leaned forward. She rested her folded hands on the desk. 'Let me explain how it works in this country, Mrs. Lewis. You're the citizen and I'm the police officer which makes me part of the law enforcement network. I ask you the questions and you answer them. If you don't then I have to presume you have something to hide which will make me more suspicious. And in the process of administering the law I see no race, gender, sexuality, or religion, just those who break the law and those who don't. Now all this other stuff you're trying to confuse matters with has absolutely no relevance to me at all so if you could get back to my original question, please?'

'Spoken to your mother lately, DI Khan?'

Khan swallowed hard. 'My mother has been dead for some years'.

'Oh yes of course I was forgetting. Spoken to your father then? Oh no, he's dead too, isn't he? So, your brothers and sisters? No, your family have disowned you. So, you don't speak to any of them. You disgraced the traditional values of your community and your religion. Just like ISIS are doing now'.

Khan glared at Angela. Daniel Lewis must have done an investigation job on her to have found all of that out and she had long ago come to terms with what had happened at her instigation. But it was the fact that they knew that was getting to her, the fact that the likes of Daniel Lewis, who probably had a hand in every serious crime that happened in Blackpool knew all about her personal history felt like she'd been violated in some way. She shivered even though it was pretty warm inside the interview room. This was getting very serious in a way that she never could've expected and what was really making her blood boil was that she'd never wanted to define herself as a 'Muslim' police officer. She wanted to be a police officer just like her Caucasian colleagues who didn't have to answer these kind of race questions. They were allowed to get on with the job of being a police officer upholding the law of the land without their background being of relevance to anything.

'Mrs. Lewis, entertaining as all of this undoubtedly is for you, we're not here for a lesson in your view of current world affairs, we're here for you to answer my questions. I want to take you back for the second time to my original question. Who is Samuel Lewis's real mother and what part did she have to play in his life if any at all? No more diversions, Mrs. Lewis. I have two murders on my hands plus one attempted murder and a suicide that I'm becoming increasingly suspicious about. Now come on, Mrs. Lewis? Why have you pretended that Samuel was yours when we both know he wasn't?'

'You mean you haven't worked it out yet?'

'Why don't you let me know if I'm on the right track?'

'Why should I make it easy for you?'

'Because you've been party to your husband's abuse of Samuel and possibly his other children, so you owe them, Mrs. Lewis. You owe them all'.

'He never touched any of our girls' Angela insisted, lying through her teeth.

'So, you do admit he beat Samuel?'

'I've already admitted that! What more do you want? My

blood?'

'Odd choice of phrase considering that blood was taken from the first two of our murder victims. Why was your daughter Deborah out on the streets that night when she encountered our killer who left her for dead without finishing the job? Is that because he knew her, Mrs. Lewis? And the murder of a familiar face was too much even for him?'

'I don't know' said Angela as she began to sob.

'Angela, I want to help you, I really do. But you've got to meet me halfway. You've got to give me something to go on. Angela, I know this must be hard, but it can't be any harder than agreeing to bring up your husband's love child?'

Angela wailed but Khan went on. 'This has been a nightmare for you, Angela, I can tell that. But it could be all over if you talk to me. Is it Vivian Blackstone, Angela? Is she the woman we should be talking to?'

'They'd had an affair for years' Angela blubbered.

'Who? Vivian and your husband Daniel?'

'Yes'

'Angela, did Samuel know that Vivian was his mother?'

Angela Lewis stared at Khan and felt utterly defeated. There wasn't any further she could go.

'I'm not saying anything more without my solicitor being present'

'Okay' said Khan. 'Then you leave me with no alternative than to arrest you for committing acts of child cruelty against Samuel Lewis. DS Drake, read Mrs. Lewis her rights would you, please?'

Drake read Angela Lewis her rights and Khan read the woman's face as it sunk in what was happening. She was a woman who clearly didn't expect to be challenged and wasn't used to it. Even on her TV and radio debates she dismissed any opposing opinions with classic Margaret Thatcher sweep of the handbag style, almost denouncing people as stupid if they didn't agree with her.

'But it's his funeral tomorrow' Angela pleaded. 'Alright, I wasn't his mother, but I cared for him and nurtured him as if he was and I feel the pain of his passing as if he was'.

'Oh, spare me. You've been putting on this act for the last fifteen years and you've covered up acts of extreme cruelty against a young boy who's now dead. Don't tell me about your pain, Mrs. Lewis. It's pathetic'.

'But you can't do this!'

'Oh yes, I can because you're so pathetic that you seem resigned to taking the rap for your husband's crimes'.

'Why have you got it in for me?'

'Because Mrs. Lewis, those who stand by and let child abuse take place are as guilty and as evil as the actual perpetrator. That's why I've got it in for you. I've got it in for you because of what you let happen to Samuel but here's the little twist. You've just been charged and now I'm going to release you on police bail pending further enquiries. Just to show that I'm not all stick and no carrot. You'll keep. And I'll come back to you when the time comes'.

Khan and Drake walked back to the office in silence. Then just before they reached the door, she turned on him.

'What is wrong with you today, DS Drake?'

'What … what do you mean? I know I was late this morning but surely you can't still be holding on to that?'

'Keith, I felt like I was alone in there! I was coming under sustained personal attack, and you just sat there like you couldn't care less'.

'That's not true, ma'am, I did care, and I did think Angela Lewis was being out of order in the way she went at you like that'.

'Well, it's no good telling me now! You should've contributed to the interview and helped me out'.

'I'm sorry, ma'am'.

'Sorry? You're sorry? Once again, DS Drake, you've let me down badly. Now, I don't know where you are this morning, but it certainly isn't here. Has something gone on that you need to tell me about?'

'What? What are you asking that for?'

'There you go, you see. You're jumpy. It's as if you're afraid of your own shadow'.

'There's nothing wrong with me, ma'am'.

'Well, I'd hate to see you when there is' said Khan. 'But look, there are things we need to get on with and I'm leaving you whilst I take Angela Lewis home. I'll be back inside an hour'.

'You're taking Angela Lewis home?'

'Ask no questions get told no lies, DS Drake'.

FIFTEEN

Khan headed out of the Blackpool police HQ with Angela Lewis in the passenger seat and headed off in the direction of Poulton.

'Why are you driving me home?' Angela asked.

'I needed a break from the office' Khan replied.

'I don't know whether to believe you or not'.

'I don't think you've got any choice, Angela'.

'Stop this car and let me out!'

'Don't be silly, Angela. We're in free- flowing traffic here. All the drivers behind me are going to be really pissed off if I stop now'.

'But where are you taking me?'

'Home. After a little diversion'.

There weren't many spaces between Blackpool and Poulton that offered an escape from being seen on the main road. But Khan knew of one and when she reached it, she turned left and drove along the gravel track.

'What the hell are you doing?' Angela demanded.

Khan pulled up down a narrow country lane that didn't seem to lead to anywhere. When she pulled up and switched off the engine, Angela tried to open the door. But Khan kept it locked.

'You've gone mad' Angela accused.

'No, Angela. I'm just running out of time, and we need to talk. Or rather you need to talk to me because I think you can help me. This will be a good opportunity for us to talk away from any distractions. Just you and me, woman to woman'.

'But it isn't what you'd call orthodox'.

'And allowing the beating of a young boy is?'

'I did love Samuel, you know'.

'I'm sure you did but you allowed him to be abused'.

'Daniel needed a son. I'd given him three daughters. He's old fashioned in that way. Oh, he's given over financial control of his business empire to our daughter Melissa, but he'd never give the whole thing over to her. But Daniel needed Samuel to be a certain kind of man. He needed him to be as ruthless as Daniel himself was. But Samuel wasn't like that. He was kind, quiet, he tried to tell his father that he'd never want to take over the business, but Daniel wouldn't listen. That's when the beatings started'.

'Did Daniel know that Samuel was gay?'

'That's when the beatings grew even more intense than they'd been before. Daniel couldn't stand to think that his son was gay. He was in an almost permanent rage about it'.

'And you did nothing to stop your husband from beating

Samuel?'

'Do you have any idea what it's like to live with a monster like Daniel? Do you?'

'No but there is a thing called divorce'.

'Like it's that simple'.

'Actually, yes, it is' said Khan. 'I know from personal experience that it's hard and it's difficult but at the end of the day you have to make a choice between carrying on in misery inflicted on you by others and taking responsibility for your own life and deciding to be free'.

'Yes, I'm sorry about what I said before. It can't have been easy for you. But you're sitting here now as a senior police officer and to have stood on your own two feet to that extent must've taken a strength of character that I just don't have. I put up with his affair with Vivian Blackstone for all those years and when she gave birth to Samuel, I agreed to taking him in as my own son'.

'Did you put pressure on Samuel the night he took the overdose, Angela?'

Angela lowered her head in shame and started crying. 'I told him that if he told the social services person who was going to be interviewing him that his father did beat him it would only result in the beatings getting even worse'.

'You went public in support of your husband beating Samuel, Angela'.

'Daniel manipulated me into thinking that we'd get a lot of public sympathy if we used it as a means of standing up for the rights of parents'

'To beat their children?'

'To instill discipline in whichever way they see fit'.

'So, you agree with your husband's beating of Samuel?'

Angela paused. She looked down into her lap. 'I didn't agree with the extent to which he went, no. It broke my heart to see Samuel struggling to get out of his bed on some days, let alone walk. But I didn't want Samuel to be gay'.

'So, you thought it could be beaten out of him? Angela, that's grotesque!'

'Yes, I know, I know it was. But I didn't want Samuel to end up like me'.

'What are you talking about?'

'I'm a lesbian, officer. I always have been. I had a lesbian affair with the love of my life that my parents found out about, and they were so incensed they virtually threw me down the aisle when Daniel proposed. I didn't want that for Samuel. I didn't want him to be forced into a loveless marriage just because he was gay. So yes, I thought Daniel could beat it out of him'.

'Even though you knew from your own feelings that it isn't possible to do that?'

'Detective, my parents have never been willing to listen when I've tried to tell them about my problems with Daniel. They'd rather their daughter lived with Hitler than with another woman. I've had nowhere to go and no choice but to comply'.

'I can see how difficult it must've been for you'.

Angela began to cry. They were silent tears full of the shame and heartache of many years. 'I didn't mean for Samuel to do what he did, but he told me that night that he felt trapped inside a life that didn't make any sense to him. He said that it only made any sense at all when he was with Ben, but he also knew that Daniel would never accept his sexuality'.

'So, he felt like he had no choice but to take his own life'.

'I called Ben's parents. Daniel doesn't know. I told them that Ben mustn't blame himself for anything. On the contrary, he brought the only joy into Samuel's life that he'd ever known'.

'But Ben became a convenient public scapegoat for you and your husband'.

'Yes' Angela confirmed.

'Angela, why did Samuel have that press clipping of the murdered girls pinned to his wall?'

'I honestly don't know, officer. And surely you must believe me after everything else I've told you?'

Khan looked at her for a moment and then asked, 'Are you HIV positive, Angela?'

'Yes. And I know that Vivian Blackstone is too'.

And that's when the case fell into its logical conclusion for Khan.

'Right. Well let's get you home. You must have things to do before the funeral'.

When Khan got back to her office, Sergeant Luke Morris greeted her with the kind of news she really wouldn't have chosen to hear.

'It's DC Beresford, ma'am'.

'What about DC Beresford?'

'She's been found dead at her home, ma'am'.

Khan thought she was hearing things. 'Say that again, Luke?'

'It's true, Layla' said a very grim looking Drake. 'We got the call about five minutes ago'.

'So, what happened?' DCI Khan asked. She felt completely

numb and very close to tears. Philippa had been her friend after all.

'Well, she was found by her mother just after ten o'clock this morning, ma'am' Sergeant Luke Morris went on. 'Her mother has a key and when she didn't get a response from ringing the bell, she decided to let herself in. She found her on the kitchen floor'.

'So, there was no sign of a forced entry?'

'No sign at all, ma'am'.

'So, what are you telling me? That she must've known her assailant?'

'There's more, ma'am' said Luke. 'The pathologist Ross Carter says the MO was the same as in the previous murders we're currently investigating, ma'am. Right down to the taking of a sample of blood'.

Khan and DS Drake made their way down to DC Beresford's house which was also the temporary home of Drake. The atmosphere between them was intense. They each wanted to reach out to the other and offer the comfort that was needed but neither of them could quite manage to bridge the gap. Murder cases are always difficult but when it's someone you know and have worked with it really does tear at your heart. This was proving to be a very untidy case indeed. When they got to the house Khan saw the body and paid her respects for a moment and then she wanted to focus on the MO used by the killer.

'I understand it was exactly the same as the previous killings?'

'Exactly the same, Layla' said Ross who'd met DC Philippa Beresford on several occasions and though they'd never been close he didn't dislike her. 'Death was by strangulation, but DC Beresford wasn't a drug addict. The blood sample was taken from the vein in her right arm and there are no other syringe marks. I'll have it tested and the results back to you as soon as possible'.

'No need' said Drake as he stepped up behind Khan. 'She was HIV positive. I know because she told me this morning'.

'Care to explain, DS Drake?' asked Khan a little more sharply than she'd intended.

'Could we talk outside, ma'am?'

'Okay' said Khan who then turned back to Ross Carter. 'I'll speak to you later, Ross. Either here or at your lab'.

Khan took Drake through the back door of Philippa Beresford's house and into her small back garden. It didn't look particularly well- tended. Khan knew that Philippa Beresford had never admitted to having green fingers. Not that it mattered much now.

'So, Keith, what do you want to say to me?'

'I don't quite know how to say it, ma'am. I'm in shock to be honest'.

'Keith, you were probably the last person to see Philippa alive. You'll be part of the investigation into her murder. I will support you all the way, Keith. But let's not forget that you could be considered to be a prime suspect here. You know better than anyone how it works and now you've revealed something very personal to me about Philippa. How did she tell you she was HIV positive? And perhaps more importantly, why did she tell you?'

'She told me because we slept together last night'.

'Unprotected?'

'Yes'.

Khan sighed and ran her hand through her shiny black hair. She thought of all they'd learned when they'd gone to the Sexual

Health Clinic and how it obviously hadn't made any impact on Drake at all. 'Oh Keith'.

'She said she was sorry for potentially exposing me to the virus'.

'And what was her excuse?'

'She didn't have one'.

'How did you react?'

'I was stunned at first and then I must admit I was pretty angry'.

'But not enough for even some bizarre accident to happen? I mean, you have been acting strangely all morning'.

'Layla, I swear!' he pleaded, anxiety etched right across his face. He was starting to sweat quite heavily too. He knew that potentially this didn't look good for him. 'I swear on my children's life that I left this house this morning and she was sitting at the kitchen table drinking a mug of tea and eating a slice of toast. I swear to you that's true'.

'I believe you, Keith. I do believe you'.

'Thank you, ma'am. I appreciate that'.

'Look, do you know who else has a key to this house apart from her Mum? There's no sign of a forced entry so whoever the killer was must've been known to Philippa and either they had a key, or she let them in like she would if they were a friend. Do you know of any visitors she may have had recently?'

'I don't know about any visitors since I've been living here,' said Drake. 'Apart from her ex-husband Andy and their son Alastair. He's got a key'.

'Who? The son or the ex-husband?

'The son,' said Drake. 'Poor little bugger. He's going to have to come to terms with his Mum dying so young and in such horrible circumstances'.

'That's one of the saddest things about this' Khan agreed. 'I know she was the first to admit that she wasn't the world's best mother, but she loved her son dearly and was devoted to him'. She shook her head and then a thought occurred to her. 'But look, Keith, have you told human resources yet that you're staying at Philippa's house?'

Keith was curious. 'No? Why do you ask?'

'And who knows that you have been staying there?'

'Well, you, my parents, Ellen and my kids, Philippa's parents and her husband and son'.

'DC Barnes?'

'No'.

'Sergeant Luke Morris?'

'No'.

'And do you have much in the way of belongings here?'

'Well, no, hardly any at all. I just brought a few basics, and I was going to get the rest this weekend. Just a bag, some underwear and a couple of shirts. Why, ma'am?'

'Then we won't say anything about you being here just yet'.

'Ma'am?'

'Leave it for twenty-four hours before we drop that little detail into things'

'Ma'am, I appreciate the gesture but … '

'… it's not a gesture, Keith. It's a risk I'm going to take to try and solve this case. But let me tell you this, if it turns out that you had any involvement in Philippa's murder, however small, I'll buy the rope and hang you myself. Do I make myself clear?'

'Crystal, ma'am. But you won't be proved wrong, I can assure you of that'.

'Good. But the next thing we're going to do is drive you over to Dr. Gillespie at the sexual health clinic. We need to get you tested and pronto. They can have the results back within twenty- four hours so come on, the sooner the better'.

'I'm terrified, ma'am'.

'Yes, I understand,' said Khan. 'But let's get down to the clinic and get the test done'.

'Thank you, ma'am. So, what are your thoughts now about the case?'

'My thoughts are in a place I don't really want to go to, Keith'.

'Ma'am?'

'I can't help thinking that Philippa knew who our killer was all along'.

After Khan had returned from taking Drake for his HIV test, she was asked to go in and see Chief Inspector Langton.

'How are you?' he asked.

'You mean with regard to DC Beresford, sir?'

'Yes. It's always hard when we lose a colleague, but in these kind of circumstances it's particularly difficult'.

'DC Beresford and I had been quite close once, sir' Khan revealed, trying not to get upset. 'And it certainly has come as a shock'.

'Well, it's turning into quite a mess, DI Khan,' said Langton. 'The killer has been able to strike at the heart of your team. In addition, you have no suspects in the murder enquiry, but you chose to divert tactics and arrest Angela Lewis, who you've now released on police bail pending further enquiries. Where the hell is this going, DI Khan? Please explain yourself'.

'Sir, we are dealing here with a killer who has one motive and that is revenge. It's been all about getting her own back on the one who's wronged her. Now, Deborah Lewis wanted to prove a very sad and twisted point to her father by going out at night to attract punters, but she unexpectedly encountered the killer who recognized her and that's why she was spared the killer's full treatment. And why did the killer recognize her? Because the killer was known to the family and a shred of compassion hit the killer to the point where they couldn't carry on with the same MO. They felt sorry for Deborah and in making their escape, we got in their way. Now, for one reason or another the killer was also known to DC Beresford, and I think I'm starting to see who that someone was. I think it was Vivian Blackstone from the boarding school where Samuel Lewis was a student. I know that Samuel Lewis was the love child of Vivian Blackstone and Daniel Lewis because Angela Lewis told me. She only took him on as her own son because she hadn't been able to give Daniel a son herself and that's what Daniel Lewis desperately wanted. With me so far, sir?'

Chief Inspector Langton sat back in his chair and couldn't help a half smile from crossing his face. He knew she'd be able to pull it out of the bag. He paused and then said, 'Go on, DI Khan'.

'Good because this is where the waters start to get a little murky. You see, it's my guess that Vivian Blackstone is the woman who according to neighbours during our initial house to house enquiries this morning, turned up at Philippa Beresford's house at around nine thirty. Philippa was seen by neighbours as having willingly opened the door to her visitor who was described as being smart, well dressed and well- turned out. That fits perfectly as a description of Vivian Blackstone, and she left about fifteen minutes later looking flushed and bothered'.

'But why would Vivian Blackstone want to kill DC Beresford?'

'Perhaps they'd been working together but fell out for some reason?' Khan suggested. 'And it could be that Philippa had been protecting Vivian from us'

'That's a high- handed accusation to make of someone who's no longer here to defend herself'.

'That may be so, sir,' said Khan. 'But I believe it to be the truth. I believe our killer is Vivian Blackstone'.

'But why would she want to go out and kill two teenage prostitutes? Why would she want to take a sample of their blood? DI Khan, there's nothing to connect her to those two murders'

'Vivian Blackstone was the mother of Samuel Lewis. That's where the connection starts but I won't be able to get down to the conclusive truth until I bring her in, sir. I've had a warrant issued for her arrest and to search her property. By happy coincidence she lives just down the road in Lytham. It's where I'm going next'.

'You'd better get on with it then, DI Khan. But before you do, did you realise the possible implications of having sent Angela Lewis back into the family home knowing that the net is tightening around the neck of Daniel Lewis, and he won't react kindly to his wife having talked to us even though we didn't leave her any choice?'

'Sir, did she realise the possible implications of Samuel being beaten to within an inch of his life on a regular basis because his father thought it was a way of somehow curing him of his sexuality? No. Instead she went on air positively boasting about it as the only way to rear children'.

'I see and I understand what you're saying, DI Khan, but our job is to deliver justice according to the laws of the land. It is not about making it possible for others to deliver retribution'.

'Point noted, sir'.

'I'm not sure about the game you're playing here, DI Khan. But it had better bring results'

'That point is also noted, sir'.

Khan was about to leave the chief inspector's office when a sudden surge of anger and resentment made her stop and challenge him on an issue or two. She knew it was disrespectful to a senior officer and quite unprofessional but for a moment she couldn't care less.

'Sir, the file that the journalist Josh Walker at the Blackpool Evening News spent months and probably years compiling on Daniel Lewis? The one that detailed everything about his unlawful doings in this town and that he handed over to us and you distributed accordingly?'

'Yes? What of it?'

'Well, it all seems to have gone rather quiet on that front and the evidence contained in that file about Lewis and his involvement in the corruption of officials is pretty overwhelming. I'm surprised Daniel Lewis hasn't been brought in by now'.

'What point are you making here, DI Khan?'

Layla took a deep breath before going on. 'Well with all due respect, sir, are you putting the same pressure on the team that's handling that as you are on me? Or are you taking a softer line with them because you all drink down the pub together whilst eyeing up bits of skirt?'

SIXTEEN

'Two things, ma'am' said Sergeant Luke Morris after she'd come out of her meeting with Chief Inspector Langton. 'First of all, Malcolm Arnott of the Blackpool HIV trust has finally returned from his holidays. He heard that we've been trying to contact him and so decided to give us a call'.

'Really?' said Khan, stopping in her tracks. 'I'm surprised

when you consider what was in the file about him that Josh Walker handed over'. It gave her a kick in her intuition. There'd been no progress on the information provided by Josh Walker and now a potential suspect was coming forward of his own volition. Something wasn't right here. 'I would've thought he'd have wanted to lie low and see where the dust settled'.

'You would think so, ma'am, but I spoke to him for about ten minutes and he was more than happy to tell me whatever he could about Vivian Blackstone and perhaps it's because, if Arnott is a close associate of Daniel Lewis and Vivian Blackstone is beginning to smell like trouble because we're getting close to her, then they've probably dropped her like a stone. She was previously part of Lewis's inner coterie but not anymore. Arnott told me they had a massive falling out about a year ago and that's when Daniel Lewis began an affair with DC Philippa Beresford'.

'You're not serious?' said DS Drake who'd been listening to it all.

'I am serious, sir'

'She was standing here with us and yet all the time she was sleeping with the enemy,' said Khan.

'Well let's not jump to any conclusions, ma'am' said Drake. 'I mean she's barely cold'.

'Well, what am I supposed to deduce from all this, DS Drake? You've got to admit that there'll be some pretty hard thoughts going through our heads when we stand there at her funeral. It's as clear as bloody day to me that she was being treacherous'

'I agree it looks bad, ma'am'

'It's about as bad as it can get'.

'I do have more to tell you, ma'am' ventured Morris. 'According to Arnott, Vivian Blackstone was a volunteer for the Blackpool HIV trust for two years until about six months ago.

She trained as a nurse originally and only changed career after a nervous breakdown ten years ago'.

'What did she do for the trust?' Khan asked.

'She manned the mobile unit that they sent out to the streets where prostitutes are known to ply their trade. Using her knowledge as a former nurse she took the blood samples from patients, and they were then sent off to an independent testing facility in London' explained Morris. 'Then the girls would come back next time the mobile unit was out on the streets for the results'

'And they kept a record?'

'They said they destroyed them once the girls knew the results of the test'

'So, for that time between taking the blood and waiting for the test they did keep records that anybody who worked for the trust could've accessed or copied?'

'Right, ma'am. It meant that the girls could then make their own decision about seeking further treatment or not. Some did but most didn't because they didn't really care that much about themselves'.

'They'd already given up on leading a long and happy life,' said Khan.

'Exactly, ma'am. Now the reason why Vivian Blackstone stopped volunteering for the trust was because Arnott accused her of stealing equipment from the mobile unit'.

'Don't tell me,' said Drake. 'Syringes? Those large bags that they keep blood in? Perhaps a couple of refrigeration cases?'

'That's exactly the sort of thing, sir, yes' Morris confirmed.

'The sort of thing you needed to take blood from people who you'd just murdered' said Khan who was still wondering why

Malcolm Arnott, who'd been such a close ally of Daniel Lewis, had been so willing to give it up about Vivian Blackstone. 'Come on, boys. We've got an arrest to make'.

Daniel Lewis asked all the guests who'd come back to the house after Samuel's funeral to please go home after they'd been there for a respectable enough time. He explained that he and his family needed to grieve in private and that had sent a shiver down the spine of his wife and daughters Melissa and Verity. Deborah was still unconscious in hospital. None of them had been to see her. It wasn't what families like them did. Both Angela and Daniel Lewis's parents had been to see her though. The grandparents cared.

Everybody had been commanded to assemble in the drawing room of the Lewis family home in Poulton. Melissa looked round nervously but also with a mixture of contempt. This house had never been a home. This house had been a place of fear and intimidation. She almost envied her brother Samuel. He'd managed to get himself out of it. That had taken guts. She'd almost thrown up at all the false emotion at Samuel's funeral today. Her father was just disappointed he'd lost a whipping boy and her mother had always been able to turn on the tears to order like the pathetically weak bitch she was. Neither of them were actually going to miss Samuel. But Melissa would. She'd got on well with her little brother and even though she could never protect him from her father's brutality he did know for his short life that he had a big sister in the family who he could rely on. They'd talked a lot about his emerging relationship with Ben Cartwright and it was the only time she'd ever seen him happy. His love for Ben had been right there in his eyes.

The three of them, Melissa, Verity, and their mother Angela stood waiting. Something would be bursting through the consciousness of the moment, and it would probably involve Daniel's fists. One of them would be punished for what he'd see as having let the family down. That was a given. But what was truly filling Melissa's heart and causing it to break was that Samuel had taken his overdose because he knew that his father would never allow him to love whoever he wanted to. Well, her father was going to get one hell of a surprise in the next few hours when he found out what she'd done to stop her father. It was just a shame that Samuel wouldn't be around to share in what she had planned.

'I don't like liars' said Daniel in his usual deep voice and looking down at the ground and not at anybody else in the room.

'None of us do, Daniel' said Angela who'd recognized the same body language in Prince Charles who also looked down when people were trying to communicate with him.

Daniel looked up sharply at his wife. He didn't like anyone speaking unless he'd asked them a direct question which he hadn't. She'd broken the golden rule. Now she would have to pay for it.

Angela tensed as her husband stepped towards her, hesitated whilst he sank a look of total disgust in her eyes, and then walloped her across the face with the back of his hand. It knocked her off balance. She landed on the floor and could feel blood coming out of her cheek. That must've been where his rings had ripped into her skin. Even though her legs felt like jelly she managed to get herself back on her feet although she was somewhat uncertain and unsteady. She tried to lift her head to stare back defiantly at him but in that moment, she saw her daughter Melissa land a punch on her father's face that made it light up with anger and the desire for retribution. But Melissa wasn't yet done. She had more poison to infect her father's mood with. She hadn't planned on using it yet but his lack of compassion for any of them destroyed her restraint.

'Mummy?' she said with her eyes firmly fixed on her father's, almost daring him to unleash more violence on her because he'd never be able to face up to the truth of what she had to say. The growing police investigation into the affairs of her father meant that more and more of his staff were starting to come out with information as a means maybe of avoiding having the finger being pointed at themselves. 'Did you know that Daddy has been screwing another woman in your bed? Oh yes, whilst you've been out and about promoting beating as a means of child rearing, which is a disgusting exercise in itself and shame on you for doing it, Daddy here has been sexually entertaining a woman called Philippa Beresford. She's a police officer, or she was until she was found murdered at her home this morning and she'd been feeding Daddy's sexual appetite since he dumped poor old Aunty Vivian. So, Daddy, are you going to beat your way out of that one?'

Daniel kicked Melissa on the backs of her knees, forcing her to come crashing down on her lower spine and causing excruciating pain. She screamed out with a mixture of terror and pain and her father proceeded to kick her unmercifully as she lay flailing on the floor like a captured animal.

'I trusted you, you treacherous little bitch!' he charged. 'And now I've got the fraud squad all over my bloody business looking into everything to do with my money and that must be down to you! Even my friends have turned their backs and turned grass in exchange for the Queen's shilling and now you've tarnished it all with the mention of poor Philippa'.

Verity and her mother Angela did nothing except whimper as they watched Daniel kick the life out of his eldest daughter, their sister, their daughter, their flesh and blood. They didn't even hold hands or huddle together for safety. In their family it just wasn't done even when it felt like the sky was falling in on them. Then Daniel deployed his usual method of humiliation and obedience by grabbing Melissa by the hair and dragging her across the floor to the door that led to the stairs. He'd drag her up there one by one and she'd feel it throughout her already pain drenched body. But he'd carry on to his study where he'd take his belt off to her and she'd be passing out by the time he finished. Melissa was crying her eyes out, but she wasn't begging him to stop. She wouldn't give him that satisfaction.

'What is he doing to her?' Katja demanded as she ran through from the kitchen.

'Keep out of it, Katja!' Angela demanded. 'It's none of your business'.

Katja slapped her across the face.

'How dare you' said a startled Angela as she stroked her cheek. 'You've forgotten your place in this household'.

'Oh, don't lecture me you stupid bitch! You stand by and watch your children being treated in this way and you expect me to respect you? Dream on!'

Katja charged for the door and Angela chased after her. She caught up with her just as Katja had opened the door and in the struggle that followed Katja, who was younger, and fitter managed to get the better of Angela and before she knew it, she had Angela's hand trapped between the door and its frame. Angela shrieked out loudly with pain, but Katja couldn't help smiling.

'There!' she sneered. 'See how you like it'.

'Katja, please' Angela begged. She thought her fingers must be broken because the pain was so intense. The two women were eyeball to eyeball and the hatred that passed between them was intense. Then Katja pushed all of her weight onto the door and watched Angela's silent screams. 'You deserve this. You deserve every bit of this for what you let happen to your children'.

'I can't breathe!'

'Good! You don't deserve to' And with that Katja pushed her entire body weight once again against the door sending sharp merciless fireballs of pain down Angela's arm and into her shoulder. Then Katja repeated the exercise just to make sure that she was causing the maximum pain possible. And from the look on Angela's face, she was certainly hitting the right target.

'Please, Katja' Angela whispered. She could barely speak.

'Sorry? What was that? You'll have to speak up'.

Katja began to think that she may have gone too far. She'd never been a violent person. She hadn't grown up amongst violent behaviour. None of her family had been violent. But Angela had driven her to exact some kind of revenge on those who'd caused so much suffering. And when her chance came just moments ago it had all happened so quickly. She didn't regret what she'd done. She wished she'd done it sooner. Angela Lewis had been in need of being taught a lesson for a long time. But she'd made her point. Time to show Angela the mercy that Angela had never shown her children. She relieved pressure on the door and Angela gasped with relief. She pulled her hand away slowly as if every movement was causing her whole body to shudder. She didn't know what to do next. This was all so new to her. The idea that someone had challenged everything Angela had accepted as normal family life, and that they'd come from outside the family, had thrown her. Now she was dealing with the most overwhelming physical pain but through the darkness of what she was feeling and the home truth of what Katja had said to her, she still had some semblance of what she'd been brought to believe what it meant to be Daniel's wife. With an energy she thought she wouldn't have she made for Katja's throat with her other hand but before she could connect Verity leapt up and smashed a vase over her head. She fell to the ground unconscious.

'We won't have long' said Katja, grabbing Verity's hand. 'She'll come round before too long. Come on'.

They ran upstairs and into Melissa's bedroom. Daniel Lewis

had gone. Katja realised that with all the commotion going on downstairs he must've been able to get away. But there was Melissa lying on the floor curled up like a baby and groaning with pain.

'Oh my God, my baby!' said Katja who then bent down and lifted Melissa's head in her hands. Melissa grabbed hold of the t-shirt Katja was wearing. She was so relieved to see her. 'Listen don't worry baby, I will sort out everything'. She then turned to Verity. 'Verity, I need you to listen to me carefully, yes? Go to your room and pack a case but just with the essentials you need to make a new start. Then come back in here and do the same for Melissa. But be quick. We don't have much time'.

'But I don't understand' Verity pleaded, tearfully. 'Everyone has just gone mad'.

Katja held Verity's shoulders. 'I know it seems that way but believe me, your sister is doing this for you and for Deborah when she gets better'.

'Doing what?'

'I can't explain now' said Katja. 'I have to find some things in the bathroom to help clear Melissa's face up'.

'But what about Mummy?'

That was when Melissa managed to break through the haze of the battering she'd just taken from her father. She pulled herself up onto her elbow although every movement sent a hammering of pain through her body. 'Verity?' she said, her voice barely audible. 'We're going to go away and get as far from this terrible life that's been inflicted on us as we can. You don't need to worry about anything. I've arranged it all. But it's all about us, Verity. You, me, and Deborah as soon as she's fit enough to travel. Katja is going to come with us too. I only wish Samuel could also come with us and it breaks my heart that it's too late to save him. But it's not too late to save us, Verity. And as far as Mummy is concerned, she can look after herself. She's always been very good at doing that'.

The classic Lytham semi with its high windows on both floors was just a block back from the seafront and home to Vivian Blackstone. Her black Renault Clio was parked in the driveway but a touch of the bonnet by DS Drake showed it was still warm and had been driven recently. The sudden presence of DI Khan and her team including a large number of uniformed officers, was causing a lot of attention on the smart avenue but she shut all of that out of her mind as she knocked on the front door.

'I'll go round the back, ma'am' said Sergeant Luke Morris.

'Okay Sergeant Morris but watch yourself and no heroism. If I'm correct, then we're dealing with a highly dangerous criminal. Take a couple of uniformed officers with you'.

'No worries, ma'am'.

There was no reply from Khan's initial knock on Vivian Blackstone's door so she tried again.

'We'll give her two more minutes and then we'll break the bloody door down' said Khan to DS Drake. 'I'm not messing around with this bitch forever'.

Then one of the uniformed officers who'd gone round the back with Sergeant Morris came running back.

'Ma'am?' he said. 'The back door was open. Sergeant Morris went in and was immediately cornered by the suspect who is now holding a syringe at his neck filled with what looks like blood'.

'She's trapped us' said Khan. 'The fucking bitch has trapped us'

Khan with DI Drake ran round to the back of the house with several uniformed officers. She stepped inside but there was no sign of Sergeant Morris or Vivian Blackstone. She assumed they'd gone upstairs and then the voice of Vivian Blackstone cut through the air like a sharp knife heading for human flesh.

'Come on upstairs, officer! I'm about to put on quite a show'.

'If you're holding one of my officers, Vivian then you need to let him go right now!'

'Oh, just do as you're told and then nobody will get hurt!'

'Once again she's giving us no fucking choice' cursed Khan under her breath. 'She's got the better of me without even trying and I don't like that, Keith. I don't like it at all'.

Khan went up the stairs followed by Drake and a couple of uniformed officers. They went in the direction of the only room with a door open and what they found was initially shocking. Sergeant Luke Morris was handcuffed to a chair. The left hand sleeve of his shirt had been rolled up and Vivian was poised with the blood filled syringe, ready to inject him. Khan held up her hand to signal to everyone behind her to back off. The room looked more like a treatment room in a doctor's surgery that a suburban Fylde coast bedroom. There was a table covered in medical equipment like syringes and large bags of blood.

'This is not something you can walk away from, Vivian' said Khan as calmly as she could, given the look of fear in Sergeant Morris's eyes. 'I don't know what you're planning to do but I can guess'

'Really?' said Vivian. 'And what's that, officer?'

'Well, I'm assuming that the blood in that syringe is HIV positive? You want to poison someone else with the poison that's going through your body'.

'You know nothing' Vivian scoffed as she pressed the end of

the needle against the skin on Sergeant Morris's arm. He flinched as she did so. 'You put yourself across as being so clever, but you really don't know anything'.

'I get it, Vivian. I get it that you wanted revenge against these prostitutes because your lover Daniel Lewis was sleeping with them too and he ended up infecting you with the virus. Isn't that the case, Vivian?'

'I had to stop them spreading their vile poison'.

'You felt betrayed. You'd loved Daniel Lewis for all those years, but he'd steadfastly refused to divorce Angela and instead of a wedding he'd given you HIV. So, in the end that's the only way you could get your revenge. He'd dumped you. He'd taken up with Philippa Beresford. You'd given him your entire life. You'd given him a son for another woman to bring up and yet he still didn't value you as much as he should've done'.

'I … I underestimated you, officer'.

'Did you step back from murdering Deborah Lewis because you recognized her?'

'Yes'.

'So why did you murder Philippa Beresford? Was it just because she'd taken your place?'

'She was furious about being infected with HIV, just like I was. But I hated her and you're right, it was just because she'd taken my place. We'd met before and when she became HIV positive, she wanted her revenge too. But when I went round to her house that morning we argued. I said she should help me more given her background as a police officer, but she wouldn't'.

'So, she did know you were the killer all along?'

'Yes, she did. We'd become comrades in arms as it were. We'd both been denied and humiliated by the same powerful man whom we'd both loved'.

Khan would've knocked DC Philippa Beresford's block off if she'd been right in front of her now. But she couldn't afford that luxury of thought. She had to save Sergeant Morris and she had to make sure that Vivian Blackstone here made her date with justice.

'So, what was the plan, Vivian? You'd collected the HIV positive blood. What were you going to do with it?'

'I was going to bring Daniel here and inject him with it' she said. 'Because you see … and this is where it gets really twisted. Daniel is the only one who isn't infected. He became a carrier. That is what is so fucking unfair!'

'And why haven't you carried it out?'

'Because I don't know where he is! I was supposed to see him today, but he never showed up. I was going to bring him back here and make sure he knew just how much suffering he'd caused'.

'Vivian, did you put the press clipping of the first murder on the wall of Samuel's room?'

The tears began rolling down Vivian's cheeks. 'My boy. My darling, darling boy. I had to remind him of his father's liking of teenage prostitutes. I told him he had to stick to his guns because his father didn't have a moral leg to stand on. He had to resist all of Daniel's attempts to beat his sexuality out of him'.

'Except it only made it worse for Samuel'.

'He was my son. I had to try'.

'I understand, look Vivian, my officer has not caused you any harm,' said Khan. 'You know the game is up for you. Now just let him go because he has nothing to do with the pain that you're in. Come on, Vivian. Let him go'.

She didn't know what came into her head but all at once Vivian was struck by the futility of what she was trying to play out and released the syringe which dropped to the floor. Khan picked it up whilst Drake rushed to release the cuffs that had been holding Sergeant Morris to the chair. He was now looking extremely relieved. Uniformed officers then reached forward and apprehended Vivian Blackstone.

Khan took great pleasure in charging her with three counts of murder, one count of attempted murder, and one count of false imprisonment

'Take a good long look at the sky, Vivian,' said Khan. 'It'll be a very long time before you see it again as a free woman. If you ever do'.

SEVENTEEN

Even though Vivian Blackstone was locked up, a call came through to the office that reminded Khan that the situation was still ongoing. It wasn't all over yet.

'Ma'am?' said Sergeant Luke Morris holding the telephone handset in the air after having pressed the mute button. 'I've got special branch on the line from Manchester airport. They want to speak to you personally'.

'Then you'd better grant them their wish' said Khan as she strode purposefully down to her small office that was sectioned off from the rest of the squad room. 'Put the call through please, Luke'.

Khan closed the door behind her after she'd reached her office and picked up the phone on her desk. 'DI Khan?'

The call was from DI Trevor Winsford who was part of the special branch unit at Manchester airport's Terminal 2. He explained that three young women by the names of Mellissa Lewis, Verity Lewis and another girl called Katja Wolinski, had checked in for the Singapore Airlines flight to Singapore that was due to depart in just over an hour's time and he was wondering if he should let them proceed given the investigations that were taking place into the Lewis family.

Khan thought for a moment. She'd already received an interim report detailing that Melissa Lewis had managed to transfer the Lewis family fortune into a series of Singapore based bank accounts and that as far as could be seen Daniel Lewis didn't have a penny left to his name. Well, that was some kind of justice as far as Khan was concerned because she didn't believe the sisters owed their father anything and they'd be better off by getting right away and making a brand new start. They deserved that. They'd been through hell and though she wondered why Katja Wolinski was with them, she didn't really bother about it.

'I want to tell you to let them proceed on their flight to Singapore'.

'Ma'am?'

'Melissa and Verity Lewis have suffered unmercifully at the hands of their violent father. If Melissa has found a way to get her and her sisters away from him using her father's money, then I would consider it justice'.

'So, what are you saying to me, ma'am? I mean, I can understand your point but if Melissa Lewis has shifted money that isn't hers then I'm sure the fraud squad will be wanting to speak to her'.

Khan breathed in deep. 'Yes, the fraud squad. I know, I know, I know. Look, tell Melissa she's wanted for questioning. I doubt the other two will go without her. And then let the fraud squad know you've picked her up on their behalf'.

'Okay, ma'am, and thanks'

Khan hit her fist against the wall out of sheer frustration. She really wished the girls had been able to get away. She really did despite the implications that would have on any future arrest proceedings. Melissa had done wrong to steal her father's money, but could you blame her given the circumstances? These were those rare occasions when she had to remind herself that she was a law enforcement officer and that the law was black and white for good or bad. But it was also the mention of the fraud squad that had her thinking. Nobody from there had bothered to contact her on any matter relating to the case. She did think that was a little strange.

She decided she needed a break from all the tension and so went to see DC Justin Barnes who was still in hospital following the hit and run on him a few nights previously and they now knew that Vivian Blackstone was at the wheel.

When she got to the small treatment room at Blackpool Victoria where they were keeping Justin she was about to wave through the window from the corridor when she saw something that stopped her. There was Justin enjoying a full- on snogging session with none other than the hunkiest pathologist in the business Dr. Ross Carter who was supposed to be fighting the immigration authorities to get his Canadian girlfriend into the country for them to get married. She stepped back. They hadn't seen her. She hid to the side until Ross Carter left ten minutes later. Then she left it a minute before she went in.

'Well congratulations DI Khan' said Justin as he embraced her with his one good arm and hoped she hadn't seen Ross. 'You cracked the case'.

'Thanks, Justin' said Layla who then perched herself on the edge of his bed. 'Although anybody would've got there'.

'Perhaps a lot more slowly than you'.

'Oh, I don't know' said Khan, shrugging her shoulders. 'I took a couple of chances and they paid off'.

'Chances that some other officers wouldn't have had the nerve to take, and you know it'.

'Even when it came to Philippa Beresford?'

'That wasn't your fault'.

'It was on my watch. I'm responsible'.

'No Layla, she was responsible for her own actions. She was sleeping with the biggest criminal in this part of the northwest. She was asking for trouble'.

'Well anyway, how are you? When do you get the plaster off your arm?'

'A week on Tuesday thank God. It aches and it's itching like mad'.

They quickly slipped into the kind of banter they always did when they were alone together and were soon laughing like a pair of little girls. Khan really needed this kind of exchange after all the heady days recently.

'I'll have to ask you round for dinner before your plaster comes off your arm,' said Khan.

'Before it comes off?'

'Well that way you won't be able to make a pass at my Steve like you did last time'.

Justin was mortified by what he'd done last time he'd gone

round for a meal with Khan and her boyfriend Steve. He would admit to having been quite magnificently drunk but after confessing to finding Steve attractive he'd then launched himself onto Steve's lips with his own.

'Oh God why did you bring that up? I wanted to die'.

Layla was laughing. 'Hey, Steve didn't mind. He's told all his mates that he's got a gay admirer. He loves it. He thinks it makes him really cool'.

'And what do you think?'

'I think it's cool too. Why not? As long as you have no serious intent on converting him because in that case, I'd cut your bloody balls off'.

'I'd never do that to a mate'.

'Good. So, if you come to dinner will you be bringing someone?'

'Who?'

'Oh, someone like the gorgeous Dr. Ross Carter with whom you were hoovering mouths with a few minutes ago. I saw you. I decided to wait until he'd gone before I came in, but I can still smell the passion in the air'.

'He's the love of my life, Layla'.

'But what about his Canadian girlfriend?'

'He finished things with her last week'.

'And now he's with you'.

'And now he's with me. He's had relationships with men before, but none have been as serious as this one with me. He says he's always considered himself to be sexually ambiguous, but that when he met me all the pieces started to fit together for the first time'.

'I am so pleased for you, Justin'.

'When I leave here, he's moving in with me'.

'And trust you to bag one of the best- looking men on the Fylde coast'.

'Layla, I look at him sometimes and I can't quite believe that he thinks I'm the one'.

'Well, you enjoy that first flush of love' said Khan who was truly delighted for her friend. 'But getting back to your physical well-being, get better soon and get back to work. I miss you'.

On her way from the hospital Khan had the lingering feeling that even though Vivian Blackstone had been charged and was behind bars, the reach of this case wasn't going to stretch as far as it should do and beat down the door of Daniel Lewis. He'd done a disappearing act. His bank accounts had been cleared by his daughter Melissa, but nobody knew where he was. Where could he have gone without being noticed by somebody? His apparent lack of money didn't concern her. People like that always have hidden resources they could pull out of the bag when the law is on to them. But before she went any further, she decided to go and see someone she'd been meaning to have a word with for a few days.

She'd been inside Blackpool town hall before and noted its architecture and decoration that were a throwback to more golden and halcyon days before foreign travel had been brought into affordable levels for the masses. She liked the way the town hall was though. It was grand and yet illusive.

'DI Khan' greeted council leader Lesley Hammond warmly as Khan was led into her office. 'It's very good to meet you'.

'Thank you and likewise' said Khan 'I've heard a lot about you from our mutual friend Josh Walker at the Evening News. He seems to be a fan of us both'.

'He must have a thing about self-assured women,' said Lesley. 'Although he is one of the good guys. There's nothing misogynistic about our Josh'.

'I'm sure there isn't,' said Khan. 'He's gone into hiding until this whole business with Daniel Lewis has blown over. I don't blame him to be honest'.

'No, me neither. Now, you live in my particular council ward I understand?'

'Yes, I do' confirmed DCI Khan. 'But that's not why I'm here'.

'Well sit down and tell me why you are here'.

They sat down either side of Lesley Hammond's desk. Lesley felt a little unsure of herself. She got the distinct feeling that DI Khan was on some kind of an agenda. She'd seen that look before on many a politician. It was when you recognized there was a snake in front of you and you wondered when it was going to strike and how deeply the venom would penetrate. It was never a politician from another party that used the serpent look on you. It was usually someone from the same side.

'Lesley, I'm looking forward to you and I working together, with Josh Walker, to keep this town clean and to never allow the likes of Daniel Lewis to ever dominate this town again' Khan began. 'But for that to happen successfully we need to build a relationship of trust'.

Lesley Hammond was puzzled. 'Well, there's no problem from me there'.

'That's what I thought you'd say' Khan went on. 'But you see, a picture has been drawn to me of you controlling those councilors who are being recalcitrant against your wishes by threatening them with exposure to their law- breaking activities. That's where I come in because it's my job to uphold the law'.

'What do you want, DI Khan?'

'I want the name of the council employee who took the money from Daniel Lewis to secure contracts for his corporation. I'm told by my colleagues in the fraud squad that you say you don't know but I don't believe that. I don't believe it for one second'.

'And if I don't?'

'Well then, I'll simply go through the voting records of your councilors and see who suddenly changed recently from being a rebel to being obedient. I've got some very talented people on my team, and it shouldn't take them long to see who you've been blackmailing. That said I acknowledge that you were severely provoked, and I understand that you took your chance to get back at the bastards. So, I'm prepared to overlook all the other bits and pieces if you give me that one name. Just that one name Lesley and then we can move on together in a spirit of co-operation'.

Lesley Hammond had thought this was all over and that she would never have to answer for the ruthlessness she'd shown in getting all of her councilors to focus on Blackpool and what's right for the people here, rather than their own positions and the cash they got from bribery. But she hadn't counted on coming up against such a thorough officer as DI Khan who she couldn't help but admire nevertheless. She must've had to be tough to get where she is. And what she was asking wasn't entirely unfair.

'DI Khan, my family have already suffered at the hands of Daniel Lewis' said Lesley. 'Our dog Patch? I'm still having nightmares about it and I had to make up some cock and bull story to my boys about Patch having been run over by a car'.

'It was evil what he did to your dog,' said Khan. 'I'm only sorry that we couldn't have prevented that'.

'Well, I just wanted to remind you who has been suffering here,' said Lesley. 'And look, alright, I'll give you the name you're asking for. It's Dean Anderton. He's our chief planning officer. I've been barely able to look at him since I found out'.

'I'll pass the name on,' said Khan. 'You can expect an arrest to be made by the end of the day'.

'DI Khan, we've got some shocking social statistics in this town surrounding young carers, teenage prostitution, young people with HIV, teenage mums, plus the under achievement of the general population. I intend to finally make a difference to all those figures and if I have to box a little clever to do it then I will'.

'We speak the same language, Lesley. We're two strong-willed women who want to make a difference, but I just want you to keep me in the loop where any potential illegalities are concerned'.

'Point taken, Layla' said Lesley and whilst we're on the subject there's been a development this morning that I believe you should know about'.

'Oh?'

'The consortium that won the contract to redevelop the town centre instead of it going to the Daniel Lewis Corporation has suddenly pulled out'.

'Reason?'

'Who can say? It looks annoyingly like it'll have to go out to tender again but I haven't been able to get hold of them'.

'Do you think that Lewis got to them?'

'I don't know about Lewis, but I know that your colleagues have been to see the leader of that consortium in recent days'.

Khan wondered if Lesley would've told her this if she hadn't come to see her this morning. If there was going to be a relationship of trust between them then it might take more work than she initially thought.

'Can you explain further, Lesley?'

'My in-laws live directly across the road from Adrian Gibson who was head of the winning Fylde Coast development bid for the town centre'.

'And therefore, a sworn enemy of Daniel Lewis I don't doubt,' said Khan. 'But what do you mean about my colleagues having been to see Adrian Gibson?'

'Layla, my father-in-law is a retired police officer. He recognized the two officers who went to see Gibson. They were both from the fraud squad'.

DCI Khan drove over to the Devonshire Arms for the end of case drinks with her squad and just as she pulled into the car park she received a call from Josh Walker at the Evening News who gave her some rather illuminating news which nevertheless confirmed her suspicions about Daniel Lewis.

'I thought you were supposed to be in hiding?' Khan questioned.

'I am but my sources still manage to get their stuff to me,' said Walker. 'So, listen up because you need to know this'.

Khan listened intently to what Walker had to disclose and it was indeed something she needed to know. The problem now was what to do with the information.

'Dr. Gillespie has given me the all- clear, ma'am' said DS Keith Drake when she walked into the bar and he took her to one side. She hugged him.

'That's fantastic news, Keith'.

'I've got to take the test again in three- months- time, but as far as it goes, I've not been infected with HIV, and I just wanted to say thanks for all your help, Layla, and all your reassurance. I can't tell you how much I appreciate it'.

'Just keep working with me Keith and not against me as you sometimes tend to do'.

'I know and I will' said Keith whose admiration for DI Khan had grown in recent days. She'd stuck to her guns and ended up with the right result all round. That had taken strength.

'Good. Now get me a drink I'm parched'.

'Diet coke?'

'With ice and a slice of lime, please'.

With Sergeant Luke Morris and a few other members of the direct and support teams they'd taken over a couple of round tables in the lounge area of the pub. When Chief Inspector Langton showed up, Khan stood up and greeted him. Langton took an order for the bar and asked Khan to help him get everybody's drink to them. Once that had been done, he ushered her over for a little chat.

'Layla, don't let my delight in your success blind you to the fact that I don't necessarily agree with the way you do things. I'll cover your back, Layla. I'll cover it as much as I can because I believe you're a brilliant officer. But try and keep to the straight and narrow. That's all I ask. Just try even if you don't succeed'.

'I'll do whatever it takes to get the right result, sir'.

'Yes, and that both reassures and terrifies me,' said Langton. 'But look, this was a good result, and you should be proud. You've also scored points with the fraud squad which, as you know, is not bloody easy'.

Layla wondered why every compliment was always back handed in some way. Chief Inspector Langton wanted her to carry on doing it her way but yet didn't at the same time.

'Sir, those points I'm supposed to have earned from the fraud squad?'

'There's no supposed about it, DCI Khan. You have scored very positive points with them'.

'They really don't know me at all, do they?'

'What do you mean?'

'Well, if they think I can be fobbed off with a meaningless compliment about my work than they really don't know me'.

'DI Khan, I don't follow?'

'Where is Daniel Lewis, sir?' she asked in relation to her call from Josh Walker who'd told her exactly where Daniel Lewis was, but she was interested in Langton's reaction. He didn't seem to have flinched. Was he just good at covering his guilt? 'This evil specimen of a man who was supposed to have been rendered destitute by his daughter's imaginative accounting can't seem to be apprehended'.

'Are you implying that the fraud squad have something to do with this that isn't legal?'

'Well, if they do then am I expected to keep my mouth shut?'

'You're expected not to accuse your colleagues of wrongdoing unless you've got proof, DI Khan'.

'So, if I told you that Daniel Lewis had been pictured earlier today alive and very much kicking in a beach bar in Malta seemingly without a care in the world then that wouldn't mean anything to anyone in the fraud squad? How was he able to escape to a country where he has friends and money in a secret account? Because you see, I've been wondering why he didn't go after Josh Walker at the Evening News and Lesley Hammond on the council who both played a big part in his downfall. Oh well of course he did go after Lesley Hammond. He abducted and then butchered her family dog. As if that was going to put off someone as strong and as determined as her, no matter how devastating the actual thing was for her and her family. Do you see where I'm coming from here, sir? Why wasn't he held up at the airport like his daughters were? There's a stench about this whole thing but maybe it stops smelling the higher up the pay grade you get'.

Langton bristled. 'Watch your language, DI Khan. And anyway, what if you are right?'

'Well, if I am right then Daniel Lewis must've had help from people who could guarantee his passage out of the country and I think any fool could see that, sir. And sir, we're talking here about a man who used his own daughters as prostitutes to secure business deals as well as using a number of very vulnerable young girls as prostitutes too. Now I certainly didn't join the police force to make deals with the likes of him'.

The Chief Inspector looked decidedly uncomfortable. 'Are you alleging some kind of corruption, DI Khan?'

'Those are your words not mine, sir, and it would be up to the public to decide, if these matters we've been talking about were ever disclosed' said Khan. 'But I'll tell you this, sir, if Daniel Lewis ever set foot back in this country I would have him no matter what kind of official protection he may have around him. What's he doing for us anyway? Are we using him to catch even bigger fish? Is he part of some bigger picture that I'm not going to be made privy to? Or is it just a simple case of someone taking backhanders, and the powers that be want to avoid a public scandal? Whatever the answer is, sir, it'll all come out one day. Some journalist, or TV reporter will dig deep enough. The story as it stands is going to be all over the papers, including the fact that Lewis is now in Malta and seemingly not worried about any possible extradition'.

'I think you've said enough, DI Khan'.

'Well, I notice you're not denying anything that I'm

suggesting, sir,' said Khan. 'So, are you saying that the fraud squad are ignoring all the evidence against Daniel Lewis for reasons best known to themselves?'

Chief Inspector Langton responded quietly but firmly. 'Let's go outside, DI Khan'.

Khan followed the chief inspector out into the pub car park. 'I thought that in these days of transparency and honest policing these little chats were a thing of the past?'

'DI Khan, listen to me. If the fraud squad does not want to go down the route of prosecuting Daniel Lewis for their own inexplicable reasons, then that's where it has to be left'.

'Sir, are you really saying that the fraud squad are deliberately ignoring all the evidence against Daniel Lewis?'

Langton sighed wearily. 'DI Khan, I'm saying that you have to consider the investigation closed. You're right. This does go way above my pay grade and yours. Whoever has taken this decision will have their reasons but they're not going to get down as far as either of us until the operation is over or unless we need to know sooner for whatever reason. But as far as you're concerned your work is done. You've got the right result. Vivian Blackstone is behind bars. Just be glad of that'.

'It doesn't sound like I've got much choice'.

'No, I'm afraid you haven't'.

'Well, these days, sir, things like this have a habit of coming out. And when it does, I really hope I'm there to see it because right now I'm beside myself with rage that Daniel Lewis has escaped justice. Especially when it's been with the assistance of people who I'm supposed to call colleagues'.

'So have you heard anything from your Aunty Layla recently?'

'Why would I have done? She's supposed to never contact anybody in the family. Anyway, why do you ask? In fact, why do you keep on asking about my Aunty Layla? It's like you've got some kind of agenda?'

'She disrespected your family'.

'Did she fuck! And in any case that was years ago, and everyone except my dad wants to put it all behind us and for the family to move on with Aunty Layla as a part of it again'.

'She sleeps with her non-Muslim boyfriend in the same bed! That's immoral. No good and decent Muslim is going to want to touch her after that'.

'You're getting close to a line here, pal. Don't forget that she is my Aunty, and I won't have bad stuff said about her'.

'But it's the truth, man!'

'She's not a bad person in my eyes, Charlie! My Mum says she's really happy with this Steve and if that's the case then I am too'.

'The faith has lost you, man'.

'No Charlie. The faith is there as a guide, but it doesn't dictate everything I think and feel. I've got more confidence in myself and my own moral judgment than that. You're like any convert to any religion, Charlie. You've been blinded by what you see as a strength that's been missing in your life all these years. Well please, in the name of Allah the blessed prophet, step back and really read the Quran. And if I hear any of your extremist mates bad mouthing my Aunty Layla with their twisted perversion of our ancient and beautiful faith, then they'll be licking their own blood off the floor'.

'Well, if you feel that strongly then why don't you try and stop them saying what they do?'

'Because this is a free country'.

EIGHTEEN

Flanked by DS Keith Drake and Sergeant Luke Morris, DI Khan led the mourning at the funeral of the still unidentified first murder victim of Vivian Blackstone. Khan had insisted that they do something to honour the life of someone who nobody had come forward to say that she was theirs. The social worker Iain Kempton was also there with them along with council leader Lesley Hammond and Khan's boyfriend Steve. She'd been lowered into her grave and then each one of them present had thrown a handful of soil down onto the coffin. Then they stood back and huddled under a large tree to shelter against the rain that had started to fall.

'Not even the sun would come out for her' said Khan who'd been close to tears during the short service. Usually, things are said about the deceased by the vicar or the priest, anecdotes are mentioned. But what could anyone say about a girl they knew nothing about? During questioning Vivian Blackstone admitted that she'd compiled a list of potential victims from when she'd volunteered for the Blackpool HIV Trust, and she'd made this girl her first target precisely because she hadn't revealed any personal information about herself other than a name. Debbie.

And that's all they knew about a young girl who was now buried six feet under from where they stood. They'd all clubbed together for a headstone that simply read 'Debbie'.

'And that the only way she thought she could survive was to sell her body to the sad bastards of this town,' said Iain Kempton. 'That's where we failed her in social services'

'We all failed her, Iain,' said Khan. 'And I mean every single one of us in this town'.

'But she chose to make herself invisible, ma'am,' said DS Drake. 'However sad that is'

'But somebody should've noticed her and realised that she needed help,' said Iain Kempton. 'Somebody should've done that basic thing. I'm ashamed'.

Lesley Hammond patted his arm. 'We all are, Iain. We all are'.

NINETEEN

DI Khan was treating herself to a couple of hours off and planned to use some of the time to get her nails done. She always went to a little salon on Highfield Road, South Shore where her nail technician, Michaela, was sweet enough but didn't have the brains she was born with and was somewhat naive when it came to the boys. But still she always had a story to tell, and Khan always left the salon still laughing at what Michaela had revealed about her latest exploits. It had been a hard couple of days to get through and she and her team still had the funeral of DC Philippa Beresford ahead of them. Nobody had said that joining the police force was an easy option but recently it had really stretched Khan to her limits.

The nail salon was also convenient for a cafe called Green's which was Khan and Steve's favourite place when they fancied a fry up. So before Khan's appointment with Michaela she took Steve to Green's where it never ceased to make her smile that when you bought the 'large' breakfast you could have your sausages 'upgraded' to Cumberland sausages for only a pound extra. They did also serve the most wonderful chunky brown toast and they were never quiet in there. It was always busy. Discerning people did gravitate towards quality and obviously didn't mind paying for the upgrading of their sausages. And they included her Steve.

They finished their breakfasts and then Steve asked if Khan was okay.

'I'll be glad when Philippa's funeral is over' she confessed. 'I'm not looking forward to that. And it's hard to know that there's something going on in the upper ranks that me and all the other DI's across the Fylde and the rest of Lancashire aren't deemed important enough to know about'.

'Well, none of any of that is your fault' said Steve, holding her hands reassuringly and then getting up to leave. 'But I've got to go, babe. I'll see you later'.

She watched and waved affectionately as he ran over to his car and headed off to his garage where he knew that his two apprentices, Rory and Helen, would already be hard at it. The two of them were both in their early twenties and now they got on like a house on fire but in the early days Steve had needed to remind Rory that just because Helen was a girl it didn't mean that she always had to answer the telephone when it rang, and she wasn't there just to fill in any gaps that couldn't be handled by either Steve or Rory. He'd also had to face down the prejudices of some of his customers, one of them, some snooty git from St Annes or Lytham or other such pretentious up its own arse type of place, had demanded to see Helen's qualifications for doing her job and said he didn't need to see Rory's because he no doubt wasn't part of some left wing politically correct movement to push women into places they didn't necessarily want to go. Steve told him in no uncertain terms that he wouldn't show him Helen's qualifications and certificates and that if that was his attitude then he could just fuck off and never offer his business to him again because just like today, it would be declined.

Khan left the cafe a couple of moments later and began walking to her car. But she didn't know that she wouldn't make it to her nail appointment.

'Dad, you've got to warn her' said Muhammad, the intensity in his voice matching the anguish he felt. 'You've got to'.

'I haven't got to do anything' Zahid replied. 'Besides, we don't know for sure what Charlie is going to do'.

'No, but we've got a good idea and it isn't about him walking up to Aunty Layla and shaking her hand. He's a jihadist, Dad. Somewhere along the line he stopped listening to whatever you or me tried to tell him, and he started taking more notice of those idiots at the mosque who think they can blame all their personal problems on the evil west'.

'Just like all the lazy, spineless white people here blame all their problems on us for just being here' his father replied.

'And we know that both of those perspectives are just not true'.

'So, what do you want me to do about it?'

'I want you to get out there with me and save your sister from a fucked- up maniac'.

'Don't you dare use those words in front of me, Muhammad!'

Muhammad ran his hands through his hair in frustration. 'It's not the use of the words that's important here, Dad'.

'Are you questioning me in my own house?' Zahid demanded.

'No Dad, I'm just asking you to really think about what's going on here'.

'We took him into our home,' said Zahid. 'His own family had let him down and we took him in and tried to steer him down the right path. And this is how he repays us?'

'So Dad that's even more reason for us not to let him take out whatever his agenda is on Aunty Layla'.

Zahid sat and thought for a moment. Muhammad was right. If he was anything of a brother he'd go after Charlie like a shot. It had only been a few hours since they'd discovered that the family file all about Layla had been taken from Zahid's desk. It contained everything about her from where she worked to where she lived and if Zahid could peep over the top of his defiance and find that little bit of clarity that would make him see the ghost through the fog, he might be able to see his parents urging him from the other side to go and see to the family business.

'Come on, Dad' said Muhammad as he held up his father's car keys in front of him. 'We've wasted enough time on this as it is'.

DI Khan was about to press her fob to unlock her car door when she was stopped by her mobile ringing. She took it out of the bag she was carrying over her shoulder and didn't recognise the number. She pressed 'answer'. 'Hello, DI Khan?'

'Aunty Layla?'

'Is that you Muhammad?' asked Layla.

'Yeah, Aunty Layla, it's me Muhammad'.

Khan was instantly overwhelmed with emotion at hearing from her nephew. How old must he be now? She can't remember the last time she saw him. Most Aunts wouldn't think twice about getting a call from their nephew. But to Khan this was massive.

'Muhammad, I can't tell you how happy I am to hear from you' she said, her voice nearly breaking. 'It really is a lovely surprise'.

'I'm just glad we seem to have got to you in time'.

'What? That sounds a bit frantic? Are you okay? Is your Dad okay? Your Mum and everyone?'

'We're fine, Aunty Layla, but you've got trouble heading your way'.

'What do you mean?'

'I think my Mum told you about a lad called Charlie?'

'Yes, she did. The one who you've virtually taken in like the good Muslims you are'.

'Well, he's turned out to be the snake who swings round and bites us. He's been going to the meetings of this hate preacher we've had at the mosque. My Dad and all the others have got him thrown out now, but the point is, Aunty Layla, that Charlie has got it into his head that you got away with breaking with tradition and that ... '

'... and that what, Muhammad?'

'And that you need to be punished for what you've done. Aunty Layla, he's been into my dad's desk, and he's stolen everything to do with you. He's got your address, mobile number everything'.

'How long have you known, Muhammad?'

'Since ... well since this time yesterday. So, he's had enough time to get up to Blackpool. We're on our way to you now, Aunty Layla. We're heading down the A50 towards the M6. Me and my dad. We're coming to help you, Aunty Layla in whatever way we can and I'm sorry we should've headed off before'.

'It's alright, let's not worry about that now, I understand believe me,' said Layla. Her heart was sinking into the ground at the thought that her brother Zahid knew this Charlie was coming after her and didn't do anything about it for twenty-four hours. At least now his guilty conscience is working through his beautiful son Muhammad who seems to have his head screwed on good and proper and was swinging him into action now. 'I'll see you both later and I'll do my best to keep you posted in the meantime'.

'He's just a stupid crazy mixed up kid who never got any real love from his parents, Aunty Layla,' said Muhammad. 'There's a lot like that, I know, and he didn't have to go to extremes, but I tried my best. I really tried my best, but in the end, it just seems like it wasn't enough to draw out his resentments and deal with them in a much different way to this'.

'Don't you worry, Muhammad. I've got the measure of it' said

Layla whose heart was breaking at the sound of Muhammad's breaking. 'None of this is your fault. Okay? Now have you got any pictures of Charlie on your phone?'

'Yeah, I've got a few. Do you want me to send them to your phone?'

'That's exactly what I want you to do young man, good thinking. Describe him to me?'

'Same height as me'.

'Which is? I haven't seen you in an age, remember?'

Muhammad stopped briefly whilst he struggled with the weight of the words his Aunty had just used. He went on to give a physical description of Charlie whilst Layla got into her car.

'That's great, Muhammad, thank you. Now tell your dad to drive carefully and I'll see you when you get up here. In the meantime, if you can think of anything else that might be important then please let me know. However small you think it might be, tell me anyway. Alright?'

'Alright, Aunty Layla. Now you keep safe too because I want us all to have a proper reunion later'.

Khan could've cried. 'I'd really love that'.

Khan looked all around her before getting into her car and locking the doors. She called Steve but there was no reply on his mobile. She called on the garage landline number but Rory the apprentice said they hadn't seen him yet this morning.

She tried not to think the worst as she switched on the engine and headed for home. It was only when she was halfway there that she realised her hands were shaking. She told herself to get a bloody grip. She was sweating and felt nauseous. If this Charlie had done anything to Steve, she'd happily kill him herself.

When she got home, she turned into the avenue and looked ahead to see Steve's car parked outside their house. What was he doing back home? Surely, he hadn't forgotten anything. Oh God this could turn out to be the worst day of all to have gone to work without something that he needed to run back home for. She parked up a little way down the street and made some calls. One was to her deputy DS Keith Drake, another was to Sergeant Luke Morris who was still temporarily attached to the team, and one was to Chief Inspector Langton who said he'd call out the armed response unit. She also sent on the pictures Muhammad had sent her of Charlie. She studied his face. His eyes were full of pain and disappointment, his skin looked pale, and his overall demeanour looked like he was struggling so hard to deal with all the demons inside him.

She got out of her car and was surprised and relieved to see Steve running out of their house in the direction of his own car.

'What are you doing?' she called out.

Steve lifted up a bunch of account files that he was carrying. 'I totally forgot these and I'm seeing Joe the accountant this afternoon. I just nipped back for them. Why, what's the problem?'

Khan started to explain what was going on to a horrified Steve when out from behind one of the parked cars in the street where they were talking, Charlie jumped and brandished a sharp butcher's knife in his hand.

'You treacherous slag! You don't deserve to live on this earth after what you did!'

Khan swung round and came face to face with Charlie who was sweating like a bullock and seemed pretty unsure of himself. She could see that he was shaking.

'Now listen, Charlie' said Khan, calmly but with a firmness he needed. 'Put the knife down and we'll talk. Come on, put it down and let's see the end to all this'.

'The end to all this will only come when you're dead and in Hell'.

'You don't mean that'.

'Yes, I do'.

'No, you don't because you don't understand. I ran away because I wanted to get my life back. I loved my parents very much, but I didn't want them controlling my life. And at the end of the day what is wrong with that? What is wrong with wanting to chart your own destiny? Charlie, you've had a bloody hard time of it, I know. But it isn't too late, Charlie. There are plenty of people who will be willing to help you make a success of your life despite everything that's gone on until now. So, drop the knife, Charlie. Drop the knife and we can start working out a more positive future for you'.

'I just want to be happy' he pleaded. 'I just want to know that there's someone there who loves me'.

'I know, I know, I understand. But this is not the way to get all of that, Charlie. You're a kid. You're a kid with a bright future if we put an end to this now and you drop the knife'.

Charlie was starting to feel dizzy. Everything she said was logical and sound and perhaps he should give it all up and start again. She says there are ways, and she might not be just saying that.

Then just as he was contemplating giving in to her, Steve grabbed him from behind and Charlie's reaction was to stab Steve directly in the gut with his knife.

TWENTY

Muhammad was crying his heart out. 'I'm so sorry, Aunty Layla. I'm so, so sorry'.

Layla swept her nephew up in her arms or as much as she could do when he towered over her. 'You've got nothing to be sorry about, Muhammad. Absolutely nothing'.

'But I'm the one who brought Charlie into your life' said Muhammad in a pitifully faltering voice. He was still sobbing. They were standing in one of the corridors of Blackpool Victoria hospital where Steve had been taken after being stabbed by Charlie. Muhammad's Dad, Layla's brother Zahid, was standing half a dozen metres away from them. He was still finding it hard to show any kind of emotion. 'If it wasn't for me, you wouldn't have known anything about him, and he wouldn't have been able to do that to Steve'.

'Muhammad, you heard what the doctor said,' said Layla. 'Steve has been very lucky. The knife didn't go in that deep and managed to miss several vital organs by some miracle and he's going to make a full recovery. He's going to be alright, Muhammad'.

'What about Charlie? What will happen to him now?'

'He'll be charged of course but he'll also receive some pretty strong professional support. He's going to be alright too, Muhammad. One way or another he's going to be alright. The people that know what to do will fix him. You made a start on him, and you should be proud. Now Steve is going to be asleep all night now with all the drugs he's on and I'll come back first thing in the morning to be with him again. In the meantime, I'm gasping for something to drink and I'm hungry'. She called Zahid over. 'Now I know I'm leaping in the dark here, but I want the two of you to come back to mine. I'll make us something to eat and you can stay the night. What do you say?'

Muhammad looked pleadingly at his father. 'This could be the only way for any of this to make any sense, Dad. It's brought us together with Aunty Layla again. It must've been meant to. Can't you see that?'

Layla could feel her heart beating. She desperately wanted her brother to agree to some sort of reconciliation. She was so taking to this wonderful young man her nephew had turned out to be and she wanted to be a real part of her family again and to introduce Steve to them all and show them how happy he made her. Zahid stared at her for what seemed like hours before he spoke.

'Okay' he said. His face turned into something like a smile. 'Perhaps it is time. I'll call your mother, Muhammad and tell her we won't be home tonight'.

Khan and Muhammad exchanged big hugs and smiles. They both knew it wasn't going to be easy, but they were about to take a tiny step forward. She held out her hand and after a few agonising seconds Zahid took it.

'Thank you,' said Layla.

'Aunty Layla?'

'Yes, mate?'

'Could we have fish and chips and sit on the promenade to eat them?'

'You've heard about my cooking then?'

Muhammad smiled. 'No, I just thought that because we're in Blackpool, you know?'

'Why not?' said Khan, smiling broadly. 'Why ever not?'.

THE END

But DI Layla Khan will be back.

And in the meantime, why not check out one of David Menon's other novels?

Like 'IT COULD BE YOU NEXT' which is the latest in his Detective Jeff Barton Manchester crime thrillers. Its available on Amazon worldwide

Here's the first chapter of 'IT COULD BE YOU NEXT' just to get you interested.

Hannah was driving with so little of what could justifiably pass as due care and attention that she found herself barely a whisker away from the back of a double decker bus as she progressed along Barlow Moor Road in south Manchester. She pulled over and stopped for a minute or two. It scared her to think that she couldn't recall the seconds it had taken for her to go from a safe distance behind the bus to being in danger of crashing into the back of it. This was getting out of hand. She sat there taking deep breaths until the feeling of nausea began to pass. It was early in the afternoon, and she was relieved that the road wasn't particularly busy. School traffic wouldn't be clogging up the roads for a good hour and a half yet. Delivery drivers would now be on a downward track of the list of items bought online that had been promised for this particular day. Everybody would be back at their desks now after lunch. Those on afternoon shifts would be there now whilst those on early shifts wouldn't quite have left yet. She looked up at the house she'd parked outside of. Standard semi-detached Victorian villa that was characteristic of the area. Probably a youngish couple who'd bought it because they'd started a family and the schools were good in the area. Middle class professional types who read the Guardian and watch Newsnight. What had probably once been a front lawn had been replaced by a car parking area and there was a short wall separating it from the pavement. The space was empty just now but there was enough space for two and Hannah supposed that one would no doubt be an SUV of some kind which had become the standard acquisition of middle- class yummy mummies on the school run. Then there'd be something that the man of the house would no doubt use to get to work and impress his mates down the pub. Something like a Merc or the latest BMW. Hannah and her partner Felix were trying for a baby. She'd gone part-time at work and thought that stepping back from full-time hours might make her more relaxed and therefore make it easier to conceive. Her Mum hadn't been best pleased that she was planning to get pregnant without being married. But her Mum had a problem believing that anybody could think differently to her about anything. That's why she and Hannah had always clashed. They were so very different.

She clicked the indicator on her compact three door Hyundai and looked back before moving off. A couple of streets later she turned left into Beaumont Avenue. She pulled up outside number eleven and stole herself. It was a journey she'd made from her home in Heaton Mersey so many times and yet she'd never had to make it under these circumstances before. Naomi had been her best mate for centuries. They'd gone to school together, grown up together, lost their virginity on the same night. To the same boy. Hannah had gone to Manchester university and got herself a degree in business studies. She was now a business consultant for a firm in town. Naomi had gone to work at her father's garden centre just outside Alderley Edge. She ran the place now after her father had retired. He seemed to spend most of his time these days taking her mother on cruises. They were doing the Norwegian fjords at the moment. The bank of Mum and Dad had bought her house for her. Hannah hadn't been quite so lucky although her maternal Grandma had given her the deposit for her place. But that had been their secret because her grandma hadn't done the same for Hannah's brother Miles. She'd always favoured Hannah but even she would be turning in her grave now considering what had happened.

'I'm not taking any of it back' Naomi charged after she'd opened the door to Hannah.

'And Hello to you too' Hannah retorted. She'd never seen such hostility in Naomi's eyes. She'd never seen it directed at her in any case. She'd also never seen that hostility mixed with such enormous sadness at the same time. But she wasn't going to be diverted by it. She'd come here to have it out with her, and she was fucking well going to. 'Are you going to let me in?'

Hannah had helped Naomi on the day she moved into her house. She'd made endless cups of tea for the removal men who'd flirted shamelessly with both girls. Hannah had lapped it up and made a real laugh out of it, but Naomi was well into her bitter about men mindset by then and was having none of it. She was actually quite rude to the guys a couple of times. Hannah had been rather embarrassed at the way Naomi had spoken to them and mouthed 'sorry' at least twice. But she'd been in there now a couple of years and, again thanks to the bank of Mum and Dad, she'd fitted a new bathroom, new kitchen, and had her back garden Japanese styled. Naomi had quite a thing for Japanese minimalism and had furnished the whole house that way. It didn't fit with Hannah's tastes though. Her house that she now shared with Felix was full of all different kinds of fabrics in all the colours of the rainbow. It was a real messy lived-in home too. Neither she nor Felix were particularly tidy. They weren't dirty but they weren't obsessed about everything always being in its rightful place and at least they didn't switch on the dishwasher until it was full. Unlike Naomi who would switch it on even for one mug and one small plate. She couldn't care less about wasting energy. She'd watch the tv news showing floods in one part of the world, extreme heatwaves in another and bush fires somewhere else, and then denounce climate change as an obsession of the bleeding heart brigade. Besides, she would claim, if there was such a thing as climate change then it had been caused by the previous generation so why did she have to do anything to stop it? It was the kind of logic that Hannah thought was beyond being just selfish. It was plain bloody stupid.

The first thing Naomi did when the two of them walked into her living room was pick up a magazine that had been lying on top of a pile and straighten the corner of the front page. Hannah had seen her do that kind of thing thousands of times. She was fastidious about everything looking neat. That kind of thing was way more important to her than dealing with a situation in which she'd upset someone and hurt their feelings. The straightness on the cover of a magazine was more fucking important than apologising after she'd reduced someone to tears.

'Do you want a tea or coffee or something?' Naomi asked of her best friend. She didn't usually ask. Hannah usually helped herself by filling up the kettle almost as soon as she was through the door.

'No. I won't be stopping' Hannah answered. She hadn't even put her handbag down. It was still hanging on her shoulder.

'Hannah, you're coming across like a stranger to me' Naomi appealed.

'Well, what do you expect?' Hannah demanded.

'For two days now, you haven't responded to my texts or my phone calls' Naomi went on. She was almost tearful. But she wasn't sorry. She wasn't sorry at all. But the way things were between her and Hannah in that moment was horrible. They'd been tight for so long and been through so much in each other's lives. She couldn't lose that. She couldn't bear to lose that. She wasn't that close to anybody else.

'It really does all have to be about you, doesn't it?'

'We've had fallouts before, but you've never not talked to me for this long, Hannah'.

'Oh well do forgive me but I've been worried sick about my brother!'

Three days previously Naomi had joined Hannah and her partner Felix at their mutual friend Robbie's house in Chorlton for an afternoon of wine, beer and snacks in the back garden. Robbie's husband Owen had been due to be there too, but he was a paramedic and had been called into work because of staff shortages. Hannah's brother Miles was there too with his wife Diane and their two young boys. Robbie and Miles had gone to school together and were best mates. Robbie had been best man for Miles when he married Diane and returned the honour when Robbie married Owen. Robbie was also godfather to Miles and Diane's two boys, Callum and Freddy.

'...it's such a shame Owen couldn't be here,' said Diane as she let her head fall back so that her face was exposed to the sun.

'I know' Robbie agreed as he put down three bottles of white wine that he'd just brought out from the fridge. 'But he's hoping not to have to work a full shift so he might be here later. But that's what you have to accept when your husband is a heroic lifesaver'.

They all laughed at Robbie's description of Owen. They all liked him and thought he was the best thing that had ever happened to Robbie, but it was also funny how they'd got together. It was on a Thursday night five years ago when Robbie had accompanied Hannah and Naomi to a straight nightclub in town. And it had been ironic that in a straight nightclub, Robbie was the only one out of the three of them who'd pulled. Owen had been on a mate's stag night and never imagined he'd meet the man of his dreams in there. But Robbie had noticed Owen and Owen had noticed Robbie and that had been that. Now, five years later, they were happily married and planning to adopt a child next year. The rest of them had all said that it had clearly been a case that night of the planets lining up in the straight nightclub to fulfil the destiny of Robbie and Owen to be together.

Robbie was with his godsons Callum and Freddy who were racing on the bikes they'd brought with them. As they raced around the garden none of the rest of those there could decide who was the biggest kid, Callum, Freddy, or Robbie.

'The boys adore their uncle Robbie' said their Mum, Diane. 'And their uncle Owen. They love it when they come here for sleepovers. Everything is turned into a big adventure and little boys love that'.

'They really do' Miles agreed, holding his wife's hand as they sat here drinking wine. 'Robbie and Owen will make great parents themselves one day'.

'They so will' Diane agreed.

'We're lucky to have Robbie and Owen because when the boys have their sleepovers here, it gives me and their Mum time to remember all the feelings we had that led to us conceiving Callum and Freddy'.

Miles and Diane then kissed. Hannah noticed the sneer on Naomi's face as she watched them being romantic with each other. She'd seen that look before. And it was making her nervous.

'So, Miles' Naomi began. 'This display is all very lovely, but can you tell Diane where you were last Wednesday night when you were supposed to be at a work function?'

'I was at a work function' said Miles a little taken aback. He hadn't seen this coming. 'I was at the Midland hotel in town. But why am I having to explain myself to you?'

'Because you and I both know that what you say is rubbish' Naomi spat. 'You were at the house in Hazel Grove of a girl called Lorraine Smith having sex with her and I know because she is an employee of mine and she told me. And she's got no reason to lie'.

Diane's face crumbled like she'd received the shock of her life. She'd never suspected Miles of playing away. He'd just never seemed the sort who would. If there was a sort. But she just hadn't suspected it of him. She just hadn't. So, what was Naomi talking about?

'Naomi, whatever has or hasn't happened here is absolutely no business of yours' said Hannah in a snarl of a voice that she wanted to serve as a warning. She'd caused a scene in front of everyone including Hannah's two little nephews. And for that she was a rotten bitch who Hannah would never forgive.

'I'm sorry, Diane' said Naomi in a sympathetic voice after turning to Hannah's sister-in-law. 'But I have to speak out when I feel that men are getting away with it. And this is one of those times. Like I say, Lorraine Smith has no reason at all to lie'.

'I am not having an affair with Lorraine Smith!' Miles insisted.

'Then you're a liar and I shouldn't be surprised because you're a man, so it comes as second nature to you. Your boys will be the same when they grow up'.

'I think you've said more than enough, Naomi and I'd like you to leave' said Robbie who was furious with her. He was holding the two boys. One in each arm. They were getting distressed at all the shouting and at how their Mummy looked so upset.

'And whether you're gay or straight it makes no difference' snarled Naomi. 'You men will stick together and cover for each other when you're stabbing women in the back'.

Hannah was so exasperated with Naomi. She didn't know why she was so surprised because this was so typical of her. Every man is a bastard on planet Naomi. And a woman only behaves badly if a man has driven her to it. A woman is always to be understood. A man is always to be condemned. That was the simplistic bullshit that Naomi lived by.

Diane ran off into the house in floods of tears. She was followed by Miles.

'Go on, Miles' Naomi taunted. 'Run and tell your wife more lies!'

'Shut up, Naomi!' Hannah roared.

'She's only borne two children for you' Naomi carried on. 'So don't worry, you don't owe her anything in the way of honesty'.

Hannah slapped Naomi across the face. 'I think Robbie asked you to leave ...'

'I ask because I care for Diane,' said Naomi.

Hannah laughed. 'You say you care for Diane after you publicly humiliated her in front of everyone on Sunday? I don't know who writes your script, but they need shooting'.

With a hand on her chest as if she was about to make some kind of solemn vow Naomi said 'I have to be honest, Hannah. You know that. I couldn't sit there playing smiley happy people knowing that your brother had been cheating on his wife'.

'My brother has not been cheating on his wife!'

'That's what he tells you' Naomi scoffed.

'Because it's true!'

'You're his sister so you've got to believe him. I'm not his sister so I don't have to fall into that loyalty trap'.

'Lorraine Smith has been fantasising about Miles for months ... '

'… oh here we go. You're going to make out that she'd mad or deluded. Typical'.

'You're the one who's mad or deluded'.

'You know the pain I went through and am still going through, and I don't want that to happen to any other woman'.

'Oh, for fuck's sake! You found George in bed with another woman and yes, that must've hurt, and yes, that must've been devastating, but it was ten years ago, Naomi. And you've held on to it for all this time and used it as an excuse not to get involved with any man and to label all men as abusers in some way. Get over it, Naomi. Can't you see how much it's blinding you to the truth of any situation involving men? Sometimes the way you speak to Felix is appalling and he's a saint for never reacting to your viciousness'.

Hannah had lost count of the number of times that she'd had to bite her tongue when Naomi spoke to Felix as badly as she did. Or when she deliberately turned her back on him when they were all together. When she first started seeing him Naomi had gone into a sulk claiming that whenever a woman is stupid enough to get involved with a man it means that she's totally rejecting the life she had with her girlfriends when they were all single. And in Naomi's case, very proudly single.

'You're not out of your smug little woods yet, Hannah. Felix will be off shagging other women. It's just a question of time'.

'No, he won't, and do you know why? Because he's with me and not you, Naomi'.

'That puts me in my place'.

'Well, if you dish it out you have to be able to take it too but that's a little home truth you've never quite understood. Now look, I'll tell you what's happened. Lorraine Smith has bombarded Miles with text messages, cards, calls to his mobile and all because she fancied him after serving him at your garden centre when he came to buy some things. She signed him up to your customer loyalty scheme which is how she got his contact details. He didn't encourage her in any way, Naomi. He's been ignoring her because he's not interested because he loves Diane and would never cheat on her'.

'So he says'.

'Yes he says! Or yes he said'.

'What do you mean? Changed his story? Why doesn't that surprise me'.

'He hasn't changed his story, he's disappeared! He didn't turn up for work yesterday and nobody has seen or heard from him. The police haven't yet started an investigation into his disappearance yet, but I gather there's been no use of his bank cards and his mobile was found near to where he works in town. It was lying on the ground as if he'd just thrown it away. Poor Diane is beside herself'. She put a hand to her mouth as a massive lump came up in her throat. She swallowed hard. She didn't want to start crying. She stepped up closer to Naomi and pointed a finger in her face. 'So let me tell you this, Naomi. If something terrible has happened to my brother, like he's had some kind of breakdown or worse, as a result of what you did at Robbie's house, I will never, never forgive you. And I will make sure that you pay'.

Printed in Great Britain
by Amazon

17387231R00139